Life From Scratch

Melissa Ford

Bell Bridge Books   Memphis, Tennessee

Bell Bridge Books
PO BOX 300921
Memphis, TN 38130
ISBN: 978-1-935661-98-6

Bell Bridge Books is an Imprint of BelleBooks, Inc.

We at BelleBooks enjoy hearing from readers. You can contact us at the address above or at BelleBooks@BelleBooks.com

Visit our websites – www.BelleBooks.com and www.BellBridgeBooks.com.

10 9 8 7 6 5 4 3 2

Cover design: Debra Dixon
Interior design: Hank Smith
Cover art: Spoons (manipulated) Chankim | Dreamstime
Interior spoon graphic: Blueee@Dreamstime

:Lsf:01:

Dedication

To Grandma Sally,
my love is your commission

Life from Scratch

blogging about life one scrambled egg at a time

June Cleaver beat the crap out of me with her rolling pin.

In my dream, Martha Stewart, June Cleaver, Bree Van De Kamp, and Marion Cunningham (who they were all affectionately calling "Mrs. C") were baking a pie together in my kitchen and arguing about the best way to pit cherries. They hadn't really noticed me lounging around by the sink until I pointed out what a waste of time it would be to pit your own cherries when there were perfectly decent ones that you could get in a can when June Cleaver turned with a maniacal gleam in her eye and started beating me on the face and shoulders with her flour-dusted rolling pin.

Just imagine what she would have done to me if I had suggested frozen pie crust.

Which brings us to my latest self-improvement project. I fear that you will all cease to believe me, that I've become like the girl who cries post-divorce-finding-myself project, but this one is for real lest I become a spinsterish, batty cat-woman without the cats that I've been fearing that I'm morphing into all year.

Unlike that stint with transcendental meditation (it wasn't my fault I couldn't concentrate! Could *you* meditate in a room while smelling the most divine marinara sauce wafting in through the air vents from the restaurant below?) or the time I mused about life as a zumba instructor or considered becoming a femivore and moving to a farm in Upstate New York so I could raise my own chickens, I'm really going to do this for longer than the typical three minutes I've dedicated to past life-improvement projects:

Rachel Goldman is going to learn how to cook.

This is the point where I publicly admit that I don't really have a lot of skills in the kitchen. What I really mean is that I don't have *any* skills in the kitchen. I can make ramen noodles like a pro, but I've never really followed a recipe (which is what happens when you don't own any cookbooks). I'm more of a jarred sauce kind of girl. I consider toasting the English muffin on par with making my own bread.

Before the divorce, we ate out almost every night or brought in take-out. If they offered a degree in Carryout Curry, I would have a PhD. Unfortunately, even if I am now only ordering for one, I quickly learned after we separated that while Hunan Chow is affordable on a lawyer-and-graphic designer's joint salary, it's prohibitively expensive for a living-off-the-money-I-got-from-my-half-of-the-condo-while-I-find-myself budget.

So, I am going to learn how to fry an egg without breaking the yolk. And do more than boil noodles. I might even . . . gasp . . . make my own Pad Thai. And this, my friends, is how I'm finally going to find myself during my Year of Me. I can't believe I frittered away weeks of my life sabbatical on ideas such as becoming a pet sitter (yes, it turns out that you have to like dogs in order to walk dogs.) You live and you learn.

Okay, enough whining, it's time to get cooking. I have armed myself with cookbooks from the library, a healthy stock of wine, and my best friend, Arianna, to be my co-taster. Please stick around; I need you guys.

Chapter One

Peeling the Onion

I am waiting at the bar, my soaked umbrella tucked under my seat, at a trendy sushi restaurant in Soho. It's the sort of place I used to go with my ex-husband, Adam. It's now, apparently, the place I go for the first-date-of-the-rest-of-my-life.

My stomach is in knots as I watch the door. I have vague recollections of what Rob Zuckerman looks like because he's the only man who asked for my number at the end of the local synagogue's sponsored Schmooze and Booze at a Manhattan bar. In fact, he's the only man who really talked to me at all that night when I showed up fashionably late thinking that a Schmooze and Booze is like a dinner party—you look a little desperate for company if you're the first person through the door. Turns out that the early birds catch the strapping doctors and the later birds catch the worms.

But it's been that long since I've had a first date.

I sip a glass of wine, trying to keep my hope and anxiety in check. Two years of dating followed by twelve years of marriage and nine months of post-divorce wound licking means that it has been a long time since I've had to shave my legs pre-date for maximum smoothness (only up to the knee—I make a conscious decision not to shave any higher until the third date.) A long time since I've had to worry about who is going to pay or whether I have lipstick on my teeth or if my life sounds exciting enough.

I wasn't even sure if I was ready for this, but my best-friend, Arianna, gave me no choice once my life-improvement cooking project started trucking along. I called her to tell her that I had made my own pancakes, and she dropped a Freudian hint that it might be a good time to work on getting myself a man-cake. Arianna is chronically single-by-choice, insisting that she is the dating type and not the marrying type. But I, she has decided, am the marrying type who needs to move away from calling myself post-divorce and start thinking of myself as pre-marriage.

I don't really have a good reason for not going on a first date up until this point. The fact is that when you've been with one man for all of your twenties and half of your thirties, it is difficult to switch gears and start thinking about a different person's body or the smell of their aftershave or whether they like the toilet paper roll facing the wall or facing away. Which, of course, is getting ten miles ahead of myself since it's only a first date. But still.

It takes Rob Zuckerman a few seconds to notice me at the bar when he pauses at the hostess stand, rain dripping off his expensive Burberry coat. I could do worse, I decide optimistically, for my first-date-of-the-rest-of-my-life. Rob still has a full head of brown hair, an anomaly in the over-thirty-five-and-unmarried crowd. He is tall and athletically built. He has good taste in clothing and even better taste in restaurants.

And to be fair, he could do worse than me. At thirty-four, I'm still carded at liquor stores, which I like to think means that I still look young and vibrant. I'm wearing my brown hair longer these days, almost to my shoulders, and my stomach is still mostly flat despite my newfound love of butter. I might not be the most striking woman in the room, but I tan well in the summer.

"Rachel!" he exclaims, finally noticing me. He comes over to my seat and we do a self-conscious dance where I don't know whether to continue sitting or stand, and he doesn't know whether to give me kiss on the cheek or shake my hand. We compromise with an awkward half-hug with him standing and me sitting so that my head presses into his Burberry coat belt.

I collect my drink, and we follow the hostess to a seat near the window. The rain is coming down harder now, splattering the glass so it's impossible to see anything more than taxi headlights and glowing storefront signs. I play with the corner of my menu cover. With Adam, we skipped talking until we had both had a chance to glance through the options, but Rob doesn't even crack the cover before launching into a series of get-to-know-you questions, the sort I had been rehearsing answers to inside my mind all afternoon while I worked out my nervous energy by learning how to julienne carrots.

"So, Rachel," he begins, "it was so loud at the bar the other night, I missed hearing if you were actually from New York."

"I'm not," I answer, "I'm from New Jersey. But I sort of knew that I wanted to end up here after graduate school."

"Oh, where did you go to graduate school?"

"Yale," I say, hoping that this doesn't sound pretentious. "School of art for graphic design."

"That's sort of cool. So you're like an artist?"

"Like an artist," I repeat.

"I'm from here. My family still lives off Riverside Drive."

I try not to let my scorching case of real estate envy flare up. Nine months in a one-room apartment will do that to you.

"So how did you end up in New York?"

This was the question I was sort of dreading. I mean, I could lie and make it about my parents—both incredibly successful and respected lawyers—living in northern New Jersey and say they wanted me to be close to home like my siblings. My sister, Sarah, is a brain surgeon, married and living in Brooklyn with her husband, Richard, and daughter, Penelope. My brother, who could be seen by outsiders as the black sheep of the family because he never holds down a job longer than a few months, has taken his multitude of talents over the bridge as well and lives close to Park Slope. But honestly, my first impulse would have been to move as far away as possible. It's hard to be surrounded by that much greatness. It makes you allergic to failure. Sans epi-pen.

The reality is that I ended up in New York due to my ex-husband and his job. And maybe getting this fact out in the open is the best way to deal with the big "D." I wish he was staring down at the sashimi menu rather than inquisitively studying my face and cleavage.

"My ex-husband. He got a job here so we moved here after Connecticut."

"So you've been married before? Wow ... divorce ... how did that happen?"

I'm not really itching to share my whole marriage saga with the first-date-of-the-rest-of-my-life, especially not the part where I talk about how he was so in love with his career that he essentially was having an affair with his blackberry. My ex-husband, Adam, trying to make partner, spent more time at the office than he did at home, choosing contracts over contact; the job over me. Over time, it became clear that we had differing views on money, despite what he led me to believe before we walked down the aisle. I wanted to be comfortable. Adam, who came from a wealthy New York family, worked to not only keep up with the Joneses, but to pass them in owning all the good electronic toys and going on the most exclusive vacations. You could say that we had a lack of shared goals.

I glance at the laminated picture of sushi standing upright on the table, teaching customers the visual difference between the toro and maguro tuna rolls.

"Oh, you know," I shrug, "50% of the population gets it wrong the first time."

"Huh … 50%. I didn't realize the number was that high."

"I think it's over 50%, actually," I say. "But luckily seventh marriages go the distance about 90% of the time."

"Those are good odds for the married-seven-times set. I wonder how polygamy rolls into that statistic. I mean, if your seventh marriage is at the same time as your other six," he points out.

"I'm guessing you were never married before?" I ask.

"Nope, I love a good first date, but I've never met the right person."

I plaster a smile back on my face and take a deep breath. I wonder if it's time yet to take a break in the small talk and see what sort of maki constitutes hip in Soho. It has been so long since I've eaten in a restaurant. But Rob Zuckerman has more questions and apparently, a non-grumbling stomach.

"Where do you live in the city? Wait, you're in the city, right? Not over the bridge or anything," he jokes.

"I'm in Murray Hill."

"Do you have any roommates?" Rob asks.

"Actually, it's a studio. It's small, but it's a great neighborhood, all things considered. I mean, I'm lucky I found it. And it's close to my best friend so I can walk to her place. Where are you?"

"Gramercy Park," he tells me.

My old neighborhood, and still Adam's neighborhood. My ex-husband bought me out of my share of our condo which was how I was able to take off this year from my old job designing pamphlets for the New York City Library. My intention was to find another job, but that hasn't happened and savings are dwindling down, it seems more and more likely that I'll return to making materials to accompany exhibits. I'm lucky I had the year to sit in my sweatpants and try out every self-help suggestion Oprah passed my way.

"That's a great neighborhood," I offer.

"I'm on the board at my co-op. It is crazy how many people want to move into our building. I feel like my life is one long series of making rejection phone calls. Seriously, there are people applying who have kids. And pets!"

I smile wanly again, wondering if I would make the cut in his building. Job-less, unmarried me. At least Adam was too busy with work to ever make a baby with me. And I have my allergy to cats going for me.

"So, Rachel, what do you want to get?" he asks, even though we still haven't opened the menu.

I throw open the cover and quickly scan my choices. I am hungry for everything. I want to taste their teriyaki sauce and see how they've worked yuzu into a salad dressing and sample their tempura batter. I want to sit up at the sushi bar and chat with the chef about different fillets of raw fish. And I want to be on a date with a guy who wants to hear the chef's answers too. Still, Rob Zuckerman is nice, and he's obviously smart and successful, and he has a full head of brown hair (one cannot discount that full head of hair). So I close my menu and ask him to suggest a few things since he has obviously been here before.

"Why don't we start with a bowl of edamame and an order of tatsuta-age chicken?"

"I made that this week," I exclaim, excited that he'd pick that off the menu since I was eyeing it. "I'm learning how to cook and it's actually really easy. You just marinate the chicken and then coat it in potato starch before you fry it." I notice that Rob is staring at me as if I've just started reciting the recipe in Japanese. "I can't believe I've ordered it all these years when I could make it at home."

"So, you like to cook?" he asks, quickly recovering from my blinding enthusiasm.

"I love to cook. I just started a few months ago, but it's amazing what you can pick up from cookbooks and few Food Network shows."

"How do you find the time?" Rob asks, motioning to a waitress that we're ready to order some appetizers. "I eat out most nights or order in. I think the only thing in my refrigerator right now is ketchup and a few bottles of water."

I try not to judge since that was my life as well only a year ago. While I miss my dog-eared copy of Zagats and hunting out new restaurants, I am intensely proud of my variations on a stir-fry and the salsa I make from scratch. I blame my lack of cooking knowledge on my mother who unhelpfully taught me that "real women don't scramble eggs."

Women, such as my mother, who bring in a comfortable six-figure salary with their husband might not need to scramble their own eggs, but cooking for myself became a necessity when I studied my credit card bills closely. My year-long vacation from life was going to be cut awfully short unless I quickly learned how to make my own marinara. There were only so many packages of ramen noodles a divorcee could eat.

Rob tells the waitress our appetizer order and I slip in a request for a green tea. We both watch her walk back towards the kitchen, and I pound my brain for a topic of conversation. I had come up with so many good ideas back in my apartment. I wish I could have written them on my hand.

"Actually, I don't even know what you do. You're an artist?" Rob asks.

"Not exactly," I admit. If he didn't run screaming from the admission that I was a divorcee, perhaps he'd be equally as gracious about the fact that I'm currently job-less. "I used to work as a graphic designer for the New York Public Library, and I'll probably return to that job, but I was taking the year to find myself. That sounds very self-helpy."

"It actually sounds sort of nice. Like an extended vacation," Rob admits.

I nod my head, feeling a bit more confident. I write in my blog every night which sort of makes me a writer, right? Saying you're a writer is a very New York thing to say—sort of like how anyone living in Los Angeles can get away with calling themselves an actress, and no one calls their bluff. So I tell Rob that I'm also a writer and sure enough, he just gives a small smile and says, "Have I read anything you've written?"

And I merely deliver the next line every wanna-be New York writer feeds their first date: "Probably not. It's just freelance stuff."

The fact is that I read blogs long before I wrote a blog, and honestly, say what you want to about social media, but if it weren't for blogs, I'd probably still be trapped in my marriage. There's something about finding someone and saying, "me too" to give you the fuel to make a similar change.

I first discovered blogs when I started Googling, "divorce laws in New York City" (always a bad sign when your Google searches include lawyer names and mediation advice.)

I started with the divorce blogs and then worked my way backwards through the sex blogs and Internet-dating blogs until I found a woman who called herself The Dating Diva on a relationship blog titled, "Before You Put on the Little Black Dress."

She offered all sorts of dating advice, analyzing the photographs of first-date outfits that readers sent her and telling women how to know when a guy is lying to them. I never commented or sent in my own questions; I just sat in our apartment every night like a heartbroken voyeur, devouring the words of other women who felt equally unhappy in their relationships.

And then one night, she was answering a question about a boyfriend who never apologized at the end of an argument even though the girlfriend was always forthcoming in admitting to her own foibles.

The Dating Diva wrote:

You can't change someone else, cookie. You can only change yourself or the way it affects you. And if you can't honestly change the way it affects you because you're going with your natural reaction to his lack of contrition, you need to get yourself out of that relationship. You're never going to be happy with who he is as a person, and shoving a square peg into a round hole has never had the good makings for stable furniture that will stand the test of time.

When I read her words and applied them to my life, I ended up sitting at the computer and sobbing, knowing bone-deep what I had to do.

I closed the Dating Diva's blog and sat there for several hours until Adam got home, thinking about whether or not our relationship could be fixed. I couldn't change his behavior and make him leave his office in order to spend more time with me, and I couldn't get past my loneliness and anger. It was better for both of us, I decided, to go our separate ways than for me to spend the next twenty years seething through every empty evening and for him to resent me.

The cockroach incident came a week after reading the Dating Diva's advice, which was the end of the end.

And soon after that, I started my own blog a few weeks after moving into my new apartment, a whim one night where I signed up for a free blogging account and started posting tales of all the things I was doing to try to fill my new life. I talked about trying to mooch free yoga classes from nearby gyms and self-help books I checked out of the library.

Learning how to cook finally gave me something to write about, because I had been itching to find a direction for my blog. I didn't want to write solely about my divorce because frankly, I thought about it twenty-four hours a day and could use a little break from obsessing. I couldn't write about my job because I no longer had one. I had stopped going to museums and shows because ironically, I could no longer afford them even if I had all the time in the world to attend them so a blog about Manhattan itself was out too.

The name of my blog was already *Life from Scratch*, and food became a natural extension. It turned out that writing about food was the perfect jumping board to discussing the rest of my life too. If nothing interesting was happening, I could talk about how I learned to roast potatoes (the trick: put the cubed potatoes in a bag; splash in the olive oil, salt, rosemary, and garlic powder; and then shake to coat each potato evenly.) But I could also write about the night my best friend Arianna gave birth to her baby, Beckett, or muse about the idea of coloring my hair, and it all fit into the cozy space I created for myself, governed by my own rules.

After being so silent through the end of my marriage—I was constantly biting my tongue when I was with Adam—and with no one to talk to in the apartment when he was at work, starting the blog was like the first breath of air after breaking the water's surface while swimming. The words came out fast and furious; I had finally found my voice again, that old friend who had disappeared over the years from disuse.

Blogging can seem a little self-indulgent; foisting your free therapy on everyone else in the world. But some of us can't afford a vacation from life *and* therapy, so free isn't half bad. Plus, the night I received my first comment was like finding life on Mars. I was this tiny voice yelling from my apartment in New York City, and someone actually *heard* me. And took the time to tell me so.

The waitress brings us our bowl of edamame, and Rob opens one shell and pops the peas into his mouth. "What do you do?" I question.

"I'm a lawyer—business law."

You know how your hair sometimes rises on your arms like a vestigial connection to cats on high alert? That was the reaction I had when Rob mentioned his job. The tiny bubble of hope I had been floating on since I first got his phone call popped somewhere over the table, and I came tumbling down into the bowl of steamed edamame.

I am *not* going to date Adam Goldman, the extended remix version, because I am never going to date another lawyer. Or a hedge fund manager—not only because they seemed to work long hours but also because I don't really know what a hedge fund is. I'm not even sure if I'd be a good match for a surgeon who could be unreachable in the operating room for ten hours at a time like my sister.

It took a failed marriage to make me realize that I had had enough of being alone. First, when I was growing up, and my parents were always off at work and then second, with Adam. I didn't need to repeat the cycle a third time.

"You must work a lot of hours," I say, cracking open an edamame.

"Oh my God, I don't get home most nights until eleven. It's murder trying to make partner."

"I bet it is," I mutter under my breath, instantly crossing Rob Zuckerman's name out of my mental palm pilot's address book. *It is also murder*, I wanted to add, *to be the wife of someone trying to make partner. It actually makes you want to commit murder, if you must know.*

"I had to cut a trip short recently to Bali and come home to work on this account," Rob went on. "I planned that trip for four months and only got to spend five hours in Bali before I came home."

I take a deep breath and nudge out of my head all the regret that I am feeling about how this is the person I'll always have to remember as my first date. It is like the Hymen Fairy giving you back your virginity and then wasting it yet again on another partner-track lawyer.

"Why don't you order us some sashimi if the waitress comes before I get back?" I tell him, trying to at least get a good restaurant meal out of this evening if nothing else.

I slide out of my chair and head towards the bathroom, giving Rob a small smile to let him know that all is well, and I'm not about to duck behind a wall and call my best friend mid-date. Except that is exactly what I do.

"I hate you," I hiss into the phone when Arianna answers.

"I hate you too," she responds. "How is it going?"

"Rob Zuckerman is a lawyer trying to make partner."

"Well that was an unfortunate choice of first date. Didn't you ask him what he did when you met him at the bar?"

"It was loud in there," I say. "I couldn't hear anything. And now I'm stuck with Rob Zuckerman being the first post-Adam date I had for the rest of my life."

"You don't have to see him again," Arianna reminded me. I could hear her washing out baby bottles in the background.

"I meant that saying: 'Today is the first day of the rest of your life.' And Rob is my first date since the divorce—the only first date I'll ever have again."

"Until the next one."

"You think I'm going to get married and divorced again?" I admonish.

"No, no, I mean that you'll have other first dates. Sweetie, calm down. Go have some kappa maki and enjoy the night. And then call me when you get home, and we'll talk about how you're never seeing him again."

"I do hate you for pushing me to do this," I say, only half kidding as I bite my lower lip and peek out at Rob Zuckerman testing out his chopsticks and dropping them accidentally on his plate.

"It was time, Rach. It was really time."

I hang up the phone and use the decorative mirror on the wall to make sure that I don't have lipstick on my teeth before returning to the table.

"Rob Zuckerman," I say brightly. "Tell me more about your five hours in Bali."

Life from Scratch

blogging about life one scrambled egg at a time

If Fernand Point, the greatest French chef of all time, wasn't dead, I'd slather him with his beloved butter and just eat him all up.

I had never heard of Fernand Point until I decided to learn how to fry an egg. Which seems like an easy-enough dish, but since I trust myself less than a nearby diner, had never attempted at home. Finances, of course, changed that, since even greasy spoons are a little too greasy, sliding money out of my thinning wallet.

It seems simple enough, right? Crack the egg into a hot pan and watch it sizzle. I always order my eggs over-medium because I can't handle even a speck of the whites uncooked, but I like the yellow part warm and runny. But my homecooked egg quickly turned rubbery except for a centimeter or so around the yolk; the edges were paper thin, clear and crisp. I tried to flip it, and it folded over onto itself as it unstuck from the bottom of the pan; the yolk broke, and I tossed the whole thing in the sink.

I tried this with three more eggs and different things happen: sometimes I broke the yolk as I tried to move it. Sometimes I succeeded in keeping the yolk intact, but had uncooked whites because I had crumpled the whites as I folded it over. Oh, and then I did what I should have done before I cracked a single egg— which was open the damn cookbook and read what Fernand Point wrote a hundred years ago.

Apparently, even Mr. Point knew that the simplest things were the ones that we most commonly botched. Such as cooking an egg. He made each of his apprentices slow down and fry an egg over a candle *after* they butter the pan.

I forgot the love that is butter.

Cooking spray and eggs should never mix. Sigh.

So I started over melting a pat of butter over medium heat, and when it began to foam, I turned down the heat to low and added the egg. Yes, you read that right: I turned down the heat. No sizzle. No pop. If I had been filming a cooking show, everyone would have yawned. The whites slowly, slowly, slowly cooked. And once the whites were set, I let it go a bit longer until the yellow part slowly firmed up. And then I gently flipped it over, and, low and behold, the butter helped it release, and it slid over gracefully like a ballerina sinking down into the swan pose.

Oh, and after the eggs were on the plate I realized that I had no bread in the apartment and was pissed off because you need bread to sop up all of that lovely yolk. They were, even without bread, the best damn eggs I had ever had. Like I said, I love Fernand Point.

Eggs are delicate things. They deserve this much attention, if not more. Oh, and butter is my new best friend.

Chapter Two

Juicing the Lemon

I push my way up the street, against the steady stream of traffic that is walking across the city towards Rockefeller Plaza and the enormous tree. Christmas is the only time of year where New Yorkers slow down and walk like zombie tourists, unable to drag their eyes away from store displays and the siren song of twinkle lights. It drives me crazy when people walk slowly.

A few flakes of snow drift in the air, as if they're unsure whether or not they have permission to land. If I didn't need cake flour this badly as well as have to give Arianna back the purse that I borrowed for my date with Rob Zuckerman, I would never step outside my apartment during prime weekday shopping hours. Within three blocks, my knees are already bruised from getting thwacked by tourists' shopping bags.

I buzz the front desk at Arianna's apartment building and step into the warm lobby, unwrapping my scarf as I make my way across the marble flooring. Her building always smells like too much perfume, as if they have washed the floors in Shalimar, and it's much older than mine. It has a delightfully creepy, Red-rum feel to the place.

Someone has wedged a plastic Santa from a Happy Meal into the ashtray by the elevator bay, and it stares at me with a frozen smile while I wait for the lift beside a mother and her preschool-aged child.

"I ate toilet paper," he whispers to me, apropos of nothing.

"Honestly, Henry!" his mother exclaims, rolling her eyes as if telling a stranger that he has eaten toilet paper is the last straw. She yanks his hand to lead him into the open elevator, and he remains silent the rest of the ride until I get off on Arianna's floor.

The truth is that I want a little boy who eats toilet paper. Food would obviously be better, but I'd take toilet paper if push came to shove.

Arianna is breathtakingly lovely, dressed more for the front row of Stella McCarthy's next runway show rather than an outing to Zabar's on the Upper West Side. Arianna is a finisher for a major fashion designer. She doesn't design anything or cut the patterns, but she does all of the hand-stitching and bead work. The designer's staff is thrilled to have her work out of her apartment rather than give her space in their crowded loft. So she has set up her life to be a full-time mother to Beckett as well as a full-time seamstress. She is currently wearing three inch kitten slides paired with a pair of expensive-looking designer jeans she probably got as a free sample from a friend in the industry. She kisses me on the cheek while she lets me into the apartment, taking her purse out of my hands.

"It's terrible out there," I warn. "Swarms of tourists, all carrying shopping bags. Seriously, every last one of them."

She shrugs a baby Bjorn over her shoulders and loads Beckett into it so he's facing outward, his matching jean-clad legs dangling in front of her. She yanks a stocking cap over his head, blindly tying the strings underneath his chin, which is sticky with drool that he has dragged out of his mouth via his hand. She puts on her own coat—a delicious, soft, moss-green pea coat, hand-sewn for her by one of her designer friends. I spend a lot of time coveting her wardrobe.

"I know Christmas isn't supposed to be a big deal if you're Jewish," I tell her as we step out of her apartment, and she locks her door. "I mean, the biggest thing I have to do that day is order Chinese food. But every single commercial is about what your husband is going to buy you."

"Diamonds," Arianna agrees.

"Or sitting on your Stainmaster carpet and opening Christmas morning gifts with your husband. Or buying a new car with your husband. This whole first-Christmas-after-the-divorce thing is making me very depressed. Television commercials are like downers."

"Imagine how single, Christian people feel," she says, motioning to herself.

"But you have Beckett," I point out. "You're not really alone in the true sense of the word. Like I am," I add dramatically, throwing open the front door of her building and streaming back onto the sidewalk to join the sea of shoppers making a pilgrimage to the subway stop.

"Seriously, you cannot borrow my feeling-sorry-for-myself holiday. You can have Valentine's Day," Arianna offers.

Beckett squeals in agreement and points at the traffic lights. "Let's just walk the four blocks to 7th," I tell her as I wind my scarf around my neck again, the flakes of snow still cautiously testing out the air.

Adam and I meant to have children. At least, we discussed having children before we were married, and it was a base understanding between us. When the time felt right, we would ditch the birth control and have two kids and live happily ever after. But the problem was that the time was never right.

For instance, it turns out to have a child, one has to have sex.

It really makes me cringe to admit this, but Adam and I only had sex a handful of times during the final year of our marriage. Maybe five. First and foremost, he came home so late every night that he practically turned into a stranger; and I couldn't roll around in bed with him as if nothing were wrong.

The other thing is that I started over-thinking whether or not we'd make good parents. I had grown up with parents who were barely around, and it sort of sucked to be their child. My parents never attended dance performances or piano recitals, and they would have missed my high school graduation due to a business trip if I hadn't gotten my favorite teacher to persuade them otherwise. My parents loved me intensely, but I wouldn't have called them *great* parents, and I seemed doomed to repeat their mistakes, since I had no other example to follow.

Plus, Adam and I hit a point where I didn't want to have children with *him*. I didn't want to become what would essentially be a single parent, though it was hard to admit that to my friend, Arianna, who *is* a single parent by choice. But even she'll tell you that if she could have found the right partner, she wouldn't have gone about parenting alone. Still, she has always had a much stronger calling towards parenthood and, as my mother puts it, "grabs life by its balls."

The woman who grabs life by its balls pushes her way down the subway stairs and jiggles herself gracefully through the turnstile, carefully lifting Beckett's legs so they clear the bar. We wait for the train next to a large group of high school students all dragging suitcases behind them.

Arianna shocked the hell out of me three years ago when she asked if I could bring her home from a doctor's appointment, and I ended up meeting her at a fertility clinic. "What is this?" I asked, as if I was living off-the-grid in the wilderness and had never heard of in vitro fertilization.

"I'm doing intrauterine inseminations," she told me. "With donor sperm."

"Why would you do that?" I asked dumbly.

"To get pregnant," she said impatiently, sitting down gingerly on a bench in the clinic lobby, as if she was scared the sperm would swim out of her body on the taxi ride back to her apartment.

"I mean, why are you trying to get pregnant?" I tried again.

"To have a baby, idiot. Listen, we're in our thirties. Your fertility doesn't exist forever. I want to be a parent. If I can do it this way, great. If I have to go about it another way, fine. The only thing I cannot accept is never having a child at all."

Which, like women synchronizing their periods, made me start thinking of the world in terms of babies and fertility too. I spent the next two years helping Arianna conceive and carry a child, while becoming increasingly bitter towards Adam, who was not filling me with his very inexpensive, readily available seed. There I was, watching my friend shell out tens of thousands of dollars to become a mother while I technically could become a mother for free, but didn't know if I'd even make a good one.

After two miscarriages, three fresh IVF transfers, four frozen IVF transfers, several months of daily Lovenox injections, a premature delivery, and a NICU stay, Arianna had Beckett, so named after the author of the most famous Godot of all times. Beckett may have been her own personal Godot, but the delay in his arrival only meant that she had built up more love for him than any one person could possibly need in their lifetime.

We jump off the train at the 79th Street station, dodging the Upper West Side nannies returning their charges from play dates and students coming home from school with oversized packs strapped to their backs like studious camels. 79th Street feels, if possible, ten degrees cooler than the packed sidewalks in Midtown. Of course, Zales has been decorated for Christmas with the requisite boughs of holly hanging over the enormous sign announcing the store's Christmas sale and window displays of heart-shaped sparkling jewelry. Arianna rolls her eyes and Beckett gurgles and slaps the fabric of the baby carrier.

We forgo bagels at H&H, and instead push our way into the throng of shoppers clogging the narrow aisles of Zabar's. We travel up here usually once a month so Arianna can get the pickles she likes and stock up on their cream cheese spreads and coffee beans. We hit the dairy aisle first, dropping containers of Greek yogurt and crème fraiche into our basket.

"Zabar's makes me hungry," Arianna announces as we pass the

smoked fish counter. I cannot think of anything more unappetizing than fish that has been pulverized into a spread.

"Seriously? Smoked fish? What are you, a seventy-year-old man? I understand if you said that back at the cheese counter. Did you see the fresh pasta that was on sale? Tri-color capelletti?"

"Their smoked sable is incredible. Not that I need to spend twenty bucks on smoked fish at the moment, but if they were giving out free samples, I'd stand in line for hours."

"Beckett would love that," I comment.

I duck past a woman reading the label on a jar of lemon curd and make my way toward the baking supplies. We stand in front of the empty space in the baking section, where cake flour would normally be stocked next to the enormous jars of active yeast and the Dutch-milled cocoa.

"Do you think the world is trying to tell me something?" I ask, shifting around bags of cornmeal and gluten-free rice flour.

"What do you mean?" Arianna asked, adding vanilla to her own basket.

"When everything is going wrong—when your husband is choosing the office over you, and you're somewhat newly divorced, and you only have a few more months left in your savings account before you need to go back to designing pamphlets, and every store is not stocking cake flour even though you already went out to New Jersey to retrieve the stupid angel food cake pan you were given for your wedding—do you think that is the universe telling you what you should expect after you die? Is this forewarning that I am heading to hell?"

"Oh, sweetie, of course you're going to hell. That's where all self-pitying drama queens go." Only Arianna can get away with teasing me while I'm down. She holds up a bag of whole wheat flour, and I shake my head.

"I can't use that to make my angel food cake. It has to be cake flour."

"So drop the idea of the cake, and you'll make it some other time."

"What other time?" I admonish. "I've had the pan for months now, and I still haven't used it. It's mocking me. It's whispering to me every night that while I may have gotten quite good at flipping over fried eggs, I will never master the art of baking."

Cake flour—not fancy cream cheese spreads—was the *whole point* of this trek to the Upper West Side.

A few weeks into learning how to cook, I took the train out to New Jersey with two empty, rolling suitcases, and I went down into my parent's basement to retrieve all of my unused wedding gifts—gifts to celebrate my now-defunct marriage.

When Adam and I were engaged, I registered for cookware like all good brides in New York, even though I didn't know how to use a roasting pan or colander. I mean, how do you admit that fact to friends and family who are so keen to buy new brides cookware? It's practically written in the Wedding Bible: Thou shall buy brides either cookware or lingerie for their shower.

So I unwrapped box after box of beautiful William Sonoma silver pots and pans and Le Creuset enamel and silicone spatula bouquets and properly ooohed and aaahed about each gift, all the while knowing that they probably would never be used. I would have loved to have thrown Martha Stewart-inspired dinner parties with linens matching the centerpieces, but emptying a pre-cooked chicken purchased in Chelsea Market into a roasting pan seems like cheating. And though Martha went to jail for some type of stock debacle, I could not see her being down with that type of cheating and sullying her good housekeeping name.

I considered just admitting that the entire idea of learning my way around the kitchen filled me with exhaustion and ask instead for other gifts—maybe lifetime memberships to various city museums or a subscription to the American Ballet Theatre. But my non-cooking mother encouraged me to register for the cookware because people loved to buy it, imagining the couple hunkering down to some warm soup in the middle of their first winter together. She also helped me repack it in boxes after the guests departed and labeled the outside of each William Sonoma box with a black sharpie. My mother is, if nothing else, practical.

She took all the boxes back to her New Jersey basement under the guise that we shouldn't use up precious New York storage space on wedding items. I think my mother was a tad fearful that I might ignore all the beliefs she drilled in my head as a teenager if I had access to those gorgeous pots and pans in my kitchen.

According to my mother, suggesting that women cook dinner

rather than order in from a local restaurant is the first step in returning all of the liberties women have obtained in the last fifty years. I might as well declare myself Amish and go sew my own clothing and can green beans from my garden. "You don't knit your own sweaters, Rachel," my mother was fond of saying. "So why do you want to cook your own meals? Let Diane Von Furstenberg make your tops and let Hunan Chow make your dinner. You have more important things to do than housework, and it's just food."

Except that, unlike her, in the few months leading up to the trek out to New Jersey to pick up my kitchenware, I really didn't have more important things to do.

It's not like Adam and I literally *never* ate a meal at home. We had cereal for breakfast, and I was fantastic at boiling up ramen noodles. But once I crossed the threshold of three or more ingredients, once the directions weren't written on the outside of a package, I sort of tossed the idea of preparing the meal back on the figurative shelf.

Through most of our marriage, I didn't think Adam cared. He liked my mother's spirit and complimented her when she ordered Thanksgiving dinner from his favorite caterer. And *he* certainly wasn't doing any cooking since he rarely got home before 11 p.m. But it was a throwaway thought he spat out during one of our final conversations while we waited for our lawyers to divvy up our possessions that gave me pause.

"You've never been supportive," he said.

I couldn't think of a way I could have been *more* supportive of his work at the office unless I'd offered to deliver his subpoenas. So that left showing support of him at home, which conjured up images of wifely duties I should have been performing instead of watching television. Of meals unprepared and shirts un-ironed and all of the things my mother had drilled into my head *not* to do for a man.

It's not as if his own socialite mother ever slowed down from her busy schedule to toss a few steaks onto the grill for Adam's family so I'm not sure where the domestic desires stemmed—certainly not from childhood. But learning to cook became a way to recreate myself— something I had never done before. I'd defy my mother's brainwashing and Adam's unspoken accusations about not being homey enough with one, single act.

So New Jersey was where my cookware rested until several months following my divorce, when I went to collect it so I could scramble my own damn eggs.

After we had coffee and bagels, my mother asked why I had brought two deflated suitcases with me. There was a fearful tone to her voice, as if she was bracing herself for me to request moving back into my childhood bedroom.

"I'm just going to take back some of my old wedding gifts to New York. The stuff in the basement," I said.

On second thought, moving back into my bedroom seemed more sane. My mother had been holding her breath for several weeks as I talked about redefining myself with a new career. I think she secretly hoped that I would announce that it was law school for me after all.

"Are you talking about the cookware?" my mother questioned. "Your father and I were talking about donating that stuff. Give it to a family who needs it."

"*I* need it," I told her.

"I really don't understand why you're bothering with that." She couldn't even bring herself to call it *cooking*. She left dishes in the sink where my father would get to them later. It was one of the tradeoffs between his love of the earth as an environmental lawyer and her insistence on rejecting any tasks deemed "housework" as an escapee from the 1950s and overworked immigration lawyer. If they weren't going to choke the landfills with paper plates and plastic forks, Dad was going to have to take care of the dishes. My mother did not touch dish soap.

"I'm bothering with it because I can't afford to eat out every night anymore," I explained as I started following her towards her office.

I wanted to add something snide like, "I'm not a big fancy lawyer like you," except I knew that would only take us into a discussion on how I could *be* a big fancy lawyer like her if I only applied myself. In her world, 35-years-old was not too old to return to the classroom and get a new degree.

I went into the basement by myself and filled my bags with salad spinners and frying pans and tiny saucier pots. I left behind the tagine, knowing that certain cookware was out of my element. At last minute, I threw a tube pan into the mix—an angel food cake pan that came with a recipe card called The Anniversary Cake, to be eaten on the first anniversary. I crumpled up the card and tucked the bakeware into my bag.

The Cuisinart and the standing mixer were too bulky and heavy to fit in the bags. But I wanted them. I stomped back upstairs, dragging one of my suitcases behind me. I found my father in the kitchen at the

3 3 3 3 3 3

3 3 3 3

sink, scrubbing a dish before he turned the water back on.

"Any chance you could drive me back into the city?" I wheezed. I motioned to the suitcase. "I have a lot of stuff I want to bring back."

"Oh, cupcake, I'm working on a brief right now."

"It's Saturday," I pointed out. "You're washing dishes."

"After this, I mean. I'm working on a brief this afternoon and then your mother and I are going out with the Perlmans."

Just as I didn't know how to say it to Adam, I didn't know how to remind my father that I am just as important as a brief. That I'm part of that environment he protects—a living, breathing human. Instead I accepted his apologetic shoulder shrug and walked through the house to find my mother. She was sitting in front of the computer, reading the *New York Times* both on the screen and in paper form simultaneously.

"You have to go online to see the comments," she explained.

"Why not read it all online?" I asked.

"I can't stand the computer. I need to hold my newspaper. Smell the news."

"You would think Dad would have convinced you to cancel your subscription by now," I said. "Chopping down trees. Bad for the environment."

"I recycle," she insisted. "Are you heading out, pumpkin?"

"Actually, I was going to ask you to drive me into the city. I have so much stuff to take back and I can't really fit it all into the bags. It's really heavy."

"I can't, honey. After I finish the *Times*, I'm getting back to work."

"And then you have the Perlmans," I finished for her.

"Right, the Perlmans," she agreed, relieved that I wasn't pushing the issue.

"Can I borrow your car?" I finally pleaded. "I'll drive into the city and then drive back and take the train back in."

"I don't see why not," my mother told me. "As long as you're back before we leave for the Perlmans." She beamed at me as if she was so proud of my self-sufficiency. One needed to be self-sufficient when surrounded by those who treasured paper over people.

That was months ago, but I hadn't been brave enough to attempt angel food cake until recently. And, of course, once I decided to try making it, cake flour disappeared off of every shelf in New York

City. This was not the first store I had traveled to in search of baking ingredients.

I lean against the wall and take out my phone, opening Twitter so I can complain about Zabar's lack of flour choices.

"I think it is merely a strange coincidence, this city-wide disappearance of cake flour," Arianna admits, nuzzling the top of Beckett's head. He twists around to try to grab the ends of her honey-colored hair.

"Blech!" he exclaims in Beckettese.

"I couldn't agree more," I tell him, hitting send.

We walk back out into the damp, cold afternoon, which is slowly bleeding into evening. I can see my breath in the air, and Arianna fusses with Beckett's hat, tying the strings underneath his chin again. He swings his little legs against her stomach as he hangs from his carrier. They're always together. A unit.

Even though he was created with sperm that came from an anonymous donor, it seems as if all of Beckett's features come straight from Arianna. Her narrow, blue eyes; her stick-straight blond hair that looks like it benefited from some obscure Japanese straightening treatment; and her thin, straight nose have all shown up in miniature on Beckett. They share the same smile down to matching dimples on their left cheek.

"Oh, I forgot to tell you. I nominated you for a blogging award," she says as we walk down the subway steps, trying hard not to knock our bulging shopping bags into the other riders.

Arianna knows how much the blog has grown on me, how much pride I take in the relationships I've built through the site or the comments I get on my posts. I turn my head slightly so she can't see my huge, slightly-embarrassed grin.

"Er . . . what sort of a blogging award?"

"I don't know. It's called 'the Bloscars.' I saw a post about it on one of the fashion blogs I read. I nominated you in the food category."

"Well, there's no way I can win," I tell her. "I mean, my blog is about frying eggs, not making soufflés. Probably one of those big-name bloggers will win. *Pioneer Woman Cooks* or *Smitten Kitchen*. People who can really cook and have a million readers."

"You have a million readers," Arianna insists.

"I have like twenty readers. Maybe thirty."

"How do you know?" Arianna says.

"Comments! I get twenty to thirty comments on a post."

"Maybe you have more people reading and not commenting. Haven't you ever read a blog and not commented?"

Er . . . like *The Dating Diva*? But that was because I thought I had nothing to say. Or I thought I had a lot to say and had no clue how to say it. I hadn't found my voice again; but now that I have, I expect that everyone who reads me probably comments at least once.

"Anyway, Rachel, you have *loyal* readers. They love that you share all the stuff about your divorce. And love life," she hurriedly adds.

"One date with Rob Zuckerman does not constitute a love life," I sigh, stepping onto the subway platform, bypassing a woman mumbling to herself.

"Give it time," Arianna promises.

That night, I Google the Bloscars and immediately see hundreds of thousands of hits including the main site. I scroll through the categories and see Arianna's nomination for my site, under Food Bloggers. Seeing my blog name makes my heart start pounding, and I cover my mouth to hide my smile even though I'm alone in the apartment.

There is a small box next to her nomination that you can check in order to show your agreement with the nomination—the point, of course, is to help the award-givers separate the wheat from the chaff. Blogs that receive more nominations probably deserve a second look. After I click it, it informs me that I am the sixteenth person to nominate the site. There is no additional information on who the other fifteen are or where they came from.

I am about to shoot off an email to Arianna when someone knocks on the door. I instantly know it is my brother, Ethan. He is the only person I know who would rather hang around outside waiting for someone to give him access inside rather than use the buzzer. It all goes back to his love of shocking me.

I open the door, and God bless the asshole, he has arrived with a bag of cake flour. "You bitched about it on Twitter that you couldn't find any. I brought this one over from Brooklyn." I hug him, crushing the flour against his shirt.

"My angel food cake!" I exclaim, taking the bag out of his hands. He shrugs his shoulders and starts rummaging through my refrigerator for leftovers. No one in my family can cook.

These are the things you should probably know about my brother.

He is thirty-two going on sixteen. He has the self-righteous indignation of a teenager coupled with the irresponsibility of a first-year, pot-saturated college student. And he is brilliant—smarter than my brain-surgeon sister and lawyer parents combined.

He is, as these types always are, redeemed by his quick, wide smile which divulges the sweetness and thoughtfulness with which he conducts our relationship. Take, for instance, the time he returned to my old apartment to pick up all of my books when I didn't feel like facing Adam. He carried those boxes up and down three flights of stairs for seventeen consecutive trips. That is love; that is redemption.

For the time being, he is a photographer. I say, "for the time being," because this career was preceded by stints as a carpenter, a first-month medical student, a dishwasher, doorman, and amusement-park mascot, and it will be followed by something equally unusual such as being someone's butler. He's smart, but he's bored easily and doesn't think it is remarkable that he can add seven-digit figures in his head instantaneously. I think he gives my mother more stress than I do. At least they can write me off as a talentless failure; with Ethan, they need to contend with wasted brilliance.

Just to be clear, when I say "photographer," I mean that he is wholly unpaid and working on a coffeetable book featuring photos he's taking at Starbucks and Mudtrucks in Manhattan. *A coffeetable book about coffee spilled on tables.* Which means that until it sells—which it probably won't—he never has any money. Our parents cut him off a long time ago. He doesn't ask me for cash because he knows I'm trying to eke out my savings to last for a year. Instead he bothers our sister for rent money and comes over to my apartment to raid my refrigerator.

Feeding Ethan is the closest thing I have to a stint in mothering.

"I have some salsa and chips. I made the salsa myself," I tell him, taking the chips off the top of the refrigerator.

"Is it any good?" he asks, bringing the bowl towards his face to sniff at the tomatoes.

"No, Ethan, it's terrible, so I saved it and offered it to you."

"I had an idea today. Do you know what you need?" Ethan asks me. "You need to have a dinner party. You've never had a dinner party."

"Adam and I had dinner parties," I say defensively.

"You had other couples over and ordered in from somewhere. It's not the same thing. Look at all the things you can make now. Eggs.

You could make fried eggs for everyone. Or salsa. You need to socialize. You're spending too much time communicating with people online. People you can't see. People who may actually be a sixty-year-old man in Kansas pretending to be a thirty-something cook in Vermont."

"I like my online friends," I insist.

"I know you hate it when people tell you what you need to do, but seriously, you need to socialize and show off your newfound skill to people who have the ability to taste your creations. Everyone will drink a lot and we'll wreck your apartment and give you tons of great ideas for things you can do with your life other than graphic design. Such as being a traffic cop. I saw a traffic cop today, and I was thinking about how you would be great at that."

"Who would I invite? Sarah?"

"Um … no … not Sarah. Because that means she'll bring Richard. The idea is to socialize, not let Richard put everyone to sleep. I swear, the only thing more boring than one surgeon is a married pair of surgeons."

The reality is that beyond my siblings, I really have only one person I consider a good friend, and that's Arianna. There are acquaintances here and there, but since I left Adam, and since I left work, most of the people we mutually knew or who I saw in the office have fallen away. I'd be hard-pressed to come up with a guest list larger than "one."

"Don't worry about that. I'll invite a few friends, and you could invite Arianna. We can call the dinner: "The Reinvention of Rachel Goldman Who Should Go Back To Calling Herself Rachel Katz But Is Still Using Her Ex-Husband's Last Name."

"I'm not ready to change my name." He stares at my left hand, and I curl it under the table protectively. "I'm almost ready to take off my ring. Almost. I swear. Seriously, it's too much change in one year."

"You know my thoughts on that," he says. He slides off his chair and seals the chip bag, returning the half-eaten salsa with chip crumbs back to the refrigerator.

"All right, Ethan. You can invite two people. Two. And they can't bring more people. I don't have room in the apartment."

"I'll invite two. And you invite Arianna."

He wiggles his eyebrows as he says this, and disappears out my front door, just as unannounced as he came.

Life from Scratch

blogging about life one scrambled egg at a time

This post is brought to you by the word of the day: substitution. I'm not just talking about out-with-the-old-and-in-with-the-new. Bumping out the past-the-expiration-date marriage for some new produce. I am talking about making cooking work in Manhattan when you are at the mercy of the local bodega.

Okay, so I'm not exactly at the mercy of the local bodega if I would get my ass on the subway and trek down to Whole Foods or Fairway. But since I tend to stay close to home, I poked around on the Internet to see if there were things you could substitute if the local market was missing ingredients.

For instance, if, by chance, you needed a shallot and you went to two markets before giving up, you could use the white part of 6 or so scallions to equal one shallot. Gelatin can be used in place of agar-agar. Lime juice and a little lime zest can be used in a pinch in exchange for lemongrass. A tablespoon of raw ginger can be converted into a 1/8th tsp of powdered ginger. Plain yogurt can stand in place—cup for cup—for buttermilk or sour cream.

And then there are the things that cannot be substituted no matter how lazy you feel about getting on the subway. You can't exchange a green pepper for a red pepper. Turmeric can turn something yellow, but it won't have the taste of saffron. The correct bean may actually matter depending on the dish. I mean, can you imagine lima beans in chili?

I know that substitutions may not taste exactly the same as the original recipe. It may, for instance, take some time for the new flavor to grow on you. You may have to let go of some of your expectations. Wait . . . we were talking about food . . . right?

Chapter Three

Melting the Butter

I wake up and realize that it is time to ditch the ring. It hadn't been the right time for over nine months, and I have made up every possible excuse to keep the absolutely perfectly symmetrical diamond-and-platinum combination on my finger. It was like a protective cloak. Removing it would make me be truly alone.

As long as it was firmly below my knuckle, the average person passing me on the street would think I was married; that someone would miss me if I didn't come home that night. My brother thinks that I continue to wear it because I can't bear the thought of owning such an exquisite diamond and not having everyone know it.

But I swear, I've never even liked diamonds. I'm a color girl. I like peridots and garnets and deep-blue sapphires. Clear gemstones aren't my thing. But neither is appearing single.

And if I'm honest, the ring is the final tangible daily reminder I have to Adam. Sometimes I find myself looking down on it during the day, and I'll suddenly remember, "I was married." It really happened. It wasn't just a dream. And as much as it leaves me gutted every time it catches my eye, and I think about him, it also privately makes me smile to think about what the ring used to mean.

But on the topic of honesty, nine months is also long enough to wear the final reminder of my marriage.

If I am taking off the ring, I am definitely going to get something sparkly and beautiful as its replacement. Which means heading to the Mecca of beautiful jewelry: Harry Winston.

Just to look. Just for ideas.

Arianna insists that we make a day of it, get tea and scones at the Plaza and try on shoes at Manolo Blahnik. She wants to get us makeovers at M.A.C. and see the new line of purses at Prada. And just to appease me and get me to let her window shop at all of the clothing stores, she promises to swing by the Crate and Barrel so I can covet kitchen equipment that wouldn't fit in my apartment anyway. In other words, spend the day pretending that we have scads of nonexistent money.

Which is not quite as nice as being rich, but is, at least, free.

By the time we get to Harry Winston, I'm exhausted from both dodging the real shoppers returning unwanted Christmas presents and upper class tourists alike. My face feels stiff from the powder Billé at M.A.C. (pronounced, of course, as Billy, though his name tag was accent aigued) promised made me look at least five years younger. I am finished with pretending to be rich for the day. It's a nice world to visit, but I wouldn't want to live on Madison Avenue. Still, we are at Harry Winston, the point of the entire trip to Midtown, so we move quietly amongst the cases, peeking at the glittering jewelry.

"This is me," I whisper, pointing towards a cushion-cut ruby ring. The band and prongs are coated in tiny diamonds. "That's the sort of thing I want to get."

"How much do you think it costs?" Arianna whispers back, her blond hair swinging in front of her shoulder. She has dressed up for the occasion in some Stella McCartney pants that she got as a gift in exchange for some work she did on her collection. They're wide-legged trousers that almost drag on the floor behind her ballet flats. Despite the fact that at least Arianna is dressed fashionably; the woman at the end of the counter, speaking to a customer, glances over at us and flashes a tight smile that says, *I know you won't be purchasing anything today so I'll take my time putting thin ankle over thin ankle to get over to you, gawkers.*

"Five figures. At least. I'm not going to get it," I tell her, as if this were ever a possibility. "I'm just saying—that's the type of ring I want to get."

We move from case to case, and I pause in front of the engagement rings and wedding bands. I can't help it; it's like watching a car accident. There is a woman paused at the case, her sleek chestnut brown hair reflecting the store's light. She smiles at me shyly.

"I think I want to try on this one," she tells the man behind the case. I lean in to examine a pink diamond ring flanked on either side by perfectly cut clear diamonds. The man takes out her ring and slips it onto her perfectly manicured hands.

The woman makes me look down at my engagement ring for a final glance. I'm going to miss it—not the diamond or the metal, but how Adam put it on my hand, how it looked sitting next to the sink when I came out of the shower, how I noticed it and thought about Adam one million times each day. And how that will no longer be the case.

"Are you looking for something?" the man asks, politely splitting his attention between the dazzling woman and my frumpy self.

"A ring," Arianna tells him as she flits past. She is in her element, surrounded by pretty things without any pressure to buy. Arianna is a serial looker.

"Are you getting married?" the man asks, glancing down at the case between us. "If you give me a moment, I can help you find what you're looking for."

The other shopper beams at me, a sister-in-arms, a fellow pre-wife. She gives me that look that expectant mothers exchange with one another, brides who bump into each other as they examine the same Vera Wang knock-offs at Filenes. *We're on this crazy ride together, and isn't it better to finally be on this crazy ride than be one of those poor people still waiting outside the ride in line?*

I mumble something about coming back after lunch and drag Arianna away from a case containing a Padparadscha sapphire-drop necklace. "I think I once saw that on Gwyneth Paltrow's neck in *People* magazine," she says as we spill out onto the street.

"Harry Winston sucks," I tell her as I start leading us to the subway so we can go south to more realistic jewelry environs. "Soon-to-be-engaged people suck and people who are happy suck the most."

"Agreed," Arianna says simply. "Unless you get engaged one day. Or you're me. We are the exception to the rule."

"Of course," I tell her.

We head straight to Me&Ro, simply because I've coveted their jewelry in the past. It seems like a good starting point and end point. It's the type of store I'd always begged Adam to duck in just for a minute and peruse the cases on our way to somewhere else. He'd stand by the doorway, scarf in hand, letting me browse while he read messages on his blackberry. If Holly Golightly had her Tiffanys, I had my Me&Ro, the sort of store where peace reigned, yoga was probably performed in a back room, and workers greeted each other with an earnest "*Namaste.*"

And yet, I not only never had breakfast there (to be fair, since the store didn't even open until 11 a.m., it didn't really seem like a breakfast-y sort of spot), but Adam had never bought me a piece of their jewelry as a gift. A thank-you-for-being-my-wife sort of gift. Or a birthday gift. Or an I'm-sorry-that-I-missed-your-work-function-yet-again-because-I-was-working-really-late gift.

It wasn't even about Me&Ro or jewelry at all, but the fact that we went from thinking-about-you moments to forgot-you-existed-at-all. When we first started dating, he noticed everything about me. He knew more about me than I even knew about me, remembering what I wore on certain dates or which book I read on which trip. But while I could still rattle off what he ordered at each restaurant, which tie he liked with which suit, the movie he wanted to see after glimpsing it on a coming attractions kiosk, he stopped noticing me. He stopped hearing what I was saying and filing it away for later use to show me that he thought about me even when I wasn't around.

Maybe he needed me to spell it out for him, have Arianna drop the hint directly before an anniversary, but it felt like it didn't count if you needed to tell the person outright. He should have been attuned to that sort of thing, looking out for dropped clues into what would make me happy, just as I was always trying to read his mind and do little things for him.

Instead, since he always had his nose buried close to his blackberry screen, I'm not sure he could have even named this store if someone put a gun to his head. I don't know if he could have named my favorite cereal (Special K) or the book I had read at least 12 times (*Jane Eyre*) or the brand of lipstick I used (always Bobbi Brown). I knew every detail about him: his choice of after shave (Gillette, picked up at Duane Reade), his favorite piece of sushi (unagi), which turnstile he always used at the 6th and 23rd subway stop (the one all the way to the left).

Which only makes the store more enticing as the place to replace my wedding band. Toss out the old, bring in the new. Be good to myself. Arianna is a patient shopper, even when she's paying a babysitter at home $15 per hour to entertain Beckett with fuzzy toys. She points out idea after idea in the case. A ring covered in Tibetan writing, one that looks like a skull with ruby eyes, a set of three, hammered, stackable rings.

"Have you ever considered online dating?" Arianna asks.

"Not exactly," I say, not wanting to offend in case she's thinking about searching for a husband herself online.

"I've actually been on a few dates through Datey.com, and they were all really good."

"Then why aren't you dating those men anymore?"

Arianna chooses to ignore this question and instead reads a tiny card propped up next to a bracelet. "You could try it. You can set up an account for free and wait for someone to contact you and go on one date before you write it off."

My eye catches on a thick cuff ring, etched with flowers and leaves and tiny designs.

"This one is beautiful," I breathe.

And just like that, Arianna hears the love in my voice and drops all other suggestions—jewelry or online dating—coming behind me to agree that it is not only love at first sight, but it is love within the first eight minutes of stepping into a store, and therefore, it is also fate that this ring and my hand be joined.

"You just know, you just know," she murmurs, like a sorcerer testing out a potion.

A woman who could have been a dead-ringer for Sandra Bullock unlocks the case and pulls out the ring for me. I slip off my wedding ring, taking my time twisting it over my swollen knuckle. I've taken it on and off before, but there is something about this time that feels momentous, as if I'm about to set it on fire or toss it into the sea, rather than place it in my pocket.

"Do you know your size?" she asks politely.

"I don't," I admit, extending my ring finger so she can slip on the cuff.

"Rach," Arianna admonishes, "you can't wear it on that finger."

"Why not?" I ask, completely taken aback by this thought. Wasn't the entire point to this outing to get rid of the wedding band?

"Get rid of it, not replace it," Arianna corrects. "You can't wear another ring on *that* finger."

I know why not. Because everyone who only does a quick glance will think I'm taken, and I'd never have a stranger propose a date when we bump into each other in the produce department at the food store. I would look married. And maybe that *Why not?* is my *why*. Why I am willing to finally take off my wedding band—because I am merely slipping on something else in its place. Having something there means I can keep the memories even if the original ring and the husband who gave it to me aren't there anymore.

"Absolutely not," Arianna tells me.

"Then where will I wear it?"

"Your middle finger. It will double as a big fuck you to Adam." Arianna explains to the sales woman, "My friend got divorced this year."

"That is so sad," the woman says in a completely unconvincing voice.

"It *is* sad," Arianna corrects in a more believable tone. "And she is finally getting rid of her wedding ring. So don't you think she should wear the cuff on her middle finger? Rings on a middle finger are bad-ass."

"I'm not really that bad-ass," I remind her.

"This will *make* you bad-ass. Please, Rach. Not the ring finger."

There is a plea in her voice, one that reminds me that she has been the listener on the other end of the phone all the times that I've called her crying in the middle of the night. She has lugged over Beckett and brought cookies and camped out on my floor.

She has given me for years what Adam couldn't even muster giving me for minutes at a time—her attention, her ear, her sympathy. She advises me not out of cruelty, but because she will be the one on the other end of the line when I call her a few days from now, crying because the new ring still reminds me of the old ring. I extend my middle finger towards the woman and hope that because it is not pointing upward, it is not offensive.

Sandra Bullock's stunt-double measures my finger with a ring of sample sizes and finally picks out the proper copy of the paisley-printed cuff to slip onto my hand. I stare at the exquisite cuff, just slightly right of the puffy line left behind by my old ring. And I choke on my words, telling her how much I love it. That I'm going to wear it home.

I should sell my wedding ring but I can't bear to do it. So I tuck my wedding ring into the back of my underwear drawer. I'm aware that the back of a drawer isn't the best place for a diamond ring valued at several thousand dollars, but it seems safer—both fiscally and emotionally—than lumping it in with the other pieces of jewelry that I keep in my night table. I won't have to ever see it again unless I run out of good underwear and need to scoop a few pairs of period-flecked panties from the back of the drawer.

I sit down at the computer, reading first through a few emails. My brother has secured two friends to come to my place for dinner and asks if I've broached the topic yet with Arianna. Comments have come in on a recent post on my blog about the best way to de-skin butternut squash—I didn't know this back when I mentioned that I needed to prep the squash for a soup, but apparently there is a long-standing peel-first-or-roast-first debate. An online friend has sent a recipe-exchange chain-letter email.

I minimize my email and open another tab and take a deep breath. I Google Arianna's suggested online dating site, and the screen is immediately filled with a carousel of happy couple photographs. Everyone has perfect teeth and perfect skin and perfect happiness contained in a rotating 4x6 image. The newly-formed couples are playing tennis, horseback riding, and enjoying dinner in front of a fireplace. Quotes from happy customers run down the right side of the screen:

Thank you, Datey.com, for helping me find Dave. He's one in a million, and so are you.

Datey.com made dating easy. And now my fiancé and I are getting married in Vail!

I write my own premature "thank you" inside my head:

Datey.com, thanks for giving me something to do with my Saturday nights beyond crying over my ex-husband and eating raw cookie dough.

I try to conjure up a good attitude and click on a button labeled "Getting Started." I create an account and jot down my password on a sticky note, and then I start going through the pages and pages of questions aimed at helping me find that Special Someone.

Name? This is easy. I am Rachel Goldman. I pause for a moment. Maybe I should write Rachel *Katz* even though I haven't changed my name back yet? Maybe I should change my name back before I fill this out? I shake my head; I can probably change my profile later, just as I updated my wedding ring this afternoon. I delete and restore my married surname several more times before moving on.

Birthday? February 17, 1974.

Location? New York City.

Religious Affiliation? Jewish. Emphasis on the "ish."

Status? It takes me a moment to understand the question, and it isn't until my cursor hovers over the drop-down menu that I understand. *Never married. Separated. Divorced. Looking for friendship. Looking for a relationship. Don't know.*

Don't know? How could you not know what your past relationship history held? Had you been married or not? What were the possible other options? That you might be separated today, maybe to be divorced by the time someone reads your profile? And who the hell comes to a dating site looking for *friends?*

I start to make my way through the various questions. What do I like to do? I like to cook, write, read . . . but these acts seem a bit too tame, too boring. No one is going to jump on a profile that essentially states that I like to live my life in solitude, like a Walt Whitman poem. I look around the apartment for inspiration.

It is easier to say what I *don't* like to do: sit on the sofa by myself deep into the evening. Write love notes to my husband that go unanswered. Endure mediation followed by divorce. Yes, that's a sucky way to spend an afternoon. I'm actually not so much into dating, either, and would love to skip straight to the established relationship, if that is possible.

I decide to come back to the question later, and charge ahead. I can feel myself losing steam with this project; my eyes wander longingly down to the tab that holds my email account—the gateway to my blog and cooking project and people who think I'm funny. My blog is easy. Dating sites are hard.

What kind of food do I like? Finally, questions that call forth my years of carry-out knowledge. I do like Indian food, and I do like standard American fare, and I do like French, very much so. I like sushi, and I like Chinese, and I like coffee, especially if it is served with cinnamon buns that have just come out of the oven so that the icing oozes down the sides. My cursor hovers over the next selection. Japanese. But I just answered 'Yes, please,' to sushi. Do they mean tempura? Teriyaki? Everything except raw fish?

I glance down the list. Dumplings have been separated from Chinese food. Falafel has parted from the Middle East. I decide to come back to the food questions.

I skip ahead and see screen after screen filled with questions, most of them unanswerable, at least not in a way that tells the reader anything about me. How you can capture the way my nose scrunches when I hear something I don't like? That was something Adam always said was his favorite face I made. How can I explain via a check box the sound my jaw makes as it clicks when I stretch it before bed?

Other unphraseable facts: The shape of my hands, the way I sleep on my side, how I am more likely to take the last brownie than offer it to you, how deeply I love, because that seems like the most important point of all for a potential suitor to know: *how deeply I love.*

I close the screen without completing the form, bypass email and head to the safety of the kitchen, where the curve of an apple is the curve of an apple is the curve of an apple. And no one is going to ask me if I like apples. If I like fruit.

I take a deep breath and preheat the oven, reading through the instructions several times, wondering if I'm starting the steak too early, if it will really taste as good as the cookbook promises if I serve it room temperature over the salad. I preheat some oil in a pan and salt the steak, having deep regrets at attempting meat. I should have stuck with just making the tomato sauce. The vinaigrette would have been a Martha Stewart-y enough touch to the meal.

I decide to make a really easy pasta dish for the dinner party—keep it simple. I buy bread from the faux French bakery down the street and dessert from Magnolia's, the West Village shop that kicked off the whole cupcake craze. I don't need to make the *whole* meal, I decide. It counts as "homemade" if you make the main dish. Plus, I decorate the vanilla cupcakes with chopped up strawberries for color. I'll throw together a salad with great butter leaf lettuce I found at Whole Foods and the extra tomato I bought earlier in the week. I'll make my own vinaigrette. And then stupidly, at last moment, I throw some steaks into my basket at the store, and now I am back home and staring down the meat with dread. The cookbook is talking about searing and finishing. About making my own garlic butter.

I drop the steaks into the pan and then step back, promising the cookbook author that I will not touch the steaks, will not fuss with them and touch them and move them around until the timer goes off marking three minutes. I watch the color crawl up the side of the meat, the top still freshly pink, the bottom half a caramelized brown. When the buzzer goes off, I smear on the garlic butter I mashed together while I waited, flip the steak, and send the whole pan to the oven. Done. Door closed. I breathe a huge sigh and pour myself a glass of water. My hands are shaking from steak anxiety.

As the steaks finish in the oven, I start on my tomato sauce, a bit more confident now that the hardest piece of the meal is out of the way. I chop my garlic, lovingly bringing the knife over it like I've seen the Food Network chefs do on television, taking special care not to slice open my fingers, because I'm *not* a Food Network chef. I mix it with a small amount of water in a cup to mellow the bite of the garlic once it hits the oil. As the garlic browns, I open a can of crushed tomatoes to get ready. I hum to myself, picturing my mother rolling her eyes at the way I am spending my afternoon.

The buzzer goes off again, and I pause for a moment, grabbing some newly-purchased oven mitts. The steak comes sizzling out of the oven, and I let it rest for a few minutes on a plate. It looks gorgeous, and I have an urge to cut it immediately despite directions to the contrary in the cookbook.

I proudly slice open the first steak and am greeted by the red fleshiness of undercooked meat. I panic, fanning back to the steak salad page in the cookbook. Can I put it back in the oven? Serve it semi-raw? Dump it and cry over the wasted money?

The chef gives no directions for this possibility, as if it could never happen if the original instructions are followed precisely. I wonder if my steak is too thick; if I skipped a step. With a deep breath, I drop the steaks back in the butter-laden pan and return them to the oven, biting my lip over this decision as if it holds the same importance as choosing which college to attend or which person to marry. Did I make the right choice?

When the meat comes back out of the oven a few minutes later, the center is a creamy pink, like the photographs. I almost cry, so incredibly proud of the steaks—my babies—and how they have browned in their own juices. I set them aside again, this time with real confidence. I am like a kitchen ninja from an Alton Brown skit, striking out on my own to stave off meat catastrophes.

I throw a pot of water on to boil. The crushed tomatoes in the sauce crackle and splash out, staining the stove top with blotches of juice. I turn down the heat, sprinkle in a bit of sugar for sweetness, some salt for bite, and leave it to putter away while I start on the rest of the salad.

I turn on some music and dance through the apartment, tucking dirty clothes under my blanket and snapping down my air-drying bras from the shower curtain bar. I touch-up my lipstick, give the vinaigrette another shake, and combine the pasta sauce with the drained noodles back in the original pot. I toss in some chopped kalamata olives, some arugula leaves for color. I rummage in the cabinets for something to serve it in.

The memories always comes out of nowhere, when I least want to be thinking about Adam. I'm about to throw my first dinner party, for Christ's sake, but suddenly, I am reminded of the day he bought me the serving dish I'm holding in a small town in Upstate New York.

We had been on vacation, a small weekend getaway to Bolton Landing on Lake George. We spent the day wandering through antique shops and drinking coffee by the water. Right before we got back in the rental car to return to the city, we stopped in a home goods store to pick up a gift for my sister's birthday.

Nestled between two teapots was a cheery, orange, oblong dish with stripes around the top edge. We often played a game while we were dating where he had to guess whether or not I liked a certain ring or dress as we window shopped. This game strangely stopped soon after the wedding, even though I was obviously dying to play it during all of those excursions to Me&Ro. But in this store, back when he seemed to care what I thought as if he was exploring every nook and crevice of my being, he raised his eyebrows at me and pointed at the dish, "Like?"

"Like," I agreed.

While the cashier was ringing up the vase we were buying for my sister, he pointed towards the serving piece and asked her to box it for us. "Adam," I hissed, trying not to let the woman hear me. "We can't afford that right now."

"I don't really think you can wait on happiness," Adam said, which was such an Adam thing to say at the time. "And when are we going to get back here?"

He had a point, and I had a dish. It was one of the things I debated leaving behind in the divorce because it made me remember that day, but it was my favorite serving piece. Remembering Adam and that day by the lake is a little bit like my longing for children when I see Beckett—this strange mixture of grief and peace and happiness all at the same time.

The truth is that a long time ago, I was more like Adam now, and he was more like I am now, and somewhere along the way, our personalities crossed and transferred like a Freaky Friday experiment. Back in graduate school, where we met, I was the one who worked well into the night. He was the sort of person who loved the minutiae of academics but dreaded applying that to the real world. He liked to argue, liked to read cases and dissect them in the same way he loved his literature books and talking about composition.

One night, he even asked me if I thought he'd be better off being a teacher. But we were too heavily in debt from law school, and he agreed—he'd find a job at a New York firm, work the requisite amount of hours so we could pay off the student loans and then have money left over for travel, the suburban house and 2.4 kids. He brought home stories from the office about other lawyers who stayed well into the night while we happily snuggled and ate carry-out dimsum on the sofa.

At first, *he* was the one who suggested that we grab matinee tickets to the off-Broadway shows or check out the latest exhibit at the Met or walk around the funky, bohemian Busker festival as if we had nothing better to do with our afternoon.

And then slowly, slowly, the wardrobe changed, and the jeans and t-shirts were replaced by suits. And then slowly, slowly, his tastes changed until he was telling me that he *enjoyed* the dinners out with other lawyers rather than finding them tedious. And then slowly, ever so slowly, he started stretching out his day until he was working more than he was not working.

At the same time, I was losing my drive and desire to become the best little graphic artist in the world. I was reading house-decorating magazines and talking about which neighborhoods had the best schools and could he *please* come home before nine o'clock so we could have some time together before bed?

And slowly, slowly, my heels and skirts changed to cords and sweatshirts. And slowly, slowly, I started to find things about Adam that annoyed me, like the way he discussed how much he missed the Hamptons with his mother or the way he flossed his teeth in the bedroom or the way he left his damp towel on top of our bedspread. And then slowly, ever so slowly, I started wearing out the sofa cushion directly across from the clock which I watched as if it held the answer to when Adam would be returning home.

These are the things I should not be thinking about five minutes before a dinner party.

I throw the noodles in my serving bowl and place the salad into a tacky dish I picked up in Bar Harbor, Maine, in the shape of a lobster. I work the serving dish a little too hard, lining up the strips of steak to look like the claws, and then change my mind and toss the whole thing together.

At eight o'clock, the table is set and the food is all cooked and no one is here. I sit down to check my email. I wade through a few comments from my latest blog post—an internal debate on whether or not I should attempt baking projects now that I am the owner of a bag of cake flour. The unanimous vote is "Yes," though no one can agree if I should begin with the angel food cake or something easier.

There is an email from a PR person wondering if I'd write about her client's product on my blog, which is ten kinds of weird, and I don't even know how these PR people find me. A few notes from mailing lists, an email from an online friend, and a recipe contest announcement from the site, *Epicurious*. And then, tucked between a note from Arianna telling me she secured babysitting for tonight and an advertisement from an online bookstore is a note from the Bloscars.

It is obviously a cut-and-pasted message to all nominees, but it congratulates me on being a finalist for the 2009 Bloscars and passes along a series of important dates (the opening and closing of voting being two of them) and a Bloscars icon in case I want it for my blog.

I am fumbling frantically to add it to my sidebar when the buzzer rings.

I buzz the person into the building by hitting the button on my wall and then go back to trying to figure out my blogging software. The icon is a plain grey box, but I am strangely proud to have made it to the finalist round. I finally get it uploaded and admire it for several moments on my site before a knock comes on the door.

"I'm a finalist," I crow, throwing the door open.

But instead of finding Ethan or Arianna on the other side, I am facing a tall, droopy-eyed man with carefully tousled hair holding a wine bottle.

So, naturally, I scream.

Which causes my next-door neighbor to instantly throw open her door as if she were waiting for this exact moment to happen and hiss at me because she has a baby sleeping. I apologize to her and to the man while my brain catches up with my body, and I realize this must be one of the two men my brother said he would bring along. Silly me, I expected them to come *with* him, as in *at the same time*, so that I didn't have to entertain a stranger in my apartment, alone. But unless you specify these things with Ethan, it's always a guess as to how things will play out.

"I apologize," the man said in a thick accent of European origin. I guess Spain. Or maybe France. Or Portugal. "Ethan told me to come here tonight? To a dinner party?"

"I'm sorry—I just thought you would be *with* him. I thought you were . . . I don't know . . . a *random* man. I'm Rachel."

"And I am Gael Paez," he tells me, as if I should have heard his name before. What I hear is *Gayle Perez*, and the only person I can think about is Oprah Winfrey's best friend, Gayle.

Except that he doesn't look anything like a middle-aged woman. He is, by far, one of the most attractive men I have ever met face-to-face (except for Adam, but I shove that image immediately out of mind.) He is about six feet tall with broad shoulders. A quick, lopsided smile, a small scar above his left eyebrow that screams "fútbol accident," and deep brown eyes that match his equally dark brown hair. The accent also helps. I step aside and give him space to enter the apartment.

"I work with Ethan," Gael tells me. "On the coffee book. I lent him some of my equipment."

"Cameras?" I ask, nervously playing with the dish towel hanging off the kitchen drawer.

"Cameras, tripods, lens," Gael ticks off on each finger. "I am a photographer."

"For books?" I ask.

"For weddings."

Of course it would be for weddings.

I pick up a corkscrew and open the bottle of wine. It is white and room temperature and Gael looks at me strangely as I stand there with the cork in hand. "I didn't mean for us to drink it now," he admits. "It's a gift? It's what you bring to a dinner party, no?"

"It is; thank you. I just . . . I meant to open this bottle of red. I'll just put this aside for a moment, and I'll drink it later."

"By yourself?" Gael asks, and I see him glance at my left hand and my bad-ass middle-finger cuff ring.

I imagine myself, hand around the neck of the wine bottle, drinking straight from the bottle and drooling in front of the television after everyone goes home. *Yes*, I want to answer truthfully, but instead I say, "We can have it with dessert."

Gael slides himself onto one of the high stools in the kitchen while I switch out his wine bottle for the bottle of red I left on the counter. I glance over at the clock; Ethan, Arianna, and the other mystery guest are now nineteen minutes late.

"What do you do, Rachel?"

I like the way my name sounds coming out of his mouth. Towards the end of my marriage, I was always annoyed when I heard Adam say my name, because he often threw it into the sentence as if it were a curse word. *What do you expect me to do, Rachel?* was a well-worn phrase that I heard every time we argued, precisely after I had complained about something. That always made me clam up for the next several hours. Adam *spat* my name, but Gael lets it rolls of his tongue as if he's uneager to let it leave his mouth.

The taste of the name *Rachel*.

I pour him a glass of the red wine and pass it to him. "I'm sort of between things right now." I've obviously practiced since my date with Rob Zuckerman. "I'm a graphic artist, but I'm taking a small sabbatical from work. Learning how to cook. Writing a bit."

"What sorts of things do you write?" He gives me a smile that says he would gladly drag this portion of the evening out indefinitely, making me volunteer every small scrap of information before he turns over whatever he has brewing behind those eyes.

My God, those chocolate-brown eyes.

And that lopsided smile.

I am saved from embarrassing myself by staring for too long by the buzzer jolting me to my senses. I ring the person into the building and stand awkwardly beside the front door. "It's probably Ethan. Or Arianna."

A few moments later, there's a knock on the door, and I can hear a cacophony of voices on the other side. Arianna has arrived with Ethan and another man in tow. She rolls her eyes at me as if to say that it was painful enough to spend time in the elevator with the stranger much less now sit across from him at a dinner table. She disappears into my bedroom area to throw her coat on my bed and adjust her bra. I know her that well.

"Hey, sweetie, this is Pete," Ethan says. "And Gael is already here."

"Hi, Pete," I say, offering out my hand. The man takes it limply, as if he has been told to apply the least amount of pressure possible lest he fracture some of my fingers. He is the polar opposite of Gael, and I do mean *polar*. His skin is beyond white, as if he has been gessoed. A piece of white meat chicken. His hair is this pale orange, as if it couldn't quite decide if it wanted to have a color or not.

And his skin is cold.

Gael's hand is warm and dry when he places it on my shoulder and asks if I want him to pour some wine for everyone. I flounder for a moment and then will my head to nod.

Arianna emerges from the bedroom area—I have a studio, so screens around the bed have to suffice—examining a stain of unknown origins on her shirt. Perhaps Beckett's spit-up or remnants of his old bottle. She leans against the counter, smiling wanly at me while avoiding eye contact with Pete.

"What did you make?" she asks, accepting a glass of wine from Gael.

"Well, Gael, I don't know if Ethan told you," I start, staring at

Arianna for confidence, "but I'm just learning how to cook after thirty-four years of eating out and ordering in. So . . . I made some pasta. And a steak salad. And I cheated and bought the bread and dessert."

I had felt like a rock star before they arrived, but now, listing out the menu, I realize that it sounds like a meal prepared by a middle school student in her Home Ec class. Noodles? Salad? The only thing this meal needs to look more amateur is an apple brown betty made in an EZ Bake oven.

I am acutely aware that Gael is standing next to me.

"It sounds great. I'm starving," my brother announces. "Let's eat."

When we get to the table, we do the dance. Where I'm waiting to see where Gael sits, and I *think* he's waiting to see where I sit. He stands with his body behind one chair and his hand resting on the one beside it while I linger by the counter as if I need to break its magnetic pull before I can venture over to a seat. I take the chair to Gael's right and stand next to it for a moment to mark my territory, even though I need to go back into the kitchen to serve the meal.

I take special care as I walk each dish over to the table—not because the bowls are heavy, but because I am terrified that I'm going to end up standing in a pool of pasta. I can't even pinpoint why I'm nervous. Is it the fact that strangers are eating my cooking for the first time? The fact that Gael Paez has a small, alluring gap between his top teeth? That he smells incredible—like cinnamon and winter and darkness and sex.

Sex.

I set the final bowl on the table—the lobster-shaped one with the vinaigrette-splashed steak salad—and take my place. I'm suddenly not hungry at all until Pete says, "It's always a bad sign when the chef isn't eating."

Really, that's all it takes before I decide that I hate Pete. Even my brother, who usually has a terrible case of oral diarrhea, gives Polar Pete a look. I wonder how they know each other or why Ethan ever thought he'd be a good addition to my first dinner party. I help myself to the end piece of the crusty bread.

"*A mucha hambre, no hay pan duro,*" Gael says, mostly to Pete.

"I'm don't know what that means," Pete replies, somehow sensing that the words are meant for him.

"It means beggars can't be choosers. It means when you're hungry, there's no stale bread. Rachel made this wonderful meal, and we should be grateful that Ethan invited us to eat this food and drink this wine and meet his sister."

I watch to see what Gael puts on his plate. Whether he's leaning more towards the salad or the carbs. I hope he's not the sort of person who eschews white flour. I try to discern whether he's smiling while he chews. It sort of looks like a smile.

"Are you from Spain?" Arianna asks.

Arianna asks all of the questions to which she can sense that I want answers. That is what dozens of years of friendship buy you— mental telepathy. I find out that he was born and raised in Madrid, moved to New York four years ago to learn English and works as a wedding photographer for his brother-in-law, knows how to speak three languages, and likes my pasta.

And he knows that I am divorced, I am single, I am in love with all things Spanish. That I visited Barcelona for two weeks with a school-sponsored group when I was seventeen. That I don't love Central Park. That I do like zoos. That I write a blog and am on a graphic design sabbatical and am terrified of baking. See, more information than Datey.com could get out of me.

We are having a fantastic time, and I can feel my body actually relaxing when Ethan yanks me out of my reverie by mentioning that the guests should rate my meal. "You know, like they do on Iron Chef. Give her points for plating and taste."

"Judging me on plating isn't fair," I say, motioning to my tiny apartment kitchen. "I don't have room for cool dinnerware."

"But this dish is very interesting," Gael says, motioning towards the lobster bowl.

"It's from Bar Harbor," I tell him, even though he didn't ask. "Anyway, cooking is just a hobby."

"Cooking is more than a hobby," Arianna says generously. "It's your blog. It's you taking back *you*. Or becoming you. Or something like that."

I hope Gael's English isn't good enough to follow this conversation, because I'm suddenly embarrassed over the idea of needing to find myself.

"I think plating is a creativity thing," Pete corrects. "It has to do with how attractive the food is arranged on the plate or if it was just tossed into a bowl."

"Well, I thought the pasta was amazing," Arianna interrupts. "It's simple; but simple is good. And sometimes tomato sauces can be too garlicky and this one wasn't."

"I dulled the garlic a bit with water before adding it to the oil," I explain.

"And the salad was delicious," Gael adds. "The steak was perfect."

I beam at the mention of my little-steak-that-could.

"The dressing was a little lemony," my brother tells me.

"It was supposed to be lemony," Arianna points out.

"Then it was too lemony," my bother continues. "But the pasta was incredible."

"I liked the bread," Pete says, almost grudgingly.

"I didn't bake the bread," I tell him.

"Next time, you will have to make Spanish food. *Habas con jamon*," Gael teases, since I admitted earlier in the meal that I've never tried pork. I'm not kosher, but Hebrew school did a number on my conscience.

I like that he refers to a next time.

"I wish I could make the blog my fulltime job," I sigh. "I don't really want to return to the library."

"Sorry, no help here," Pete says.

You can say that again, Polar Pete.

"Write a book," Arianna says decisively, as if publishing a book is as easy as learning how to fry an egg.

"Travel," my brother tells me. "Become a travel writer."

"I can't just become a travel writer," I say with a hint of exasperation. "If writing a book isn't very realistic than writing a travel book is less so. I don't even think my passport is up to date."

"Why not, Rachel?" Gael says to me. "You can do anything, right?"

"What do *you* think Rachel should do?" Arianna asks, because she knows I can't.

"I need to think about it. I will call her with my answer," Gael says.

While I'm making a small pot of coffee, he writes out his name and number of the back of the ingredient's receipt. G-A-E-L, I notice. Not Gayle. Not a middle-aged lady's name at all. I tear off the other half of the paper, hoping the toilet paper I bought isn't listed on the back, and scrawl my own name and number. "Rachel," he says again, repeating the numbers on the slip of paper before tucking it into his pocket.

Is it terrible that I'm thinking, through bites of my cupcake, about how this will make a fantastic blog entry? How I can't wait to write about him which is just an adult substitute for writing *Mrs. Rachel Paez* one hundred times on the inside of a math notebook? That I wonder if I have it in me to try cooking ham just to have an excuse to have him over again? Which is the most sex-worthy pork—serrano, jamon, or chorizo? I pluck one of the tiny chopped strawberries off the top and hope I look sexy eating it. Aren't strawberries supposed to be an aphrodisiac?

And at that moment, Pete's voice breaks into my thoughts with "Who the hell eats Canadian bacon?"

Which seems to end the party. Polar Pete knows how to cool off a conversation. Arianna collects her coat, my brother gives me a quick kiss on the cheek while he slips the leftovers out of my refrigerator, and Pete gives my hand a final limp shake. Gael grabs me in a spontaneous hug before he catches the waiting elevator with the rest of them. He thanks me for the dinner and conversation.

I realize after everyone has left that I forgot to tell Arianna about the Bloscar email. Though it doesn't really matter, because the phone rings once she gets home and relieves her babysitter. We spend an hour on the phone dissecting the dinner party, until Beckett howls for his midnight bottle.

Life from Scratch

blogging about life one scrambled egg at a time

. . . And that is how I made the pancakes. I'm never going back to a mix again.

Off the topic of pancakes, I'm trying to keep this as vague as possible in case he ever stumbles upon my blog, but I met the most delicious man in the world recently. Literally, I could have eaten him. He smelled like cinnamon and coffee and chocolate and sex, the man just reeked of sex. Not that he smelled like he had just dismounted, but he had that Marlboro Man without the cigarettes, soccer player who just scored a goal, sprouting stubble manliness about him that made me realize that if I were a different kind of woman, and I met him on the street, we would have ended up doing it in the alleyway.

Not that I've had great sex in . . . oh . . . almost thirteen years. Fine, Adam and I had some early good years, but the last few caused a fine layer of dust to settle on my nether regions.

So these are my questions, oh brilliant people of the Internets: (1) if you just had dinner with said man, how long would you wait for him to call you before you tried his cell? (2) Would you ever call his cell or would you take his lack of phone call as a sign and just polish off the entire stack of pancakes by yourself in a pity party? (3) How many dates do you need to have before it's kosher to have sex these days?

Not that I'm thinking of taking a bite of that chocolate, cinnamon, soccer-playing concoction or anything . . .

Chapter Four

Preparing the Thyme

I am actually humming. I am walking through the food store, collecting the rest of the ingredients for the angel food cake I'm finally going to tackle this afternoon. My first true excursion into the terrifying world of baking, and yet I'm humming. This is the hum of a woman who is in that zone where it is probable that the man she gave her number to will call her.

Two days post-dinner-party. Which is a very different window than the five days post-dinner-party time period, which is not hum-worthy. That window contains obsessive Googling and ice cream eating. But I'm not in that window of time; I am still in a happy, full, self-satisfied place.

It has been a long time since I've been in this place. Anyone married who laments their single years is only thinking of this chunk of the continuum. The excitement of knowing that someone is holding your telephone number (okay, perhaps he isn't literally holding it, perhaps the paper is on his night table, or in his pocket, or . . . shit . . . at the bottom of a garbage can . . .), that they *could* call any minute. I think that's why people love to check email or go to their mailbox—just because the chance of human connection exists. But what married people forget is the anxiety that creeps into that space, the self-doubt, the frustration as the minutes tick over to that next chunk of the continuum—the five-day-post-telephone-number-exchange window.

I grab some bags of frozen berries out of the freezer case and toss them into my basket, wondering if it would be too forward to call Gael and invite him over for cake even though this cake may be a complete disaster. I take out my cell phone and the scrap of paper I've been carrying around in my pocket in case an emergency occurs where caller ID does not record his phone number, and I am unable to call him back if I have bad reception at the grocery store. (I am also in that window when you plan for any possibility no matter how far-fetched.) I call Arianna instead, which is the safer choice.

"Any word?" she asks.

I can hear the sewing machine humming in the background. In addition to her freelance work for the designer, she is a sought-after seamstress, hemming the swingy pants legs of many a New York socialite. Beckett gives his greeting by screeching in the background.

"Nothing yet. Can I come over tonight with an angel food cake?"

"You're baking? Good for you. Why don't you come over after Beckett goes down, and we can eat it and get fat together. I'll take you down with me if you're going to ply me with sugar."

"It does have a lot of sugar. An inordinate amount of sugar for something that is supposed to be angelic," I say, glancing at the shopping list. "If I stay home, I'll just stare at my cell phone and the clock."

"Then come over here. Are you in the zone?"

Arianna, of course, knows all about the zone. She is the one who labels every increment of time from the moment you hand over your phone number to a period of time two weeks later without a phone call.

"I am in the zone, and I'm alternating between humming and feeling dizzy."

"That's bad, sweetie," Arianna tells me, and I know that it's true.

This is very *very* bad.

A single, divorced woman, not completely over her ex yet, pining after a Spanish photographer.

This is bad bad bad.

He calls while I am reading the recipe for the third time, moving my lips as I go through each step. *Preparation is the key to success*, my high school gym teacher once told us, as if knowing the rules of field hockey would get us anywhere in life. But it's not terrible advice overall, especially in baking, where it's sort of in the same genre of "Measure twice cut once."

I stare at the caller ID, heart pounding. Gael Paez. Two days. In zone terms, this is perfection. Any time before the second day and the guy seems too desperate. Rob Zuckerman, for instance, started calling the day after our date. I have been letting his calls go to voice mail for two weeks because I am too chickenshit to pick up the phone and tell him that while he is really nice, I'm just not interested in dating another lawyer-trying-to-make-partner. Perhaps I should come up with a better strategy than avoidance, since five phone calls later he still hasn't gotten the message.

I've already fallen back into bad dating habits of wanting the kind of man who makes me wait.

Gael says hello as if he isn't quite sure whose number he has called, and my heart sinks. "Hello?" I ask back. There is a moment of silence and then Spanish spoken at rapid speed and finally, his voice returns to the line at full volume. "Right as I dialed your number, a friend asked me directions. Hello, Rachel Goldman, how are you?"

"I'm fine, Gael Paez," I say, closing my cookbook and sitting down on the stool in my kitchen. We are on a full-name basis. Which can be formal or it can be intimate. I decide that I'd rather have it be intimate. I wonder if Gael still smells like cinnamon and sex. "How are you?"

"I have been giving a lot of thought to your desire not to go back to work at the library," he admits. "To be a cooking travel writer, instead. And I think I have some solutions."

"A cooking travel writer who juggles?" I suggest.

"Well, these solutions are quite wordy. Maybe it would be better if we got together, and then I could tell them to you."

"But what if they're no good?" I flirt. "Getting together could be a complete waste of time."

"Oh no, I worked hard on these ideas," Gael says with mock seriousness. "I will make it worth your while."

"Are you going to cook for me?" I question. "I cooked for you."

"I will do my version of cooking. It's called going to a restaurant. I may not know how to make pasta, but I can buy it quite well."

If I had only waited a few weeks, Gael Paez could have been the first-date-of-the-rest-of-my-life instead of Rob Zuckerman, who spent five hours in Bali. That's the whole problem with this not-knowing-what-the-future holds thing. Arianna is always talking about trusting that the next step will become obvious, but I'm not so sure this is the best way to live. A few weeks—that's all that separates me from the best first-post-divorce-date story of all time from the most boring story of all time. Just as a few hours a day was all that separated Adam from the home life, the married life, I'd thought we both wanted.

Wait, I am not supposed to be thinking about Adam right now.

I am on the phone with Gael Paez, Madrileño photographer, who smells like sex. I am supposed to be concentrating on that.

So I imagine my ex-husband on a dark, empty sound stage, standing there expectantly as if he's waiting for the right time to shout his lines. I picture my hands, triple the size of his tiny image (think Mike Teavee after he shrinks himself in the original *Charlie and the Chocolate Factory*), shoving him off the stage while he trips over his own feet and shouts out feeble, silent protests.

Well that's what he gets for popping into my head at an inopportune time.

"Oh, I know all about that whole restaurant thing. I used to be that way myself. So you're an armchair chef?"

"What is that? 'Armchair chef'?"

"It's like an armchair traveler. Someone who reads about traveling rather than doing it," I explain.

Gael likes this term and repeats "armchair chef" several more times before he finally gets around to asking me on a date. "How about this Saturday night?"

Shit. I have plans with my sister, Sarah, which I would normally cancel, but the lunch date includes her husband, Richard, and my niece, Penelope. I do some math in my head, calculating out the time it would take to return to my apartment in Murray Hill from Park Slope, shower, and get dressed in something that says, "No sex tonight, but it's a definite possibility in the future," with Arianna's help.

"What about a late meal? Eight?"

"That is late?" Gael asks. "Eight is perfect. I'll come to your apartment, and we will go be armchair chefs."

"I'm a real chef now," I remind him.

"Okay, real chef," he corrects. "I am looking forward to this, Rachel Goldman."

"So am I, Gael Paez," I respond.

And I mean it. He doesn't realize how much I truly mean it.

Despite being angel cake-less (how can I be expected to attempt baking after securing a date?), I head over to Arianna's apartment after Beckett is asleep, carrying a package of Pepperidge Farm cookies and a bottle of semi-expensive wine. We are toasting my return to the dating scene as well as becoming a finalist for the Bloscars as well as celebrating the fact that I don't need to take my blog commenters' advice ("Call the guy after three days," was their consensus), because he has already called *me*.

Plus I have decided not to write about him again. It is too risky in case we don't end up married with 2.4 kids, and he finds my blog posts in the future while I am licking my wounds. He knows already, at the very least, that I do have a blog, even if he hasn't asked for the url.

That is the whole problem with using blogs as free therapy. At least in therapy, you state your situation, and you get to hear the words outside your head and receive feedback from another person. But how can I discuss the anxiety I feel over spending the evening alone with Gael, of finally being attracted to a man other than my husband, in a public forum such as a blog? What if he's secretly reading it, and we sit down to dinner, and he knows exactly what I'm thinking and feeling in the moment?

"You can tell if he's reading your blog. I don't mean definitively, but there are ways of figuring it out," Arianna tells me mysteriously, turning down the volume on the baby monitor. The baby monitor is completely pointless in a small, New York apartment. I can hear the "monitor Beckett" gurgling at his mobile in unison with the real-life Beckett in the other room.

"How? And how would *you* know? You are more computer-deficient than I am."

"I obviously knew about the Bloscars when you didn't," Arianna points out. "I read blogs. I read articles in the *New York Times*. My finger is on the pulse of the World Wide Web."

"Hardly," I say, cracking open the Milanos. "So how do you know?"

"You can install trackers on your blog, and then it tells you who has been on."

"Wait," I tell her, suddenly panicked. "Do other people know that I've been on *their* sites?" Though I haven't gone back in months, right after the divorce, I spent more than a little bit of time still visiting Adam's photograph over at his law firm's website. Now I imagine the IT staff gathered around the computer, cracking up as they see my name popping up every night around 1 a.m. when I couldn't sleep.

"You don't see a name," Arianna says, "but you do see an IP address. I'm not exactly sure what that is, but you can tell where the person came from. Do you want to find out if Gael's reading?"

Arianna, it turns out, knows exactly what she is talking about. We turn on her computer and it boots up slowly, giving us time to eat through a layer of cookies. She takes me to a site called Sitestalker, which sounds dirty, as if I'm by the window in a trench coat waiting to flash everyone who visits my site. I set up a profile and follow the instructions to add the tracking program to my site. It's relatively easy even if my computer skills are limited to being proud that I've learned how to add hyperlinks to my blog posts. We sit there, staring at the counter on zero.

"Why isn't it adding *us?*" I ask, clicking back and forth to my blog open in a separate window. "Did we do it wrong?"

"Try closing down your blog and reopening it," Arianna suggests. Lo and behold, the counter refreshes with one, lone visitor. I chew on my lip, hitting refresh a few more times, but we're the only people reading my blog tonight.

Seeing that in black-and-white feels quite lonely. I poke around on the site and see that we're logged as coming from New York, New York. We figure out a way to label Arianna's IP address, and she comes up on the main screen under her name instead of a series of numbers.

"It makes me feel better to see that it's you reading instead of a string of numbers. It feels more human . . . less mechanical," I tell her.

"But *you're* reading right now."

"I don't mean now. I mean, in the future, when I log on to check who is reading, and I see your name. I'm trying to have a sweet moment here, connect as humans rather than allow the cold plastic-and-metalness of computers to come between us."

"Hit refresh again," Arianna commands.

I hit refresh and stare at the number on the screen. Twenty-one. Not just me and Arianna. Twenty-one people have been reading my blog while Arianna and I figure out Sitestalker and eat through two levels of Milanos. *Holy shit.* I click through each of the links, staring at the different lists of information. They have been on for a range of two seconds to fourteen minutes. They are from London, England; Reston, Virginia; Brooklyn, New York, and elsewhere. They are entering from blogrolls and comments and links inside posts. Who the hell are these people, and why didn't I know they were reading before this point?

We hit refresh again, and the number jumps. Forty-nine. As we sit there, making our way through the final layers of Milano cookies, the number jumps into the hundreds and then two hundred, finally hovering close to three hundred before Arianna tells me that she's getting tired.

"But who *are* these people?" I ask for the fortieth time.

"Sweetie, people love your site. You can't go by the number of comments they post. I *knew* there were more people reading it than you thought. First of all, your blog is funny. I mean, you really are a great writer. People connect with your story, with how honest you are and how much you lay your heart out there. It's not just your cooking stories. It's the divorce and when you write about Beckett or me or your life now in New York. People want to connect with a whole person, and you let them. Some of the cooking blogs are so boring. They're just dish, dish, dish, recipe, dish, dish. But you tell stories. You have meat *and* potatoes. Did you like that? Was that a clever food reference for your writing?"

Hearing my blog, my writing, described this way makes me blush. I bury my hand back in the cookie bag, trying to make myself busy searching the Milano crumbs.

"I didn't know anyone was reading," I say, again, for the forty-first time.

"That's why you should have loaded this software on your blog ages ago. I *told* you that people were reading."

"How many do you think there are in all?" I question, hitting refresh again.

"You'll know in a few days. Let it run for a bit, and you'll see a trend in how many visitors you get on average."

"But how do I know which one is Gael? If any of them are Gael? There are too many from New York to know."

"I thought of that too," Arianna says, suddenly remembering the second part of her plan. "You need to create a fake site . . . well, not a fake site . . . a real site but one you'll only use for bait. Load the Sitestalker stuff on it. Make the site something about ideas for future dinner parties. Then send a link to Gael making it sound as if you're sending the url out to a bunch of people, but only send it to him. When he clicks over, you'll be able to see his IP address."

"You're a genius," I tell her. "A complete genius."

"And all of my brilliance is wasted on hem lines," she laments. "Anything to help a girl out as she dives back into the dating pool."

"Do you think Gael's reading my blog?" I ask, the other question that has been returning all night. I check my stats one last time then log off on her computer.

"There's only one way to know," Arianna tells me in her best secret agent voice. "Set up a sting."

Life from Scratch

blogging about life one scrambled egg at a time

I know you're not supposed to say this, you're not even supposed to think it, and anyone in their right mind would whisper it into a pillow rather than broadcast it to the world via their blog, but here goes: I don't like Park Slope.

There.

I said it.

Now that those of my readers who are deeply offended by that admission are gone, clicked away to go write another ode to the neighborhood, I can finish the thought. I don't like the tempo of Park Slope.

It's like Brooklyn is pudding to Manhattan's ice cream. Manhattan has bite, it has substance. It holds in your mouth. Brooklyn? It sort of slides around on your tongue. There's a little flavor, and then it's gone. It doesn't even change with the temperature. Brooklyn is always Brooklyn, just like pudding is always pudding.

But Manhattan? It's an overly sparkle-lighted mess in the winter and it's sweat stains under your arms in the summer and it's dodging the weirdoes in Central Park in autumn and spring. It's three scoops of Heath bar crunch one day and a pool of ice cream soup another and . . . well . . . I like it like that.

I am thinking about Park Slope because I have to go out there today to meet my sister. She and I will undoubtedly have the Manhattan/Brooklyn argument,

57

so I like to warm up here, get my verbal boxing gloves on so to speak. Can you believe two people I'm related to live over the bridge? You would think that we'd get an equal portion of the common-sense gene, but unfortunately, that gene seems to have skipped my parent's first and last borns.

The largest reason why I hate Park Slope is that there is no place to get a good vegetarian egg roll in Brooklyn. Before you get all up in arms and start screaming something about your favorite Chinese restaurant over the bridge, notice I said "egg roll," not "spring roll." Not even Tofu on 7th—a vegetarian haven—has a vegetarian egg roll: the chunky golden jewel of the Chinese restaurant menu.

If I could, I would wear one around my neck like a lariat necklace, with shredded cabbage as the chain. Fatness and the dough are the main differences between an egg roll and a spring roll, but I only like the egg roll version of the appetizer. And egg rolls traditionally contain pork. While I've never kept kosher, I've also never been able to overcome my Hebrew school teacher's voice in my head that starts shrieking every time I go to take a bite of something that contains swine.

I would love to learn how to make my own egg rolls, since I rarely get to order one since I realized how much carryout actually costs. Does anyone know how to make one like the ones at Hunan Chow? An easy recipe that will not make me weep and shake like my angel food cake recipe?

Chapter Five

Snapping the Carrots

Over the next few days, I see just how popular my little blog is as each reader is logged by Sitestalker. I have readers from around the world—from American Samoa to a telecom call center in India. They stay for an average of five minutes on the blog, which doesn't seem like a long time at all, but Arianna promises that is eons in blog years.

I feel like an average girl who was just told by someone that she's popular. You know the rule of the average girl, right? Popular girls always know that they're popular. They don't need to ask, and they really don't need you to tell them, but they're always glad when you do because it just confirms what they already know.

But average girls can never believe it when they're told that the cute boy likes them or that they've been nominated for homecoming queen or that their blog is being read by thousands of people each day. It seems a little surreal, as if they're part of a joke and now they need to cringe and wait for the punchline. There are average girls who have been working successful jobs for years and are still waiting for the other shoe to drop. Movie stars who can't believe their luck that they married their gorgeous, rock-star husband, and so they are still checking *People* magazine religiously to confirm that their entire life is not a dream.

I am an average girl.

So who are the three-thousand or so readers who stop by *Life From Scratch* each day, downloading recipes and checking out my photographs of onions caramelizing? How many of them are people I know; neighbors in the building, old friends from the library, potential boyfriends that hail from Spain?

It is a bit unnerving. I am well-aware that the entire point of a blog—the very fact that you put your journal online instead of tucking it between the box spring and mattress—is to get people to read it. But now, seeing them swing by the site, sometimes three times a day, makes me uncomfortable. What have I said that will bite me in the ass later? I don't remember ever writing about anyone other than Arianna or Adam or family (well, except for a few hints about Gael because he is so incredibly delicious that he is the human equivalent to food), but what if I've upset someone along the way? And, on that end, what if Adam ever finds my site?

Sitestalker gives me a PhD in paranoia.

I follow Arianna's plan and send out an email written to a fictional group of people announcing my latest site, a dinner party blog where I'll be talking about all the dinner parties I'll have in the future. I send the link to Gael without mentioning the fact that I'll be seeing him that weekend, which I think is pretty damn clever since it's supposed to be a group note.

And for once in my life, everything works out according to plan. He clicks over, I label his IP address, and then scrawl it on a post-it note hidden under my pocket dictionary on the table so I can look it up in the IP search bar every time I log onto Sitestalker.

But for the thirty-six hours preceding the date, Gael's name doesn't pop up on my main blog, and I don't know if I'm disappointed or relieved. I chew my way through a baguette with the cheapest brie I could find at the market. It tastes like cheap brie. "Don't you think this is a sign that he's not really interested?" I ask Arianna as she flicks through the clothes in my makeshift closet, Beckett sleeping in a carrier on her chest.

"No, why?" Arianna asks absentmindedly, considering a little black dress with a deep neckline.

"Because he knows my blog exists; I mean, you brought it up at dinner. He knows the name of the site. If you were going on a date with someone you were really interested in, wouldn't you read up on their thoughts by going on their blog before the date?"

"Yes, but I'm a girl," Arianna says. "You're attributing girlie behavior to a boy. Boys do not poke around blogs like that."

"What about all of those tech blogs? The political blogs?"

"I didn't say men didn't read blogs. I'm just saying that they don't cyber-stalk their potential love interests like women do pre-date."

She picks out an outfit for me that falls between all worlds—it's not hinting at sex and it's not denying it either. It doesn't scream responsible mother-type but it doesn't dismiss the desire to nurture. It is not risky or exciting or too far out there or too common. It is between everything and therefore nothing at all.

And therefore, it is perfect for the second first-date-of-the-rest-of-my-life.

Before I can go out to dinner with Gael, I must endure a trip out to Park Slope in Brooklyn to have lunch with my sister, Sarah, and her family. Usually I'm able to talk Ethan into joining us, but he claims he has some photographs to take of cream pooling up on plastic table tops.

I love my sister to pieces, and I know that she always has my best interests at heart, but she also knows how to push my buttons even more than our mother and takes every opportunity to remind me of my foibles—purposefully or inadvertently.

Sarah is very successful at what she does. She is a surgeon—a brain surgeon at that. Which means that she is very smart, though the tradeoff is that she is also slightly socially awkward. She prefers her operating room to be silent instead of playing light music like the other doctors. She keeps her Park Slope apartment much in the same way she keeps her operating room, impeccably neat and organized and silent.

She managed to find a husband who is the exact replica of her except in male form and with a specialty of heart surgery. She even reproduced herself in Penelope, a solemn child who prefers steamed edamame to fried burgers, and whose most daring moment came when she announced she wanted to be Madeleine for Halloween instead of a doctor for the third year running.

My sister also has a rabid love of her neighborhood and an inability to find anything redeemable about anywhere else in the world. She would love to bring me over the bridge into her whole wheat pancake world and thinks that it is only a matter of time until I come around.

The topic du jour is how much more difficult it is to get Penelope into a good preschool in Park Slope than it is anywhere else in the city, state, or country.

"I thought I read that preschool enrollment was down," I say as we walk down the street. We pass four or five perfect acceptable restaurants where we could park ourselves and get this meal in motion, but they study each menu carefully, debating all the past meals they've had at the establishment and sighing about how many choices there are in Park Slope. As if picking a restaurant is akin to *Sophie's Choice*.

"Not at the g-o-o-d schools," my sister says carefully, spelling the word "good" as if it's on par with a curse word or sex position.

Sarah finally decides that a small panini place will be the perfect place to deliver her monthly "Do you know what you should do with your life?" speech. These speeches started a long time ago, back when we were in high school and I was busy reading teen magazines while my sister read science journals. "Do you know what you should do?" she always began, placing her hand gently over Johnny Depp's face. "You should spend some time in the library figuring out what you want to study once you reach college."

In college she told me that I had to pick a better major, go out more, go out less, and apply for summer internships. She always knew best. She just didn't know *me*.

I order a roasted eggplant sandwich and study Penelope as she pretends to read the menu. She finally orders slowly and carefully, as if she's unsure whether her tiny voice is translating into English for the server. "I'd like a peanut butter and jelly sandwich on whole wheat bread with potato chips on the side, carrot sticks, and a juice box."

"Hold the potato chips," my brother-in-law tells the server. "Can you substitute a yogurt stick? Sweetie, you have to think about heart health."

Penelope looks down at the table, examining a small crack on the edge, and my heart breaks for her. It cannot be easy to live with two surgeons who live their lives like a test for a clinical cholesterol study. Penelope has never tried a potato chip in her life unless the nanny has been sneaking them to her on the side.

Even I'm not that brave to overstep my sister's iron grasp on her child's triglycerides levels.

"Do you know what you need to do?" my sister asks when our food arrives. She immediately removes the innards of her sandwich from the bread and discards the roll into the general bread basket. She proceeds to cut up her grilled chicken breast into tiny pieces with the precision of a surgeon, for lack of a better description.

"Join a gym?" I guess. "Drink more water? Spend less time outside? Have a colonic?"

"No, what you need," my sister tells me, "is to return to a job. Having too much time at home without structure can lead to depression. Which can lead to all sorts of other health issues."

"But I'm not depressed," I say defensively. My taciturn brother-in-law stares off into the middle distance. Penelope watches me as she methodically chews her sandwich. I can see that she's counting with each bite. "I'm having a great time. I'm trying to find a job that I'll feel passionately about, and I *do* have a structure to my day. I wake up, I check email, I cook, I write about it, I go out at night."

"Cooking and writing a blog is not structure," my sister tells me.

"I have three thousand readers," I respond, grateful the Sitestalker software has clued me in. "Three thousand people who don't agree with you. They think the blog is great and . . . I am actually nominated for an award this year. And beyond all of that, I'm dating again. I'm making baby steps."

She rolls her eyes at the term "baby steps," and doesn't congratulate me on my award or date.

"Have you considered what you're going to do when the money runs out?" Richard asks me. He questions not out of a true concern for my well-being, but out of a fear that I'm going to start bumming off them, like Ethan.

"Honestly, if nothing magically drops into my lap in the next few months, I'm back to work as a graphic designer. I know that," I reassure them. "I'll go back to making pamphlets until I grow old and die at my desk surrounded by 'I heart New York' mouse pads and Pantone color charts."

"Is Aunt Rachel going to die?" Penelope asks, her voice saturated with fear.

"Aunt Rachel," Richard says, "is speaking in hyperbole."

I notice that Penelope does not need the term "hyperbole" explained but instead seems placated enough on the topic of my health to go back to her peanut butter and jelly.

"Will that make you happy?" my sister asks.

And how can I answer that? The idea of abandoning my blog makes me want to place my head on the table and cry. If I could somehow translate my three thousand readers into subscribers for articles strategically placed in magazines or newspapers that would pay me enough to continue living in Manhattan, I'd take the job in a heartbeat. The reality is that I'm happiest when I'm writing.

"I do like design work," I answer because it's easier than vomiting out everything that just happened in my brain. "Listen, I'd love to be a writer, and I'd love to parlay cooking into a job. I am really happy in the kitchen, and I can't believe that I waited thirty-four years to learn how to make my own hummus. So, yeah, I'd love to write and cook, and if I could make that into a job, I would."

"Watch out," Sarah says drolly. "You may even end up with a career."

She pronounces the word in such a way that she conjures up every fight I ever had with Adam over the hours he worked. She makes it sound like I consider *career* to be a venereal disease, but I don't have the energy to set the record straight. And regardless, the whole thing is mixed up in my mind as is. It's suddenly too confusing to consider why our marriage ended over his emotional isolation or how I feel about work or what causes a husband to spend more time in the office than at home. Or why, oh why, I couldn't have found my writing voice while I was with Adam. I could have used all of his late nights working to blog.

"Don't you want to know about my date?" I ask, realizing that I am still trying to convince them that my life is good. Can't she see my enormous internal smile, radiating happiness?

Maybe they didn't hear me because they launch into a long story about a fundraiser at the local synagogue, the numbing effects of religion on the masses, and preschool tuitions that cost more per year than my college. There is no graceful way to bring Gael up again, so I finish off the afternoon watching my niece sit, straight-back and crumb-free in her chair, like a little robot. An edamame-loving, never-scuffed-shoe, loveable robot.

Lunch with my sister before the second first-date-of-the-rest-of-my-life was not the best idea I've ever had. No one can punch down my self-esteem or make me question all the choices of the last few years quite like my family in Park Slope.

I slip on a jangly Peruvian red-shell bracelet, match it to my matte red lipstick, and walk a tiny path between my bed and sofa to work off my anxiety.

I am really nervous for my first second date.

I sit down at my computer and try to center myself before the date by checking my stats. 2544 people disagree with my sister, I note. 2544 people think that I'm funny and sassy and make a damn fine stack of pancakes. Actually, it's 2,546 people by the time I log out of the stats after taking a quick peek to see if Gael's IP address has shown up in the log.

It isn't there.

At eight o'clock I decide to go downstairs and meet him at the front door even though he has been to my apartment before. It seems presumptuous to ask someone to take the elevator up to your apartment when you are perfectly capable of meeting them downstairs.

Unfortunately, I do not account for the possibility that someone has let him into the building, so he receives a second shriek from me when I turn around from locking my door and find him standing behind me. My neighbor must spend her whole life with her hand on the knob because she throws her door open again and barks out some words about babies sleeping in a voice reminiscent of the banshees screeching about your certain death.

"I am so sorry, Diana," I whisper loudly. "We're actually leaving."

She makes a face, as if I've only said that to rub her face in the fact that I can go out and she has to stay home with her sleeping child. I fumble for a moment, trying to think of what to say, but at that moment, the elevator doors open again, and Gael beckons me inside as if we're exiting for a clandestine affair.

The doors close, and we start our descent. Gael discreetly looks me up and down while allowing his eyes to wander to the lit-up floor numbers between glancing at each body part. "You look very beautiful," he tells me, not in a voice that suggests he wants to get into the pants he just appreciated visually, but simply as fact. I am beautiful.

My face burns, and I mumble something gracious. The fact is that I'm not the kind of woman who gets whistled at on the street. I don't have men following me down into the subway with their eyes glued to my ass. I don't even have men give up their seats for me when I'm juggling five bags of groceries on my way home to cook. The last person to tell me that I looked beautiful was Adam, and that was years ago.

It feels nice to have someone else concur that I look good, especially after so much thought was given to choosing an outfit between every possible statement. We step outside, and I shiver for a moment, the shock of the cold shooting down my spine into the three-inch heels Arianna convinced me to wear. *Height*, she informed me, *is sexy*. Especially next to a tall, Spanish man.

"You go out in winter without a scarf?" he asks, pointing at my neck. "The cold doesn't bother you?"

"The cold bothers me a lot," I say, uncrossing my arms to show him that I'm shaking. The scarves I own don't go with the look I'm trying to convey. He puts his arm around me in a way that could be construed as brotherly but I choose to take as romantic. I lean into his partial hug, and we awkwardly stumble down the street together. We could use a little practice.

"Have you lived here a long time?" Gael asks. "In Murray Hill?"

"About nine months," I say. "Almost ten months."

"It's a great neighborhood," he tells me. "It must be nice to be on the same side of the city as the museums. Easy to get to the Guggenheim from here."

I decide in that moment that I love him.

Adam and I used to trek out to the Guggenheim early in our relationship, back when we made time for taking advantage of New York—the art museums and shows and myriad of restaurants. We even had a Picasso poster in our living room from an old 1999 exhibit.

Adam let our dual Guggenheim membership lapse a few years later, claiming we didn't have time to use it anyway. That loss probably contributed to my bad moods. There is nothing better for staving off seasonal affective disorder than the clean whiteness that falls across the museum when the winter sun comes in through the glass roof.

"I love the ceiling," I tell Gael.

"Me too," he agrees. "We'll have to go sometime."

"There's a Kandinsky exhibit right now," I say, his hip awkwardly bumping into my side as we walk.

"There's also the Museum of Sex," he mentions, grinning like a nine-year-old boy who has just found his father's *Playboys*. "That's even closer, right?"

"It's a happening neighborhood," I say dryly.

Luckily he has chosen a tiny Italian restaurant two blocks away. He holds open the door for me, and I cross under the small walkway of sparkle lights the owner has attached overhead. Normally when I'm here, it feels like any other Italian restaurant in the neighborhood. Tonight, it feels a little bit like we've entered a fairy's cave.

Do fairies live in caves?

We're seated by the door, and Gael looks with concern at the table. "I'm worried my date will be cold," he admits to the waitress, as if this were one of the many things worrying him before the date. Possible floods, tornadoes, door drafts. She motions to a table towards the back of the restaurant, as if she doesn't mind that she is giving up a table in her section and the tip money that accompanies that. Or perhaps she remembers me as being someone who sticks firmly to the fifteen-to-eighteen-percent range.

"Let's order wine," Gael suggests. "We have to toast everything."

"Toast?" I ask, handing him the wine list which was placed inside my menu. He scans down the list.

"The ideas I have for your future career as a traveling, juggling, cooking writer. We need to toast my grand ideas."

He picks a bottle of red and asks me if this is okay. I notice that the skin around his eyes crinkles when he smiles his lopsided smile. He picks at the small bowl of olives the waitress placed on our table in lieu of the usual bread basket.

"I like this place because they have olives," Gael admits. "That is very Spanish, serving olives instead of bread. A small bowl of marinated olives, right?"

"What else is Spanish?" I ask. "Besides ham."

"Besides jamon?" he laughs. "Late dinners. No one goes out before eight or nine in Madrid."

"And then where do you go?" I question. I am still freezing, but I don't want to cross my arms over my chest to keep warm because it pushes my boobs into a strange position. I try to increase my body heat by jiggling my leg under the table.

"You get a small meal somewhere. And then you go to a club. Like a music club? A dance club. And then you'll go to a bar for a drink. What did you do when you were in Barcelona?"

I like that he remembers the small details. "Well, I was only seventeen. I was there on a school trip. So no bars."

"No bars at all?"

"No bars. Not even any restaurants. I think we ate in the hotel most nights. It was a place that catered to large school groups. They made this awful vegetable soup every night we were there. It was this pureed vegetable mixture. We called it *culo*."

Gael almost chokes on his olive and starts laughing. "You say that very well. Are you sure you don't know Spanish?"

"Only the curse words," I admit. "And *gracias*. And, strangely enough, *cacahuete*."

"Peanut?"

"Yeah, I don't know why, but I remember *cacahuete*."

"You know *hola*," Gael prods. "And *bueno*."

"But those are words that everyone knows. That's not knowing Spanish. I'd like to learn Spanish. It has always been on my to-do list."

"To-do list?" Gael questions.

"Like a list of things you want to accomplish."

"Aaaah, a to-do list," Gael repeats as if he's trying to commit this phrase to memory.

"I'm just impressed by how well you know English," I tell him. "I've always been jealous of people who can speak more than one language. And you know so many. Three?"

"Well, English, you have to learn in school. It was a requirement for graduation. And you learn it for a long time. Many years. But my mother speaks French; she is from France, so we spoke French in the house too. French and Spanish, depending on who was winning the fight."

I imagine Gael's parents, an older male and female version of himself, yelling at each other in their respective languages over the breakfast table. Our bottle of wine arrives, and the waitress pours Gael a small taste. Without lifting his glass to try it, he motions for her to fill both of our glasses. Then he lifts up his glass and clinks it against mine.

"*Salud*," he says.

"Yes," I answer, waiting for him to continue. But he simply places his glass down and takes another olive. I try to think up something to ask him, but my mind keeps returning to the scar on his forehead. I wonder how that question will sound. That I only notice his flaws? But if I tell him how I love his heavily lidded eyes, even without telling him how they make me daydream about how they'll look after sex, do I reveal that I've spent way too much time thinking about him? Picking apart his many gorgeous features? I stare at the menu mindlessly while I rack my brain for something non-physical to ask.

"What are you going to order?" I blurt out. That was definitely not the astute, sensual question I was aiming to concoct within the silence.

"I am going to get the wild boar. *Pappardelle al cinghiale.*"

"You know Italian too," I say softly, glancing down at the table.

"No, it was written in the menu," Gael says, pointing at the words. He repeats the words, this time with a terrible Italian accent. A man at the table next to us glares at him as if he were personally offended by the imitation. "Have you ever eaten wild boar?"

"No. The whole Hebrew school thing," I say by way of an explanation. "I'm not kosher, but I can't seem to try pig."

"Maybe you'll take a bite of mine tonight. Try something new."

"Really, I know it's all psychological, but I can't. I can't try wild boar or tame boar."

"What about kosher boar?"

"There is no kosher boar," I tell him. "Pigs aren't kosher."

"What is this kosher thing if it keeps you from tasting anything good? What, can you only eat white bread and . . . what is the most boring food, I can't think of something else like white bread."

"Tuna fish. That's pretty boring."

"Oh, I don't like tuna fish," he says, wrinkling his nose. "What is the strangest thing you've ever eaten, Rachel Goldman?"

He doesn't know how loaded this question is for me. Little Mike Teavee Adam dances back out onto my mental stage. That was always my question to Adam when he returned from a trip or checked in with a phone call. "What was the strangest thing you ate today?" I'd ask. Because there was always a good answer. Scorpion during a business trip to Vietnam. Blood sausage during a vacation with friends. Cactus apples sent from a client who took a trip to Arizona. The fact that he would put anything and everything into his mouth was always a point of awe, something that attracted me to him. It was urban daring. Urbane courage.

I've never been very adventurous with eating. I like all the standards, as much as sushi and the like can have standards. I am more *pho* than tripe, more *kappa maki* than *unagi*, more matzo ball soup than *gribinis*. I'm not even sure if Adam enjoyed choosing the most outlandish offering on the menu or if he did it for me, but before he would order, he would get this small smile as if he was trying to appear serious and run his finger across his pick on the menu very slowly so that I would flip back open my menu and try to figure out which item he was lingering over.

"The lamb heart and kidneys?" I'd ask. "The calf's tongue? The sweetbreads?"

I loved having a good story to tell the next time we were with friends. I loved watching him take the first bite without a moment of hesitation or consideration. *It's just food*, he always told me. He had the same attitude about travel. The same attitude about calling the credit card company to fight a claim or calling the cab driver on a wrong fare or asking someone if they'd stop talking in the theater. It was a confidence that made me feel as if he were getting more out of life than I was. His willingness to put himself out there and try anything made me fall in love with him. That was the real Adam.

But his attitude had its dark side. It's just food, it's just a place, it's just a company. It's just a marriage. *He's just an ex-husband*, I repeat to myself.

Whoa, I have got to get myself out of my head.

I blink several times and then place my finger against some random words on the menu, as if I've been trying to decide what to order.

"Snails." I tell Gael. "In France. Is that weird? It's actually this awful story," I tell him.

"Snails are quite good," he tells me. "Salty."

"Well, these snails were not quite good. It was New Year's Eve, and we were in Paris."

"With your husband?" Gael interrupts.

"With my husband," I agree. "We forgot to make a reservation, so we were going from restaurant to restaurant, trying to find someone to seat us. Every place was, of course, filled, and we were starving. We finally found this place on a random side street that had an open table. Adam kept goading me and goading me to try something crazy so I picked the snails. I think I made it through two before I quit. About an hour after the meal, I started feeling queasy, so we left the bar we were at and went back to our hotel room. I ended up in a Parisian emergency room with food poisoning on New Year's Day. It was awful. Really really awful."

I give a small laugh that I hope conveys just how glad I am not to be with a man who would take me to a nasty-ass restaurant that gives me food poisoning, but I'm not sure Gael is convinced. It's probably not the best idea to talk about your ex-husband ten minutes into the second first-date-of-the-rest-of-your-life. I should have waited until the dessert course to trot out my little divorce shadow.

"I'm sorry, Rachel, that it didn't work out with him," says Gael in a voice that is definitely more brotherly than romantic.

I really know how to turn a guy off.

The entire walk home, I am hoping that he'll kiss me. It's not just that I want to be kissed by Gael, but it seems like an important step—getting that first kiss on the first date with him. Like a skater nailing that first triple lutz right at the beginning of her routine. When we pause outside my building, I take my keys out of my pocket because I don't want to be presumptuous, but I tuck them into my hand. My keychain peeks out from the valley between my thumb and index finger. It is a hula girl I purchased on my honeymoon in an airport gift shop, originally meant for Arianna. I try not to think about my honeymoon, about Adam.

Gael makes small talk about the weddings he has lined up for the next few weekends. About a restaurant that was recently replaced on my block. I twirl the hula girl, watching her plastic grass skirt become a blur. I wonder if we're ever going to make it to the Kandinsky exhibit at the Guggenheim.

It happens while I am looking down at the sidewalk. First he strokes my cheek, my left cheek, with his ungloved hand, which is still warm from being jammed in his pocket while we walked back. Then he cups my cheek gently and tilts my face towards his. I help him out the rest of the way by straightening my back and leaning into his lips. They are softer than I thought they'd be, softer and gentler than Adam's. More uncertain. Slower. Present. He smells like wood and winter, and the heat from the restaurant is still embedded in his scarf.

He breaks free first and pulls back to smile at me. My God he is gorgeous. He kisses me again, and I know that if I invite him upstairs that we'll end up having sex on my living room floor. And I cannot have sex on my second-first-date-of-the-rest-of-my-life.

When he realizes that I'm not going to invite him up, he mumbles something that I think might be in Spanish that I want to ask him to translate and promises that he will call the next night. I don't watch him walk down to the subway even though I really want to, because I am trying very hard to play it cool. I smile to myself the whole elevator ride up to my apartment.

What good is having a really great first kiss if you can't blog about it? I mean, I *could* blog about it, but then he *could* read about it and then there probably wouldn't be a second kiss. Reading about how much your date is into you after one kiss is a little uncool. I practically have to sit on my hands when I get to the computer. I log into my account and stare at a blank post box and then close it again.

I open up my stat page and stare at the number of people who have read about my life in the last 24 hours. 3,576. I bypass scanning the list by location, already aware that my readership stretches to the far ends of the earth, and instead look at the referring pages. A lot of visitors come through the Bloscars, but there are also a host of other food blogs that have all linked to me either in posts or on their sidebar. I click through to Bakerella and bookmark her recipe for cake pops, even though the instructions are way beyond my capabilities.

In the dark recesses of the stat counter are the more technically advanced searches that come in the form of initials. Search IP address. Scan by ISP. I choose the button for Internet Service Provider and smile when I see that the top visitor is coming from the Department of Justice. I picture Ruth Bader Ginsburg at the bench with a laptop, searching for directions on caramelizing onions. From little old me. Maybe she's like my mother and has never held a spatula. The next visitor comes from Comcast in Ohio. Another from Sloan Kettering, here in New York.

I scroll down the list until my eye catches on a name. My body feels like it is moving so slowly that it doesn't get the message until I'm well past the entry. I scroll back up, not sure that I saw it correctly. I could just be seeing things, a name that is close but will turn out to be a few letters off. Or maybe I imagined the whole thing, that I'll spend the next ten minutes scrolling back and forth and finding nothing that could have ever been misconstrued.

But then, my heart pounding in my ears until I can't even hear the hum of the computer, it jumps out of the screen. I feel like *I've* just been caught with my nose in someone else's diary instead of the other way around, because there, on the screen, unmistakable, in Sitestalker's familiar courier font, is Adam's law firm of Brockman and Young.

Life from Scratch

blogging about life one scrambled egg at a time

One of the things I used to love to order was artichoke and spinach dip. It's so gooey and yummy. It is healthy love. It has to be healthy—right? I mean, it has vegetables in it and protein. It's green. Green things are good.

Since I no longer have the funds to go out and drop ten bucks on an appetizer (and before you start, I am not ordering that on a date. Are you kidding? Admit that I enjoy eating what amounts of green liquefied fat that leaves a stringy cheese beard hanging from below my lip? Attractive!), I thought I'd see if I had the skills and equipment to make it myself. Not that my hips need unrestricted access to artichoke and spinach dip.

So I Google the recipe and Alton Brown's smiling face comes onto my screen. Frozen spinach? Check (and thank you, Mr. Brown, for not suggesting fresh spinach). Frozen artichoke hearts? Check. Cream cheese for lovely smooth cheesiness? Check. Sour cream. Um, okay, not my favorite thing but fine. And then, like finding a cockroach in your salad, I let out an internal scream: MAYONNAISE?

There is mayonnaise in spinach and artichoke dip? There is mayonnaise in the dip? Why didn't anyone tell me? How could they let me put it in my mouth—on a chip no less? Were they trying to kill meeeeeeeeeeeeeeeeeee?

73

I hate mayonnaise. Hate it, hate it, hate it.

Further Googling brought me to recipes that did not contain mayonnaise, but here's the rub: how do you know if the spinach and artichoke dip placed in front of you contains my edible kryptonite? Obviously, in some situations you can ask, but how do I know if a waiter is telling the truth or if they're just telling me what I want to hear?

It made me really sad that there isn't a rewind button, a way to undo knowledge. Because I'm not sure I can ever eat spinach and artichoke dip again.

Chapter Six

Rondelle the Celery

Let me get this straight. Adam ignored me for the last several years of our marriage, never got home early enough so we could share the events of our day, and now—NOW—after we're divorced, he is taking the time to read my blog so he can see what I'm doing?

Hell hath no fury like a woman once ignored, who is now receiving attention several years too late.

I can't really explain why I'm so bothered over the idea of Adam reading my thoughts. If he wants to learn that I now know how to use the waffle maker we got for our wedding (and that my waffles are better than anything I've ever gotten in a restaurant; seriously, he's missing out on the best breakfast ever), let him. The divorce is over and done with and nothing I've written up until this point can be used against me. Who cares if he knows that I missed him sometimes? If he knows that I have dipped my toe in the dating pool? Good, he should be up all night thinking about another man's hands all over my body.

I am so over him.

Except a tiny voice in the back of my head coolly asks: "Well, are you?"

Yes, I am. I'm so over him that I'm dating other people. I'm telling complete strangers about my life, and they love it—three thousand of them love it. They think I'm funny and smart and . . . so yes, I am over him. I *think* I am over him. I think about him sometimes, usually when I least expect it, and sometimes I miss him . . . all of that is normal. So yes, I think I am over him.

I sleep on the fact all night, tossing and turning as if it is an uncooked pea hidden under the mattress. In the morning, I throw on some clothes and head out to Arianna's to bitch about it in person. The point, I decide to make, is that reading my blog means that however distant, Adam is essentially involved in my life. And the whole reason we divorced was because he wasn't part of my life. And frankly, he missed his chance to know me.

Someone is coming out of Arianna's building right as I get there, so I slip inside, waving to the woman at the front desk, and jump in the elevator, taking it up the six floors to her apartment. The elevator doors open and I see Ethan talking to Arianna at her door. He is holding Beckett and standing in the open door jamb. They both startle when they see me, and then look back at each other as if they're equally surprised that they're there.

"Hey, Rach, Arianna asked me to come over this morning and help move some stuff," he tells me.

"Oh," I say, watching Arianna take Beckett out of his arms.

"I actually have to get going. Photos to take," he tells me.

"Can you stay for a second?" I ask. "Because I need to talk about the fact that Adam has been *reading my blog.*"

I expect this news to elicit the same gasp that I gave last night, but they both stare at me a bit blankly, as if they're trying to grasp why this news would need to be discussed, not to mention, delivered in person. I try again: "Adam? As in my ex-husband? The one who never asked me how my day was or came home before 11 p.m. and complained every time I suggested that we spent time with one another? Who flipped out every time I suggested we go on a vacation and actually relax with one another? Ringing any bells? Well, he was on my blog last night."

Ethan shrugs but clearly gets the message that more is expected, because he turns and heads back into the apartment. Arianna begins to clean up the kitchen, setting coffee mugs and plates into the sink while Beckett gurgles at me from her hip. She sets him in the playpen with a few toys and then pours me a cup of coffee without asking first if I want any. She knows me that well. I slide an enormous vase filled with chrysanthemums to the side and squint at them for a moment, wondering why she bought herself such an enormous bouquet of flowers.

"So I was playing around on the computer after I got home last night. I had a date with Gael," I tell them, catching my brother up on this new development with his friend.

"With *my* friend, Gael? The one I brought to your party?"

"He asked me," I say defensively, as if I hadn't been attracted to Gael's lopsided smile and droopy eyes.

"I just thought you might have told me first," Ethan starts, but he's silenced by Arianna.

"How was the date?" Arianna asked.

"It was fine. I'll tell you about it in a second. So I was on

Sitestalker, and I looked at the ISP list, which I never do, and there was Brockman and Young."

"It's a big firm," my brother offers. "It could be anyone."

"Anyone? Seriously? How many people do you think work until eleven or later at night and read cooking blogs in that office? Wait, scratch that part about working until eleven. But the part about reading cooking blogs? Lawyers do not care about mastering risotto. I don't even understand how Adam found me."

"Sweetie, your name is all over the site. Your *full* name. Google yourself—you're the first entry that pops up."

"Are you kidding me?" I ask, wondering why I hadn't been a little cleverer with my sign-on name. Rachel Goldman is the most common Jewish name in the world. There has to be at least eight million Rachel Goldmans in New York City alone. I cross the room to Arianna's computer and Google myself. Sure enough, my blog is the first, third, and fourth entry for Rachel Goldman. I wish I had known more about search engines and how Google works before I started the site.

I return to my coffee cup and stare at the layer of oil glistening on the top. "Assuming this wasn't his first time on the blog, I think I've pretty much stated that I'm a complete loser and still miss him and think about him. So he knows all that, and yet he hasn't reached out at all? I . . ."

I *what?* I put my heart out there? Not directly to him. But it feels like I've been more open, more forthcoming than he has, and in return, he has gotten to bask in the fact that I haven't moved on, while I have no clue how *he* feels about me. Except for a handful of conversations after our divorce, we haven't had a phone call in months.

Which just makes him ten kinds of cruel. It's one thing when I stopped telling him about my dreams and wants a few years into the marriage. It's another thing to know that he has now *seen* what I've wanted in my own black and white words, yet he has still chosen to ignore it.

What's the point in him reading my blog if he doesn't care enough about me to actually reach out and let me know that he misses me too? Or if he doesn't miss me, that he at least knows that I miss him. I know that doesn't make a lot of sense, I mean, it would be equally cruel to call me and say, "Hey, Rach, I just want you to know that I don't miss you, but I couldn't help but notice how much you miss me when I was showing my new girlfriend your blog, and we were laughing about you."

On second thought, perhaps I'd rather not receive a phone call.

Fine, let him read. I'll just deliver him tasty morsels of how great my life is without him. My life *is* pretty great without him. I just had a wonderful first date with a gorgeous Spanish man—who is more endearing and attractive than Adam *and* has time for the Guggenheim. Gael may not have Adam's brilliance, but he's funnier than Adam was towards the end of our relationship. And he doesn't read my blog without telling me, as far as I know so far, so that's ten extra points right there.

"I think my next blog post has to be titled *Adam Goldman Has a Very Tiny Penis*," I tell Arianna and Ethan.

"Don't bait him, Rach. Just ignore him. Why bother communicating directly with him on any level—even snarky? I mean, really, would you ever want him back?"

I glance at Arianna and then at Ethan, as if they know the correct answer. The Adam I left at the end of the marriage? Not a chance. The Adam from graduate school who brought me lattes while I studied and listened to me complain about my classmates and came up with nicknames for our professors? A little bit. I'd like that guy back.

But he's gone, evolved, changed. And no, I wouldn't want to be the old me again, waiting for my husband to come home, wearing a hole in the sofa across from the clock, gritting my teeth and hissing out hellos when he kisses me awake in the middle of the night. I wouldn't want to be that silent, lonely woman again.

As promised, Gael calls that night while I am trying to master risotto. I hadn't been worried about trying the rice dish until the cookbook mentioned that most people are afraid to attempt risotto which, of course, pressed my red, Terror Alert button. I've been told to constantly watch the rice, so I am constantly watching the rice as if it is a baby crawling towards all of my uncovered electrical outlets. I am nervously adding liquid like a bartender fearful that the belligerent drunk at the end of counter is going to ask for another drink.

It is very hard to concentrate on the rice when someone is speaking with a sexy Spanish accent in my left ear.

"I had a very good time last night," he tells me. I can hear a camera clicking and rewinding in the background. "I've been smiling about it all day. One of my jobs asked me why I am so happy."

"What did you tell him?"

"I told her that I met a pretty girl."

Oh my fucking God, *I* am the pretty girl.

All thoughts of Adam Goldman flit out of my brain like the end of a dust storm.

"What was the job today?" I ask, not addressing the fact that he has just called me pretty.

"A singer. She is a guitar player. She wanted head shots taken for her envelopes she sends out. What are you doing right now?"

I touch my hand to my messy hair, hoping beyond hope that he isn't going to suggest that we get together right now. I have spent most of the day glued to an *Iron Chef* marathon, and my sweatshirt has the potato chip crumbs to prove it. I'm only attempting the broccoli risotto because it seems like the sort of carb you can pass off as healthy. My face is pre-period blotchy and greasy, my hair limp from lack of shower.

"Cooking. Broccoli risotto," I add.

"I don't want to bother you," Gael says.

"You're not bothering me," I hurry to add. I don't want him in my apartment, but it certainly doesn't hurt to hold him on the phone. "How do people find you? You know, for jobs?"

"Some through the wedding work or my brother-in-law, Paolo. He is friendly. He walks up to people, just starts talking. And that is how I get a lot of jobs."

"Because he flirts?"

"No, no, not flirting. He's married to my sister! No, it's another word."

"We call it schmoozing in New York."

"Is this where you're from? New York City?" he asks me.

"Near here. In New Jersey. But everyone from my town ends up here at some point. Do you go home a lot?"

"To Madrid? No, no, too expensive. It costs a lot of money for the plane ticket. I've been back once. I miss it a lot."

"What do you miss?"

"Madrid has a different energy. If New York is a pale ale, Madrid is a dark stout. New York is thin. The energy is thin."

"How can you say the energy is thin here! New York is *gordo. Muy gordo.*"

I like thinking about places in terms of food. I start to wonder about the edible make-up of the places I've lived and visited. If this apartment is a Cheerio, my last apartment was cinnamon toast. If New Jersey is a peanut butter and jelly sandwich, New York is a roasted eggplant panini. I give the rice another stir and tip a small amount of simmering broth into the pot.

If Adam is stale toast that is looking more unappealing by the hour, Gael is a cup of salted almonds.

He says, "I've found many other Madrileños in the city, and we are like a little family."

"What do you miss the most?" I ask.

"In this little café near the Bilbao metro stop, the . . . " the rest of the sentence is garbled Spanish that sounds like "Kramer's cats a-lunging." I grab a piece of paper and scrawl it down, determined to surprise him with the best plate of lunging cats he has ever had. "It is so thick that you can turn the spoon upside down, and it doesn't fall off." I jot down a few more notes: *thick, soup?, sticks to spoon.*

"I want to make dinner for you," I say spontaneously. "I want to cook for you again. Something Spanish."

I can figure out Spanish food, right?

"Jamon?" he teases.

"Not jamon. I'll figure out something. Are you free on Thursday?"

"Thursday is perfect," Gael tells me.

I stir the risotto, and we make our plans. I use my thumb to rub at a spot on my left hand's ring finger, and I realize that I am feeling the callous left behind by my old ring. Out with the old, in with the new. Gael's Madrileño accent purrs into my ear.

Heart, do you hear that? I have a new boyfriend and a bad-ass Me&Ro ring. Because it's all about showing your heart who is in control. And while mine may dart around, slipping out of my hands every time I try to grab it like a greased pig, even the heart will succumb to a good, old-fashioned, extended-foot trip.

I stand in front of the bag of sugar, a small bottle of vanilla extract, and two dozen eggs, still in their fragile shells. I set down the recipe next to the standing mixer and fit on the whisk attachment. If this were a boxing match, a little bell would be sounding in the corner of the ring. It's on.

I decide that I'm going to master the angel food cake tonight, photograph it for the blog, and perhaps engage in a bit of hyperbole over how easy it was for me to make it; how delicious it tastes. You know, I'm just your run-of-the-mill Betty Crocker, whipping up a cake for her new boyfriend and writing about it so her ex-husband knows just what he's missing out on these days.

The preparation is what has been my downfall, keeping me from actually getting to the point where the cake goes in the oven. I've learned that I'm terrible at separating eggs. I can do the first few, but then I start getting sloppy and soon, there are bits of shell and threads of yolk trailing through the whites, and I need to start over yet again. This time, I am taking it slow, using multiple cups to transfer only the clean whites into the mixing bowl.

I tap the first one against the rim of the glass bowl and gently pry open the crack that appears across the shell, gutting the inside. The white slides serenely into my bowl, I discard the yolk in a nearby cup, and move the first egg white to the mixing bowl. One down, eleven to go.

I went online before attempting to bake and looked up the dates of the Kandinsky exhibit. It's coming to an end in the next few days, and I consider buying two tickets, but it seems forward, considering I've already asked Gael over for dinner. I consider buying one ticket and taking myself there on a date, my own private self love affair, but it would be too lonely to walk through the stark museum on my own. I associate the space with being in love; with wanting to show another person something I've found, something I've noticed. I can't think of anything lonelier than going to an art museum on my own and having no one to discuss it with afterwards. All that unused excitement. I'd rather miss it than see it in a vacuum.

It's a shame that I'm so unevolved.

I neatly open two more eggs and the whites travel from bowl to bowl, the yolks discarded wastefully. This isn't a time to feel badly about chickens-who-might-have-been. The stakes go up with each egg. I break the yolks in the next four eggs, as if I've jinxed myself by simply considering how I'm almost a quarter way towards starting my cake.

I considered cheating; considered buying a carton of egg whites straight from the dairy section, but that isn't a challenge. Even if no one else knew that I had used store-bought whites, *I* would know that I used store-bought whites. It's like the art museum. Even if I could get something out of it by going alone, even if no one knew I spent eighteen dollars and the afternoon by myself, walking by all the other couples who probably met on Datey.com, *I* would know that I spent my afternoon alone, alone, alone.

Eating lunch alone, seeing an exhibit alone. It's one thing to be alone in my apartment; it's another thing to be alone and out on the town. People always ask "Who did you go with?" when you tell them about a movie you saw or a concert you attended. "Just myself," I'd have to answer. And beyond that, even if I never volunteered the information, *I'd* know, and that would be bad enough.

I get six egg whites in bowl and face down the final six eggs in the carton, a killing field of egg yolks and whites still in their cracked shells scattered across the sink. There is no more room for mistakes, not unless I want to run back out to the bodega and admit that I ruined twelve extra eggs in the process of making one damn angel food cake.

I work slowly, tapping the shell gently along the circumference, watching the enamel-like surface splinter apart. I divide four in a row perfectly, sliding the whites into the mixing bowl, which looks like I have filled it with gelatinous water, splashing against the sides each time a new egg white guest enters the mix. My thumb darts into the fifth egg yolk, and I try to beat time by quickly dripping the white out of the egg, but a long thread of yolk comes with it.

Shit.

I try to scoop out the yolk with the tines of a fork, but it mixes deeper into the egg white, practically disappearing into the ether. Shit and shit.

But what can I do except hope for the best and continue on because I'm not going to trot back to the bodega—not for a cake. Maybe for a pre-period chocolate bar, but not for extra eggs. I break the final one, holding my breath as I peer at the egg whites slipping into the bowl. All clear. I dump them in the mixer, add the water I've already measured out and the extract, and turn on the beaters.

The eggs foam and whiten, coming together somewhat, though not in the way that the recipe shows in the how-to pictures. My egg whites are a runny mess, grainy and lumpy. The egg whites in the photograph have a beautiful, unblemished sheen. I whip them longer, turning up the speed on the stand mixer. Every time I turn off the mixer and consult the book, the egg whites start to disintegrate, turn back into water. I add the sugar anyway, even though the whites are not forming the stiff peaks I was promised.

This is all the fault of that stupid thread of yolk.

I walk away from the stand mixer and check my email, return and peer into the bowl and back to the recipe. And that's when I notice the unopened container of cream of tartar, the plastic safety wrap still in place over the lid.

I turn off the frothy whites, dump in the flour, which bubbles around the top of the egg mixture before sinking down towards the bottom of the bowl. I take the mixer off the stand and dump the whole thing in the sink over the broken and discarded eggs.

I should have just gone out and purchased a cake. Photographed it and lied. I snap off the preheating oven and drop the angel food cake pan back into the cabinet. I would have been the only one who knew that I hadn't even tried to make the cake, the only one who knew that it was courtesy of some nameless Manhattan bakery.

Perhaps this is the universe's way of telling me that I should use my cooking powers for good, and not engage in spite baking.

I try to put my cake disaster out of my mind by preparing for my next date with Gael. I sit down on the library floor with four Spanish cookbooks and scan all of the indexes for recipes that begin with the letter K (Kramer) and quickly switch to the letter C (Cramer) when it becomes clear that the Spanish are not big fans of the letter K.

I look at the italicized titles that are interspersed between the English ingredients. *Codorniz asada en escabeche. Cocido de pollo con chorizo y garbanzos.* I repeat my phrase over and over again: Cramer's cats a-lunging. Cra Mer Cat Za Lunja. *Cramacatzalunja.* Unfortunately, there is no recipe that resembles my perfectly constructed, made-up, Spanish word.

This is like the dating woman's version of nesting. Hominess from food. It feels like a bit of a cheap shot, an obvious choice, to cook Spanish food for him when I know he misses home, but I convince myself that I'm just giving the man what he wants. I want him to know that I am the kind of woman who will give my time to another person, listen to what they want, pick up on small clues as to what would make them happy.

I do, in other words, everything Adam didn't do.

And I hope that this meal is enough to warrant a third date.

I drag two of the more promising books up to an information desk and search out the one librarian I know who is most likely to know Spanish. Miguel is in the back, working on a re-shelving cart, so I wait semi-patiently for him to make it out to the front desk, trying not to notice how overheated I'm becoming in the library nestled inside my winter coat.

"Hey, Rachel!" Miguel says, pushing his cart aside to come over to give me a quick kiss on the cheek. He turns back to another librarian and tells her the cart is ready for one of the volunteers. He joins me in the vacant chair and peers at the cover of my book. "You're working on Spanish food now? Mastered all those basic books?"

"Mastered . . . well, I wouldn't call it that. But I'm trying to find a recipe. It's Spanish . . . as in Spain Spanish. But I thought you might be able to figure it out."

"Shoot," Miguel tells me, and then scrunches up his face in confusion as I slowly tell him about Cramer's cats a lunging. "Are you kidding? Seriously, is your Spanish that bad?"

"Miguel, I don't know *anything*. Help me; I have to find this recipe. All I know is that it's something thick that can stick to a spoon."

"So it's like a stew?"

I pull my note out of my pocket. "It's thick. It may be a soup. It sticks to a spoon when you turn it upside down."

"Say it again."

"Cramer's cats a-lunging. *Cramacatzalunja.*"

"Wait, say it a few more times fast like that."

"*Cramacatzalunja. Cramacatzalunja. Cramacatzalunja.*"

"Crema? Crema something?"

I flip to the index and scan the list from the bottom up aloud in what I hope is passable Spanish. *Crema de Salmorejo. Crema de Purrusalda. Crema de Esparrago. Crema Catalana.*

"Say your word and then read the list of choices again."

On our second run-through on the list, we reach the same conclusion at the same time. "*Crema Catalana. Cramacatzalunja.*"

"Brilliant, *chica.* Though you have to work on the pronunciation," Miguel tells me. "You're making this for someone?"

I flip to the recipe. It seems to be like a Spanish version of crème brulee. Thankfully, one that doesn't require the little blowtorch. And one that I could actually follow. "Yeah, he's just a friend."

"I wasn't accusing you of anything."

I look up from the book. "No, no, I meant that I have this friend, and he's from Spain, and I just wanted him to feel like he's at home because he can't get back very often, and he told me that this is his favorite—"

"Rach, you don't have to justify it to me. You've been divorced for a year. You're allowed to go on a date," Miguel tells me.

"It's only been nine months," I say, not sure why I feel the need to correct him. But it feels like under a year is different from over a year. Or just a year. A year. My ex-anniversary is luckily a few days after my divorce date so I get all the mourning over with during one week of the year.

"Nine months, whatever. All I'm saying is that I'm happy for you if this friend is more than just a friend."

I shrug my shoulders and stand up. "Thank you. For helping me find the recipe."

"No problem," Miguel says. "I'm here for all my Spanish-deficient friends."

I don't know why I feel so defensive with Miguel. I mean, I *do* want Gael to be more than a friend. And it's not like I want to reiterate that I'm single so Miguel will ask me out. I can't really explain my general unease of admitting that I'm dating someone to Miguel when I gleefully squeal about my upcoming date to Arianna.

At the checkout desk, I notice a pamphlet that has been discarded, probably originally picked up from the racks by the door. *Are you going through a divorce?* it asks in bold red letters. *¿Usted está pasando por un divorcio?* And what else can I do but see it as a sign because the answer is that, Yes, I guess I still am.

Regardless of in which language you ask the question.

I unload the groceries I've purchased on the way home: a carton of milk, a bag of oranges, a steak I'll make for dinner. I sift through the mail and set it back down on the counter unopened. I am feeling restless since I blew off Miguel. And thinking about Miguel makes me think about Adam, and the last thing I want to do is think about Adam. And yet, I can feel myself inching towards the computer to check if he's on my site even as I am internally slapping myself into sense. It is like trying to convince yourself that your teeth aren't sensitive when you're craving a dish of ice cream.

I don't care about Adam.

I don't care about Adam.

I don't care about Adam. But I just need to check.

I log into my Sitestalker account and blink at the screen. The number is enormous—more enormous than possible even if someone was really excited about my recent discovery of stuffed, baked apples. *The visitors are nearing on one hundred thousand since midnight of the night before.*

I skip checking if Brockman and Young is on the list and head straight for the referrals to find the source for the tremendous traffic.

The list is a solid stream of traffic from the Bloscars site. I click on one, and in a separate window the Bloscar website opens up, slowly, as if millions of other people are nudging to get a view of the screen. It feels like the Louvre in front of the Mona Lisa. I read the congratulations post filling the front page. Best Blog, Best Literature Blog, Best Humor Blog.

Best Food Blog: *Smitten Kitchen.*

My heart sinks, not really understanding why there would be traffic coming from the site if I wasn't the winner. I mean, who the hell wants to go over and check out the losers?

I keep scrolling down, and there, towards the bottom, is Best Diarist.

Which, as you've probably guessed, oh my freakin' Lord, was *Life from Scratch.*

Life from Scratch
blogging about life one scrambled egg at a time

Well . . . I sort of didn't expect so many new visitors. I would have liked to have baked a cake for you all, except that I don't really know how to bake a cake. Tidy up the typos. Scour out a few old sentences such as the one about dust on my nether regions. But you have found me straight from the figurative shower, answering the door in my bathrobe, so I guess there's nothing more to do except welcome you in and thank the Bloscar people for choosing this site as Best Diarist.

In all seriousness, I don't really know how I won. I mean, I know how I won—you guys picked me. But I had no clue that the Bloscar people were considering me for Best Diarist because, well, I've always thought of myself as a food blogger. Not that I expected to win in that category. So, what I'm trying to say (poorly) is that while I'm honored, I am also feeling like this is a big April Fool's joke a few months early.

This has been a bit of a trippy evening. I have gotten requests for interviews and travel offers and about one hundred emails from PR people asking me to review their book, kitchen equipment, or food product (why yes, Tim's Turkey Jerky, I would love to taste your new smoky, low-fat alternative to traditional jerky.) All of this is a little new for me.

Um, by which I mean that this whole thing has been really cool. So thank you—thank you for nominating me and voting for me and thank you to the Bloscar people for holding this contest and running it and (I'm getting all weepy now) thank you to Arianna for encouraging me to start this site and to my brother for always eating my creations and my sister for providing fodder for my anti-Park Slope posts and . . .

Deep breath.

Back tomorrow with more stories and recipes.

Chapter Seven

Cube the Potatoes

It's not like I had been expecting to win best food blog, but I really couldn't wrap my mind around the "Best Diarist" moniker. That was the sort of prize reserved for bloggers such as *The Pioneer Woman*, *Dooce*, or *Amalah*. It only took me a few seconds to catch up and within minutes, I was standing in front of the mirror, brushing my teeth, while saying, "Hi, my name is Rachel. I'm a diarist." It had a nice ring to it.

Having never won an award—not even one of those bullshit "best attendance" awards in elementary school—I wasn't sure what happened next. The prize turned out to be a check for fifty dollars, which seemed like a strange amount based on the scope of the award—several million people voted daily for a week, which must add up to some serious ad revenue on behalf of the site.

But the money didn't really matter because there were also the emails from the contest heads wanting me to come out to the Sundance Film Festival the next month to collect my prize as part of "the concurrent and related Sundance Technological Conference." Not that I had the money to fly out to Utah or book a hotel, but still, an invitation to the festival was something. Their friendly email warned me to come equipped with business cards because people were going to want to learn about my brand.

My brand? Business cards?

Had they missed the fact that I was between jobs? A cat woman without cats? A divorcee learning to cook at thirty-four?

Then there were the requests for interviews. I received a perky email from the technology editor of the *LA. Times*, one from the *Chicago Tribune's* food section, and another from the *Austin American-Statesman*. There were emails from the people at *Zagats* and *Chow*, which would have been cool ten months ago when I was the Carryout Queen, but now were just a tad confusing. *Gourmet* pitched an idea to have me as one of the judges for their Easter dinner contest, despite the fact that I'm Jewish. Though, the crème de la crème, at least in my mind, came from Jen Dellman, who writes for the *New York Times* magazine, who wanted to meet to brainstorm ideas about an article on rebuilding your life post-divorce.

My initial reaction was panic—what if someone I didn't want to find me discovered my blog because it was featured in the *New York Times* magazine? And then I realized, *the only person who mattered had already found me.*

So much for anonymity in a city of eight million people.

The email that mattered most was a simple, sweet note that came from a junior agent at a major New York literary agency three days after I won the award.

> *Hi, Rachel—*
>
> *My name is Erika Ledbetter. I'm an agent at Rooks LTD. I think your writing style is wonderful—brash, funny, unapologetic, and honest. The strength of your platform is how deeply you connect with readers. (I am actually the recipient of more than one email exchange with you, except it was under my anonymous blogging email address, Ms. Duncan-Hines.) I was wondering if you had ever thought about putting some of your experiences into a book; perhaps a hybrid cookbook/essay/advice manual. The Divorced Woman's Guide on How to Cook Your Life from Scratch?*
>
> *Please let me know if you'd be interested in speaking further about book proposals and literary representation.*
>
> *Thanks,*
> *Erika Ledbetter*
> *Junior agent, Rooks LTD*
> *Rooks knows Books*

And then I realize why people care if they win this contest. It isn't about a fifty dollar check. It is about opportunity.

I quickly write back that I am indeed pulling a proposal together and would love to talk about representation despite the fact that the first part is a lie and the second part I want to tell her while groveling. I forward both emails over to Arianna. And then I grab my wallet, keys, and winter cap and walk over to Arianna's with a small skip being added every few sidewalk slabs.

"Hello, hello, Mr. Beckett, hello," I sing as she opens the door to her apartment, child in tow.

She raises her eyebrows at me, and I raise mine back at her. "Hello, Ms. Diarist. Ms. Bloscar-winning writer who is now getting emails from agents."

"So you checked your email," I say, taking Beckett out of her arms. He snuggles down against my fuzzy sweater and sucks his binky contently for a few moments before he switches to yanking my necklace forcefully.

"Are you going to do it? Write a book? I told you to write a book weeks ago."

"I wrote that back because I didn't want to miss the opportunity. Ari, I have no clue how to write a book proposal."

"As of ten months ago, you also had no clue how to fry an egg. You'll learn. You can go to the library and check out a book." Arianna always has an answer to every question, and she states it in such a way that it sounds doable.

No husband in the picture? You use donor sperm. Fertility problems found? You use IVF. No money for daycare? You just change your job around so you can work from home. Every solution looks simple, but I've learned from past experience with Arianna that while *she* may have the resolve to put plans into action, the rest of us are usually left with a huge, tangled mess when we dip our foot into solutions.

"And then who would buy it? People want to read about what Pioneer Woman is cooking. Or *Chocolate & Zucchini*. Who the hell wants to hear what I have to say about divorce or cooking or how to furnish a new apartment for under one thousand dollars when you leave all your furniture with your ex-husband?"

"There's a blog called *Chocolate & Zucchini*? What a disgusting combination. Regardless, several million voters voiced their opinion that they're interested in what you have to say. Not to mention your regular blog readers, which have now increased five-hundred fold."

This part is true. I thought there would be a sharp spike and then it would drop back down to my usual three thousand per day, but it has remained up near one hundred thousand for several days, only fluctuating by a thousand or two each day and sometimes climbing above the original high that came on the first day of the award announcement. About one hundred thousand people are sitting on the edge of their computer seats, waiting for me to update my feelings on the lasagna I made.

"Listen, Rach, you have a great platform. *Of course* publishers are going to be interested in buying the book."

"'Platform,' listen to you. Where did you even get that term?"

"The agent's email, and then I Googled the term. But it's true. Here, I have two hours before I have someone picking up their pants. Let's go down to the bookstore, and I'll get you a book on writing book proposals to celebrate."

"Do you think buying a book would jinx it? I mean, she may have sent that email out and then changed her mind and will never write back. And I could get myself all excited, working on this proposal, and have it come to nothing."

"Well, honestly, I think you should write a book proposal and try to sell it. Whether she ends up as your agent or someone else is beside the point. You have a good story and people love your writing and frankly, I think you need a new project. Especially if you return to the library when the money runs out. You'll need to have something back at home to distract you—something that is entirely your own."

"A baby. An ink-and-paper baby," I say softly.

We both look at Beckett, who has returned to snuggling, and Arianna, not entirely pleased that the tone of my voice, veers towards wistfulness, grabs her purse and diaper bag before I can get too far down that path.

When I consider how my life looked before last week, it feels a bit surreal to be going to a book store to purchase a text on writing book proposals and to have someone possibly interested in representing the book. All the clichés are true. Beckett bobs his head up and down a few times as if he can hear my thoughts, and he wholeheartedly agrees.

Just wait until Adam sees me now, sneaky blog lurker that he is.

It occurs to me, several minutes into reading the book on book proposals, that in order to write one, I'm going to have to lie.

I'm supposed to ask myself if I have something to teach my future book readers? If I *had* any advice to give, I would follow it myself. I haven't really moved on, or seeing Adam's ISP on my computer wouldn't have sent me trotting off to Arianna's apartment that next morning. Women who have moved on just archly raise one eyebrow at their ex-husband's shenanigans and click off the screen. Women who are still hoping for something hit refresh seven-dozen times while eating a pint of ice cream. I think we all know that I'm part of the latter more than the former.

The author of the book on writing proposals asks me to answer this question: "Why are you the best person to write this book?"

If I answer honestly, I'm not the best person to write this book. At least not right now. Not while I'm still thinking about my ex-husband while on dates with potential boyfriends (especially those of the sexy, Spanish persuasion. If Adam is cutting into my thoughts while I'm with someone who smells like leather and cinnamon and sex, you know there is a deep problem.) Not while I'm driven to eat a pint of ice cream while I stare at Sitestalker wondering what Adam's presence means. Not if I am considering, even for a second, to slip out The Box.

Which means I'm either going to have to lie in my book proposal, because I really want to get published, or I'm going to finally get rid of The Box.

The Box contains all of the sentimental stuff I saved from my marriage. The stuff you trot out when you're already feeling weepy and you need that extra push to get you to a good cry. The Box came from a grocery store and originally held a case of crushed tomatoes; now it holds the remains of my crushed marriage.

I take it out from its hiding place in the back of my closet and set it next to the writing-a-proposal book. This feels like one of those positive-thinking moments, where, if you knew how to really channel *The Secret*, you could get rid of all these mementos that only make you feel like garbage and clear the way towards thinking up some really good fodder for writing your own self-help book.

I open The Box. There are photos—the worst sorts of photos: vacations, unposed shots catching a moment in conversation, outtakes from snapping a picture for our engagement announcement. In all of the photos where we are conscious of the camera, we are smiling, huge dental-commercial-like smiles. These were real smiles, times that we were really happy. The photographs taken towards the end of the marriage, the ones where my shoulders look tense or my eyes do not match my mouth, were all discarded when I cleaned out our apartment. I threw them out or left them behind in drawers so Adam could find my tense, fake smile when he least expected it.

The Box contains a smashed penny that he made for me in a rest stop on the New Jersey Turnpike. It has an imprint of the Statue of Liberty superimposed over Lincoln's head. We had stopped to get frozen yogurt on a drive down to Washington, D.C. I secretly thought I might be pregnant—my period was late and I was ravenous—but I hadn't told him yet. Unprompted, he made me the penny while I was using the restroom, and when I emerged, he pressed it into my palm and said, "Lucky penny." I carried it in my pocket until I got my period a few days later.

There is an old concert t-shirt in the box, a button that says, "Kiss me, I'm Irish," a postcard from Berlin when Adam went there for a conference, and a ring purchased on Portobello Road during a trip to London. I take out each item and dramatically place them in a semi-circle around me, as if I'm performing a Wiccan love ceremony.

I ball up the concert t-shirt and throw it in the trash can. I grab a few chatty old postcards and toss them in too. But I'm not getting that cleansing high I had hoped to achieve, the one that I was going to translate into a "You can do this too!" message for the book. I fan myself with a handful of photographs and re-read an old shopping list.

Beer

Duck sauce (the one in the orange jar . . . do you know what I'm talking about?)

Cheerios

Roach killer

Shampoo

Toothpaste

And then, in Adam's loopy script under my handwriting:

Things that make my wife horny: kisses on her neck, being fed strawberries, having her husband do the shopping so she better be ready for him when he gets home . . .

That was true. Having him take care of things did make me horny. Perhaps that's why we had so little sex in those later years—he never had time to do the shopping.

I refold the paper and place it back in the box. I save half the photographs, the penny, and fish the t-shirt back out of the trash can. The box is about one-fourth lighter than when I began, and that seems good enough for now.

Maybe my book will be The *Anti*-Secret. How negative thinking and still mucking around in your past can actually be quite healthy and bring all sorts of good stuff your way. How you don't have to let go and trust the process, but instead can do whatever you need to do to get through the day, whether it's stare at your ex-husband's office website for a few hours or keep a box of stuff in your closest that tortures you emotionally, or still keep your married name.

I start jotting down notes on the inside cover of my proposal book. How to be a good divorcee: (1) do whatever you need to do to get through the day. (2) don't get rid of stuff until you're ready. (3) find your voice and use it. (4) learn to love IKEA.

I decide to send another note to the agent even though she hasn't answered my first one. I tell her how hard at work I am with the proposal, and how it will probably be finished soon. I send the note off before I chicken out and then sit down and start working on what I hope is the advice I need to hear in order to get over Adam once and for all.

Because the reality is that if he really missed me and was reading my blog for the right reasons, he would reach out to me. The Adam I know is keen on taking action, and the fact is that we're still in the same city. His office is near my neighborhood. We still order from the same Hunan Chow (the deliveryman tells me this every time I splurge on dinner and he drops off my order.) If Adam missed me, he could pick up the phone and call me. He could send me an email. He could even hang out around my apartment and "accidentally" bump into me; ask me out for coffee to catch up.

But he doesn't, and that fact makes me type even faster.

Life from Scratch

blogging about life one scrambled egg at a time

Meatloaf is something everyone loves. It's like a really good third date—things feel comfortable and familiar, but each meatloaf is a little different, so it has a kick that keeps you alert. I've wanted to learn how to make meatloaf for a while since I stopped shelling out $15 for it at Cafeteria (but I miss Cafeteria so much . . . those garlic mashed potatoes . . .) I've put it on my calendar. I've put the idea on the top of a shopping list. I've talked about it with Arianna.

I am really good at getting excited to do something.

I'm not quite as good at actually doing it.

This morning, I opened up Mark Bittman's cookbook, *How to Cook Everything*, and saw that he did not lay it out in black-and-white for me. He gave me choices. And choices are my downfall.

He writes that while you can make a meatloaf from one kind of meat, meatloafs work best when you blend beef, pork, veal, or lamb. But how much? How much beef to how much pork (for the love, I'm not putting pork in my meatloaf) to how much veal? I mean, is it equal parts of each? Or double the beef and less of the others? And you can't ask Mr. Bittman, because it's not like he's a blog writer where you can leave him a comment with the question.

And it's hard to put on your big-girl panties and trust your instincts. It's easier to just keep putting off making the meatloaf.

So what would you do, blog readers? Admit that while you really want to make meatloaf, it's not worth pushing your personal boundaries as it comes to making meat decisions? Take Mr. Bittman's recipe to the butcher and ask the butcher how he'd divvy up the meat ratio? Please tell me, sweet Internets, how would you go about blending beef, veal, and lamb if you need it to total two pounds and didn't want to waste money on using up meat on an inedible meatloaf?

Chapter Eight

Chopping the Parsnips

Practicing her own version of positive thinking to distract me from the looming nervous excitement about my second date with Gael, Arianna tells me that she wants to plan a great party for my quickly approaching thirty-fifth birthday. A woman cannot be sad, she figures, over the idea of turning thirty-five and earning the cursed medical title of "advanced maternal age" if she is eating really good food in an expensive restaurant, especially after the sparse restaurant life I've had since the divorce. She holds out a copy of *Zagats* coupled with a recent article from the *New York Times* magazine detailing the hippest new spaces to eat in the city. It's like a drug dealer offering a sample.

"I figure a restaurant is the best place for your birthday party,'" she says, adding another name of a restaurant to her growing list. Beckett watches us from his highchair, squeezing cubes of sweet potato between his fingers. I scan the possibilities, noting that most of them are well out of my budget range. "Built-in activity," Arianna adds. "Who do you want to invite?"

"You," I tell her.

"Do you want Ethan there?"

"Sure, Ethan. Which means you should also invite Sarah. And Richard."

"And Penelope?" Arianna asks, her pen hovering over her list.

"No, they should get a babysitter. Maybe make that clear in the wording if that's possible? Um . . . and put down Gael."

"Gael Paez?" Arianna says in a terrible Spanish accent that sounds more Madras than Madrid. "What is the Spanish equivalent to 'Ooh la la?' Is he coming over tomorrow?"

"We're cooking dinner together," I tell her, stooping down to mop up the orange mess that Beckett has dribbled on the floor. He laughs and bangs his hands on the tray, sending a spray of tuberous vegetables into the air.

"Six people," Arianna says. "I'll get a reservation for six. Ooooh, what do you think of Butter? We always read about Butter on Page Six."

"Do *you* want to bring someone?" I ask.

Arianna stares at Beckett and then looks down at her list for a long time. "No, I don't need to bring anyone else."

I wonder if Arianna is lonely, if all of the talk about Adam and Gael has been difficult to hear. I try to imagine the situations reversed, how it would feel if Arianna was dating a totally hot Spaniard while still longing a little over her ex-husband. It sounds downright *annoying*, when I put it in those terms. But there doesn't seem to be a delicate way to ask her if being alone bothers her. I vow to stop complaining, to just date Gael and not dissect the relationship so much and try to forget Adam altogether. I had a nursery school teacher who used to always chant as she passed out stickers at the end of the day, "You get what you get and you don't get upset."

And that seems to be as good a philosophy as any to live by.

I sit down at the computer, the proposal book turned upside down on the desk with the pages fanning out. I am supposed to be writing an overview of the book, but instead, I am clicking over to the website for the restaurant Arianna settled on. This must be how parents feel when they're given the promise of free babysitting and a night out. After nearly ten months of mostly home-cooked meals, I am absolutely salivating over the idea of eating in a fine-dining restaurant, with real cloth napkins and pats of butter.

Arianna goes for a dark horse; a "molecular gastronomy" restaurant where they serve a single grape and call it a "Teardrop from the Sky." I'm a little dubious to give my sole outing to a trendy restaurant over to a newcomer, but beggars can't be choosers, and I feel badly asking Arianna to pick Le Bernardin when I peruse the prices on their menu.

Arianna chose the restaurant mostly because it's so brand-spanking new that the owner offered her a special tasting menu at half the price of the normal prix-fixe menu. Arianna mentions that she might have let slip that I'm a food blogger with one hundred thousand readers each day. She promises me the restaurant will be hot. Full of movie stars and models all slurping down the same emulsified concoctions.

Before I can get to my big night out, I need to think about all the nights I spent in, waiting on the sofa for Adam, because I still have to work on the proposal. I want to get it to the agent as soon as possible. Before she forgets that she sent me that first email, since she hasn't yet sent me a second.

I grab a handful of pretzels and look at the notes I've jotted on the inside of the how-to-write-a-proposal book over the last few days. I try to think about what I would have wanted to read immediately following the divorce. Or what I would have wanted to read while making the choice to leave Adam.

I would have wanted something comforting. Like a meal of roasted chicken and potatoes. Something your mother would make you (or, in the case of my mother, something she would order for you). I would have wanted a book that told me that everything would be okay in the future, even if everything is not okay now.

Because things are okay for me now, right?

I set my hands down on the computer keys and let them rest there lightly. Is it right to encourage someone to take that first step, even knowing that you feel miserable after the fact, that divorce is like having a limb severed from your body? That I felt lighter without the diseased portion of my body while simultaneously mourning the loss? That divorce was really really really painful whereas sitting on the sofa every night waiting for Adam to come home was merely miserable? That I spent a lot of time asking myself had I done the right thing or wondering why I hadn't demanded marital counseling (as if Adam would have taken time out of his work schedule to squeeze that in). When there isn't abuse—simply unhappiness—is divorce the right answer?

But the answer is "yes," because even if I was miserable those first nights alone in my Murray Hill studio, it *was* better than being miserable in that old space. With Adam, it felt like there was no room for movement and change, but here, anything is possible. Perhaps nothing will happen, but anything *could* happen too. And lives need possibilities.

I start typing out an introduction, something that is the verbal equivalent to the hot cups of tea Arianna made for me those first nights alone. I acknowledge the awfulness of the pre-divorce state, the frustration with your partner, the agony of signing the papers. I don't make empty promises, but I do offer hope. I tell my old self—my ten-months-ago self—that I don't need to fix everything all at once. That it's okay to be sad, it's okay to take a night or two or three to feel sorry for yourself. That *sadness* isn't a dirty word. In writing the introduction, I also tell this advice to the "me" right now. This could really be it, the chance to set things on a new path, meet a new person, build the life I want to be living at thirty-five.

I type all afternoon, only pausing to run out to the grocery store before the early evening traffic and pick up all the ingredients I'll need for tomorrow's dinner with Gael. I return to the apartment and pour myself a bowl of cereal to eat in front of the computer, so I can keep typing. It is an amazing feeling to watch all the words pour out of me and see the page counter at the bottom of the screen grow.

As scared as I was to start, because I didn't want to fail, writing the proposal is the easiest thing I've worked on in a while. It's time consuming, but it isn't like the first time I caramelized onions and stood over the pot, terrified to move from the space lest they burn. I may not be a natural in the kitchen; I may need to work hard between the sink and the stove to put dinner on the table. But writing the proposal is simple. It is like popping bubble wrap; it is satisfying and straightforward. Just as one bubble leads to the next, each section leads to another until, around four in the morning, I crawl into bed, fully depleted, with the proposal and first chapter of the book neatly waiting for their first edit on top of my computer.

My head is foggy, like I've been existing in a different pool of time for the past twenty-four hours. I don't know if the act of writing completely agrees with me right now. It is as if I have indigestion; as if I've been gluttonous with words to pour out an entire book proposal in the course of a single day. I spend the next day editing my words, tweaking and twisting and changing and deleting. I sit on the sofa and twirl the end of my hair around my pen, composing future book signing table chat in my head: *thank you, thank you so much! I'm so glad you loved the book. What? You're a television producer, and you want to make a sitcom about my life? Sure, I'd love to do lunch and talk.*

Before Gael comes over, I run downstairs to pick up the mail: a few bills, an invitation to an old friend's open house for her new apartment, coupons for a local pizza place. The open house invitation is in the shape of a house even though Laura has moved into a new apartment. She is someone I used to work with back at the library; a fellow graphic artist who kept pictures of her cats framed on her desk. She is the type of person who always has her office supplies lined up neatly in her drawers and all of her computer files marked with properly capitalized file titles. And, at the same time, she can drink everyone under a table and often tells stories that end with her panties missing. She is a study in contrasts and a poor chooser of invitations.

I muse for a moment about going to her party. She hasn't seen me in months, has no idea that I'm about to be the most famous author in the entire world or that I've landed myself an extremely attractive Spaniard. The last time she saw me, I was mascara-streaked and packing my desk. It would be fun to catch up and hear what's been happening at the office since I've been gone. But I am terrible with parties. I never want to go; always feel awkward while I'm there. I throw the invitation into a desk drawer and keep working, bringing the proposal into the kitchen so I can cook and edit at the same time. I edit until I hear Gael's knock on the door, and then I shove the pages away in a drawer.

He hands me a bottle of good Spanish wine when he enters the apartment and gives me a quick, friendly kiss on the mouth. We have already settled into the hello kiss stage that follows the goodbye kiss stage. I take this as a good sign.

"It smells good," he tells me, peering into a pot where I'm browning the chicken. "What are you making?"

"What are *we* making," I correct. "Well, I wanted to make you something Spanish. So I went for the most obvious dish."

"*Paella,*" he says, motioning to the bag of rice on the counter. "With seafood?"

"Er . . . no. With chicken. It may not be the most traditional *paella*. It may sort of be very similar to a risotto recipe. But it's Spain! This is a taste of home."

"My mother makes *paella* with rabbit," Gael admits. "And chorizo."

"Well, this is not your mother's *paella*," I purr, hoping that I sound sexy when I say that. The point of tonight was to make him horny and grateful for me bringing Spain to him, not make him think of his mother.

We fall into an easy banter as I drain the chicken on paper towels and sauté the peppers. He sits on my counter and pours me a glass of wine. He pops a CD in my stereo of some Spanish rock group. I don't understand one thing they're growling. There is something easy about being with Gael; he doesn't take himself too seriously, never appears to be in a rush. Even this meal, I can't tell if he is hungry and eagerly anticipating it or annoyed that he has been invited over for dinner and it is still being prepared. He just exudes an air of relaxation, as if it doesn't matter if he eats the meal in the next few minutes or in the next few days; it is all good.

I become braver the more I drink. I slide my pan into the oven and turn around to face him. I take a step forward, tilting back my head, and slosh some wine onto the floor as I kiss him. He tugs lightly on the hair he has gathered by the nape of my neck. I have not kissed a man like this in many years. It has been too long since I've last had sex in a kitchen.

The buzzer goes off, and we pause so I can take the *paella* out of the oven. Gael takes the opportunity to remove his sweater. I push my hand against his chest, bringing him down to the floor, away from the steamy oven, almost on the living room carpet. I haven't adjusted my shades for this occasion. The whole of New York City may be enjoying our show.

I roll onto my back, guiding him on top of me. He is even easy-going in sex, pausing to murmur things to me or stroke my cheek. I want to tell him to hurry up before I lose my nerve, but he is taking his time, making things last. He gently pulls off my jeans and runs his finger over the inside fold of my knee.

I undo his zipper, and he asks me if I'm on the pill. I try not to laugh, worried that he'll misunderstand and think that I'm laughing at him. You don't need to pay for birth control if you're not having sex. He shyly pulls a condom out of his pocket, apologetic for assuming that we'd somehow end up on my floor, half in the living room and half in the kitchen, my panties discarded underneath one of my bar stools.

He slides off his own jeans, and they land beside mine. The empty legs of our pants lie entwined near their owners. I am about to have sex with Gael Paez, an incredibly attractive Spanish man with droopy eyes and a lopsided smile. Almost as if he is reading my mind, the corner of his mouth turns up in its charming asymmetry.

And then I look down.

This is my first time with an uncircumsized penis. Which shouldn't be a big deal, except that it is. It nods its way up to me, looking just this side of not-quite-right. I mean, it's sort of like a veggie burger—which looks like a hamburger and yet, there is also something about it that screams out its difference from any burger you've eaten in the past. Mrs. Gestlemann, my third-grade Hebrew school teacher, *tsks* me from inside my brain. "Rachel, honestly. Didn't I teach you about the *chuppah*? And the *ketubah*? And not to taste unkosher beef?"

But didn't I once say that the point of this year was to get myself an entirely new life? I learned to cook for the first time in thirty-four years. I'm writing a successful blog and working on a book. I kill my own spiders. Isn't having sex with an uncircumcised penis the last great frontier I need to conquer? I *can* be the sort of woman who has sex with non-Jewish, European, uncircumcised men. Like this, non-Jewish, European, uncircumcised man; an olive-skinned, cinnamon-smelling man with a soft accent, slowly rotating his fingers over my inner thighs. I moan in spite of myself.

And then the decision is made, the deal done, check it off the list, because he is in me, and we are moving together. He is darkness and corners and sound and something beneath the cinnamon . . . photo chemicals and wool and the memory of detergent. He is rough and slow and cautious and racing. I orgasm slightly before him; it doesn't take much. It has been so long since I have had sex that someone probably could have accidentally brushed up against me at Zabar's and gotten the same response. He is slightly out of breath as he pulls out, and we lie next to each other, the scent of the completed *paella* washing over us.

I never know what to do after sex. I mean, after sex with your husband, you talk about the people you bumped into during the day or a particular bill that came in the mail or something you saw on the television. Ordinary stuff. Everyday stuff. But sex for the first time in years with someone who is barely one step up from stranger? It feels like it requires special words; poetry read over the incongruent rock music that is still pouring out of the stereo or proclamations of a sort. Instead, after a few moments of silence, Gael grins and then gets up from the floor. He points at his condom. "I'm going to remove this thing, okay?"

Maybe I'm a bit disappointed, but I'm also relieved to slip back on my clothes, wash up at the sink, fiddle with the *paella* pan. To have the pressure removed to mark the occasion. I spoon the rice into two bowls and place it on the table.

"*Mi amor*, it smells wonderful. I'm starving."

"Thank you," I say shyly, watching him sit down at the table as if he has just conquered a country. I slide into a chair myself, suddenly uncertain about everything. He has seen me naked. He knows the paths on the inside, their counterparts on the outside. It feels like we should be very intimate, except that we don't really know each other all that well. I awkwardly shovel some rice into my mouth to give me a reason not to talk and wonder what I just did.

Half of my brain is on the unfinished *crèma catalana* in the refrigerator as he tells me a story about some restaurant in Madrid that has butterflies encased in glass as their front door, and the other half of my brain is replaying how our jeans looked with their legs entwined together.

What the hell did I just do?

"Would you like to help me with something? A few weeks from now?" Gael asks, spearing one of the peppers, as if we haven't just had sex on my living room floor. As if that whole portion of the evening was just part of my imagination. "I have this wedding to shoot; to photograph. Would you like to come with me? Help with the cameras?"

"Don't you have a helper?"

"She can't make this party. I just thought it would be fun. It would be interesting. You would get, of course, a meal with the rest of the staff. The same one the guests eat."

"How fancy," I say dryly.

"And I would take you out afterwards. We'd be dressed up so we could go somewhere dressy." He smiles his lopsided smile and motions to his plate. "This is quite good. Not my mother's *paella*, but quite good."

Seriously, could the boy go a half hour without mentioning his mother?

When he smiles his lopsided smiles, the corners of his eyes crinkle closed, until I can only see a small sliver of deep brown beneath the folds. I need a do-over. I would like to stop eating *paella* and have sex on my bed. Try to last beyond a few minutes.

"I'll go to the wedding," I say.

"You will?" he asks.

"You sound really surprised," I respond. What I want to ask is if the pre-dinner sex marked me as a different sort of girl; the kind who didn't accept date invitations that were really work favors. If rolling around on my carpet and getting to use the condom he stashed in his pocket before heading over here changed how he viewed me.

"I didn't know how you would feel about it being a wedding,"

Gael admits.

"It doesn't bother me," I lie, waving my hand in the air as if I'm swatting away all of the bad feelings I have when I see white gowns, morning suits, or cream-colored one-hundred-and-ten-pound cardstock invitations. "Seriously, my marriage is over and done with. I've moved on. Anyway, you'll make it up to me by taking me to the Guggenheim."

"Absolutely," Gael agrees. I wait for him to suggest a date, but we both sit there without speaking for a moment, the rock band wailing about something in the background.

"Actually, *you* could do me a favor and come to my friend's open house."

I regret it right after I say it. Why the hell did I fill the silence with that?

"Sure! When is it?"

"It's next weekend. What I meant to say is *if* I go. I don't know if I'm going yet. I mean, she's an old work friend, and she had this desk drawer that was too neat, and she never knew where her panties were at the end of the night," I babble.

"This is sounding better and better. Neat home and no underwear," Gael says.

"I don't even know how many people will be there, or if I can bring a guest. Let me talk to her first and ask her if that's okay."

Suddenly, I am so tense that I am getting a headache. I should be the opposite of tense. I should be jelly. I just had my first orgasm by something other than my hand in the last few years. I should be buzzing and humming and whatever else your body does when it has finally been satiated sexually. But I am tense, with a headache that is creeping around my forehead like a tight sweatband. I am missing every third word that he is saying: *I didn't . . . she was . . . to do . . . but I . . . happy anyway.* I want to ask him to repeat it, but I can't get the words out of my mouth.

"Do you feel okay?" I interrupt.

"Okay? Yes? Why?"

"I think I have food poisoning," I gag and run to the bathroom. Except I don't vomit. I lean against the sink and try to catch my breath and look in the mirror. I look like I am on the brink of tears. This is it: I am having a nervous breakdown. Surely this must be what movie stars mean when they sit with Barbara Walters and talk about their nervous breakdown. It must start with a panic attack over *paella* and end with crying in the bathroom.

"Are you okay?" Gael asks on the other side of the door. There is an edge in his voice as if he is checking for the answer. If I'm not okay, he's going to bolt. But if I tell him I'm fine, he'll stay for dessert.

No one wants to deal with someone having a nervous breakdown.

I promise I'm fine; that the feeling is passing. And then I silently mouth some tough love to my reflection in the mirror: *you idiot, there's no crying after sex. Old Rachel is a crier. You are the new and improved Rachel, the one who has sex before the paella she made from scratch. Who has sex, more importantly, with hot Spaniards rather than boring lawyers. Pull. Yourself. Together.*

I splash some water on my face, take a deep breath and return to the kitchen table.

"Is everything okay?" Gael asks again.

"I'm fine; I don't know what that was. I thought I was going to be sick, but I'm fine. Do you want to have dessert?

"Do you think that's a good idea if you were just sick? You haven't eaten your *paella*." Gael asks dubiously.

I am coming off as crazier by the second.

"I wasn't really sick," I tell him. "Can we . . . can we just reboot? Start the night over? I'll go place our plates in the sink and then turn around and we'll pretend that the night is just starting. Can we do this without me coming across as completely unhinged?"

"Unhinged? I don't know what that means."

"I need to start over tonight."

"Is this about the sex?" Gael asks, motioning to the space where we were rolling about a half hour ago.

"It's everything; yes, I mean, no, it's not just about the sex. But yes, can we start over? Can we start everything over about tonight? I made dessert and . . . "

I turn on the broiler and pull one of the two *crèma catalana* dishes out of the refrigerator. I set it on the table in front of him as an explanation. "I just have to do one more thing—caramelize the sugar on top. You told me that it's your favorite."

For a moment, it looks like Gael Paez is going to cry. That he'll have his own personal breakdown, and we'll at least be on equal footing. The CD ends at that precise moment, and after a whirl and click, it is silent in the room. Without saying anything, I move our *paella* plates into the sink. I sprinkle sugar over the top of the custards and slide them under the broiler, opening the oven door every few seconds to make sure that it is caramelizing and not burning.

I remove the dishes from the oven and bring them back to the table along with two spoons. Gael cracks through the sugar crust and scoops up a small spoonful of custard. He turns the spoon upside down and nods at me. "Look at this—perfect. It's your first time making it?"

"First time."

"And you remembered that I said that?" Gael asks.

I nod my head, suddenly not trusting my voice.

"This was a really perfect night, Rachel. I've never had someone do that. Hear what I said and then make it like this." He finishes the rest of the thought in Spanish, and I nod as if I understand what he's saying.

He stands up and takes my hands and leads me from the table to my bed. I get my wish for the do-over as he undresses me, very gently, very carefully, as if I am a flower and my petals may blow away at any moment.

He finishes and sighs and sinks down onto me. I don't have the heart to tell him that I'm not done yet, not when he is so grateful for the *crèma catalana*, for the attention. I want to thank him for the do-over; good things come to those who ask.

Life from Scratch

blogging about life one scrambled egg at a time

I seem to be on a rice kick as of late. First it was the risotto. Then I made paella, which is essentially Spanish risotto. Finally, I made rice pudding last night. With raisins and a little cinnamon on top. Just like . . . well . . . was going to write just like my mother used to make, but my mother never made rice pudding. Just like my mother used to buy. Except that's the whole point—it wasn't.

I used to love to get rice pudding from this diner by our house. I know it's sort of a gross dessert to love, but they'd serve it in these glass sundae dishes with a long thin spoon and a graham cracker on the side. So my mother never made it, but she often bought it, and I expected Meyer's recipe to be similar to the one at the diner—a big wedge of creamy love.

Except that it wasn't. Maybe I made it wrong, but the texture was off, and the taste was different, and it wasn't what I expected at all. I'm not enough of a cook to know how to tweak a recipe to match something in my mind, but it was this strange sensation, not knowing if I liked the new rice pudding on its own merits. I mean, it was good, it was sweet, but it wasn't the rice pudding I thought would be on the spoon. My mind was expecting one thing, and my tongue was experiencing another.

I once dated a guy who said all the unhappiness in the world is tied to expectations, and if we could live without expectations, we'd live in a state of perpetual bliss because we'd always be happy with what we have.

Except if I hadn't had the expectation of how the rice pudding would make me happy, I wouldn't have tried the recipe in the first place. Whatever. That guy smelled like patchouli and wanted to be a professional hackysack player. What the hell did he know?

Chapter Nine

Splashing the Wine

I wake up in the morning to the telephone ringing. It takes a moment for my mind to untangle itself, especially since I'm trying to beat the answering machine from picking up. *I had sex last night with Gael. Twice.* I finished the proposal. I think. The telephone is ringing.

My sister immediately launches into what she needs. That is one of Sarah's best traits—she doesn't waste your time asking questions or making small talk. She tells me that her nanny has an emergency eye doctor appointment, Penelope has no ballet class due to a gas leak at the studio, and could I please come out to Brooklyn and watch my niece while Sarah opens up a man's head.

"You want me to cross the bridge?" I ask. "Today?"

"Could you? Could you be here soon? Ethan can't."

I start dressing before I hang up, debating whether I have enough time to swing by the post office on my way to the subway and mail the proposal. Erika finally wrote back an apology last night for not contacting me again sooner and promised to read it as soon as it arrives. The agency office is a few blocks away, but I thought it would be creepy to show up at Rooks LTD (*Rooks knows Books!*) holding a stack of papers, nervously telling the receptionist, "This is my proposal," as if I'm handing in a high school essay assignment. I swing by my local post office instead on the way to the subway and choose a nondescript manila envelope from the wall, filling in the local address and paying several dollars to have it walked a few blocks away.

"It's a book proposal," I tell the postmaster as he rings up the sale.

"That's great," he tells me, not bothering to even try to sound convincing.

I take my receipt and fold it carefully into my pocket. I'm not a big scrapbooker, but perhaps I should start—keep the receipt from the very first time I mailed something to an agent, use the scrapbook as a storage space for reviews when they come out.

Dream big.

Outside it is still bitterly cold, and I treat myself to coffee. If I'm going to provide free babysitting for Penelope, I'm going to need fortifications.

Sarah is already gone by the time I arrive, and the nanny hurries away once she has established that Sarah will be back by two. Before she leaves, she passes me Sarah's Dos and Don'ts list.

Do make sure that Penelope fits in some form of exercise. Acceptable forms of exercise include 20 minutes of play in the park, jumping jacks, or going to the indoor playzone if it is particularly icy outside as long as I follow up the playtime with what amounts to an alcohol sanitizer bath.

Don't allow Penelope to eat any processed foods, especially those containing dyes. I wonder if the nanny has broken her glasses on purpose—anything to get a free afternoon away from jumping jacks and dye-free foods.

I find Penelope in her room, playing with the dollhouse Ethan, and I bought her for her last birthday. "Hello, Aunt Rachel," she says.

"Hello," I answer back, sliding down onto the floor. She looks at me in surprise. "Can I play too?"

She stares at me without blinking and finally hands me a doll. The mommy. I fluff out the mommy's apron and make her walk around the living room.

"She should be in the kitchen," Penelope solemnly tells me.

"Why? Can't she relax on the sofa? Catch up on her television shows? Can't a mommy watch some *Sesame Street?*"

This makes her laugh, but she shakes her head. She pushes my hand towards the kitchen, and I oblige. I put on my best Julia Child voice and pretend the mother is chopping up chicken parts for an udon noodle dish. "La la la, red meat is better, but in a pinch, you can add chicken to your udon noodles making a most delicious dish. Lovely lovely noodles."

"Aunt Rachel, are you a chef?" Penelope asks.

"No. Yes. I am a cook."

"Mommy says that you think you're a chef, but you're not."

"Oh, does she," I say smoothly. I love that Penelope is still at an age where she speaks in absolute truths. "That's because Mommy is a little jealous that she doesn't know how to make delicious food like me. What does she say I am?"

"She says you're a writer."

I tuck my face down towards my shirt so she can't tell that I'm smiling. I move the doll around the kitchen like she has suddenly broken out into an ecstatic dance. "Yeah, I'm a writer too. I'm a writer who cooks."

"Mommy doesn't know how to cook."

"None of the Katz women do. Grandma Katz—terrible cook. But I am breaking that fate. I am going to be a great chef. Even better than Julia Child."

"Is she a kid?"

"Julia Child? Oh…child . . . kid. No. She was a famous chef."

"Why don't you have children?" Penelope asks. She looks up at me, honestly interested rather than judging. I push her bangs out of her eyes and stare at the perfect curve of her cheek, the dark thickness of her lashes. I purse my lips together, trying to come up with an acceptable answer, one that doesn't make me want to raid their liquor cabinet so that the nanny comes home to find me drunk on gin.

"How do you know I don't have children?" I finally ask, to buy myself time.

"Because I've never seen them," Penelope admonishes.

"That's because I keep them in my pocket." I slip my hand in my jeans and wiggle it around a bit. Penelope laughs. "There is Molly; no wait . . . that's Peter."

"Let me see," Penelope says.

"Absolutely not. If I take them out, they're going to want to play with your dollhouse and mess it all up. They'll move the toilet to the kitchen and the sofa into the bathtub. Hey, I've got an idea. Henny Penny, let's go out."

"Where are we going?" she asks.

"We are going to a paint-your-own-pottery place that I just saw on the walk from the subway. And we are going to make me a big udon noodle dish. And then I am going to have you over for the most fabulous noodles you've ever tasted that I've never ever made before."

She is easy to convince, easy to distract and malleable. She puts on her shoes and unhooks her coat from the rack by the front door. She stands politely on the welcome mat while I raid the kitchen, pushing aside the boxes of flax seed crackers to find something edible and failing that, grab a few dollars from the semi-secret envelope in my sister's desk to buy myself a bagel at the Dunkin' Donuts.

At the pottery place, I have Penelope sit quietly at a table—she is definitely the master of quiet sitting—while I talk to the owner and pick out a rough white dish. It has a lot of potential, the wide, shallow slope of the bowl, the unusual crimping of the edge. I bring it back to the table, and Penelope chooses the worst colors imaginable. A murky green, a sterile grey, beige.

"This bowl is supposed to celebrate noodles," I tell her. "You love noodles. Dark green doesn't say noodles. It says 'receptacle for overcooked beets.' What about pink? What about this sparkly purple?"

"What about blue?" she says, pointing to some more palatable shades.

"What about sunshine?" I ask, pointing to a cheery yellow. She smiles and squishes her finger over the same square on the color chart. I pick up her hand and give it a kiss. "What about reds and oranges and colors that are happy?"

"How do you know if a color is happy?" Penelope asks.

"It just makes you feel happy," I explain. "When you're looking at it, you feel happy."

"Dark green makes me happy. It's my happy color," Penelope agrees.

"Okay," I say slowly, my artistic vision being ruined as I struggle to be the adult. "We'll use tiny accents of dark green."

The owner brings us the paint on a small ceramic dish, and we each tackle separate sides of the bowl, making swirls of color and dots and lines as we paint towards the middle. She tells me about how her nanny cries while she watches soap operas in the afternoon and how her best friend at the park once swallowed a goldfish. She tells me all the words she knows in Japanese and how her mother told her that she could wear lipstick to her Bat Mitzvah when she's thirteen. And slowly, slowly, our heads come together as we both bend over the bowl, our brushes crossing, and my hair touches her, mixes together until you can't tell where we begin and end.

I leave before my sister returns home, after having peanut butter and jelly sandwiches with Penelope and her nanny. I make a mental note to return to Park Slope the next week to pick up my dish and promise Penelope that I'll take her with me to get it. The nanny lets her try on her new pair of cat-eye glasses, and Penelope waves at me from the door, her already round eyes even more enlarged behind the frames.

I pick up a few ingredients for a tofu sesame stir-fry and call Laura on my walk home. She doesn't pick up on the ambivalence in my question about guests, the way I give her one too many outs and tells me that she's "thrilled" that I'm bringing my "beau," and she's just "ecstatic" that I've finally "moved on." She tells me that she can't wait for me to meet her new boyfriend as well, a "brilliant" man who quotes Shakespeare to her and takes her "picnicking indoors." I'm not even sure what that means, so I thank her and try to keep my voice breezy. I call back Gael and tell him to pick me up on Saturday at seven. It's a date.

I make dinner and eat it on the sofa in front of the television, checking my email at the same time. I know it would be too soon to receive something from Erika, that the postmaster didn't heave himself around the counter and walk the few blocks to her office to hand-deliver it that morning. I just wish that I had thought to ask her if I could email the proposal. My good ideas always come too late.

The buzzer startles me out of the zen state I have entered, watching Cat Cora do bizarre things to ostrich meat on *Iron Chef*. First, I hit the entry button and second, I realize that I have no clue who I've just let into the building. It could be my brother, finally bored with waiting for someone to exit the building so he can make a surprise entrance. Or it could be a rapist who is going to wait in the stairwell until *I* come down the steps in the morning, forgoing every other woman who lives in the building. Not that I have a self-important, pessimistic imagination.

Someone knocks at the door, and I peer out the tiny peephole. Gael's face looms like a reflection in a carnival mirror. He is staring at a spot on my hallway ceiling.

I actually mouth the word "Shit," to myself, as if I'm trapped inside a romantic comedy movie. This has never happened to me before, the unexpected guest who is not kin—fictive or otherwise. My apartment is a mess. I left this morning without time to wash the dishes that are piled up in the sink. My bed is unmade and covered with my clean laundry that still needs folding. I am eating ice cream straight from the carton in front of the television.

"Rachel?" he asks. He knows I'm inside. I mean, I've buzzed him in. Unless I can pretend that it wasn't me. It was someone else. The rapist, for instance, from the earlier worry who is lying in wait in my apartment, kind enough to buzz someone into the building but not wanting the company while he waits for me to come home.

"Give me a second," I yell out, throwing the lid on the ice cream and stuffing it back in the freezer. I scoop up the clothes and toss them in the laundry basket and dump the basket and its contents into the dry shower, snapping the curtain shut. I kick a pair of shoes under the bed and give the blanket a shake. There is no time to fix everything wrong with the sink.

I throw open the door, and we both stand there for a moment, not saying anything. I am trying to catch my breath from running around the apartment, not wanting him to see just how out-of-shape I am that I can get winded by a 30-second clean-up spree. He has a look on his face as if he doesn't quite know how he has ended up standing inside my hallway.

He pulls out a cookbook from behind his back. It is a thick volume, part of the "Cuisines of" series. This is *Cuisines of Spain,* and it looks a little dog-eared and *paella*-splattered. "I was at a bookstore today. A second-time bookstore? And I found this in the cookbook section," he admits. I step aside so he can enter my still-messy apartment.

"What were you doing in the cookbook section?" I ask.

"It was next door to the Spanish section," he said. "I thought of you."

His honesty is like swallowing a chunk of jalapeno. I busy myself by flipping through the table of contents. He hasn't removed the sticker from the bookstore. He paid eight dollars for the gift.

Is it a gift?

"Do you want to sit down?" I ask. Even though it is quite clear from the way he surveys my bed to the way he stares at the remote control as if he is waiting for me to turn off the television that sitting is the position farthest from his mind. *Do you want to lie down? Do you want to recline? Do you want to loll about in my bed making small talk and then ravage me?*

It takes me until this point to realize that this is a booty call.

I have never been the recipient of a booty call. There are no booty calls when you're married, and I haven't dated anyone since in order to have a booty call. I don't know whether to feel offended or honored. On one hand, it feels a bit humiliating to have someone show up at your apartment for the sole purpose of having sex. On the other hand, it has been so long since anyone has found me remotely sexy that I'm not going to allow a little meat-market emotions stand in the way of enjoying this.

I help him out by turning off the television and sitting down on the edge of my bed. I stare up at him with what I hope is a come-hither look. He sits down next to me like an overgrown school boy—a guilty one at that—and leans casually back on his elbows, as if it is simply understood that we're only sitting here because it is the only surface in the apartment. He ignores my leaning tower of kitchen equipment in the sink, and I ignore the way his shoe is now touching my socked foot.

"What were you doing before I came?" he asks.

"Watching television. Eating ice cream."

"Where is the ice cream now?"

"Back in my freezer," I tell him.

"Is that what you were doing while you made me wait in the hallway? Putting the ice cream away?"

"Something like that," I admit.

I really don't need any foreplay this time. He could just hurry it along and start, but he is taking his time, running his fingers through my knotty hair. I was so busy worrying about how the apartment looked that I forgot about how *I* look. My hair is back in a messy ponytail, I'm wearing jeans that have a stain of paint from this morning above the knee. I touch my own hair self-consciously, stopping his hand from working through a particularly large knot.

"I didn't realize that I was going to see anyone tonight," I admit.

"I think you look beautiful," he tells me. "I like it when women are undone. Natural."

He finally kisses me, a kiss that falls somewhere between the hungry ones that came pre-*paella*, and the thoughtful ones that came post-*crèma catalana*. He pushes me back lightly, and I land on a lump in the bed, my pajamas that I tucked under the blanket. He takes a condom out of his pocket and puts it on the bed above my head. I crane back to look at it. It begs for acknowledgment.

"You always come prepared," I tell him. "Like a boy scout."

"I don't know what that means," he says.

"It's just a saying."

"We had a scout organization in Madrid," he said, his voice barely above a whisper. I realize that he has been slowly getting quieter, as if his voice were on a dimmer switch. "*Federación de Asociaciones de Scouts de España.* But I didn't belong."

"Why?" I whisper.

"Because I thought it looked stupid," he tells me with an almost silent laugh.

He finally picks up the pace, removing my top while

simultaneously tugging out my ponytail holder. Sliding off my jeans until I am underneath him, bra and panties against his sweater and pants. I help him off with his clothes, but I'm at an odd angle, where I can only get each article of clothing started, and he needs to finish it off. He rubs my inner thighs, his fingers brushing underneath the elastic from my panties. I slide them off for him, undo my own bra, toss both articles of clothing out of my sight range onto the floor.

He hovers over me for a moment, working the condom on. It is like that plateau on the ride, where the train car has been ticking upward, ever so slowly, and now we are in that moment right before the plunge. He stares at me, and for the smallest moment, I think that he's not going to do it. He's going to roll off of me and unsheathe his uncircumcised penis, pack up his toys, go home. I tilt my head to the side, as if I am inviting whatever question is ricocheting around in his head. *Are you sure we should be doing this? Are you sure you're not too neurotic? Should I have bought you that cookbook or just left it back at the used bookstore, my own secret consideration?*

And then we are hurtling down down down.

I drag Arianna along to a tasting at a new chocolate bar opening up in Gramercy Park. I tried to bring Ethan too, but he insisted that there was spilled coffee to photograph somewhere in the city. Since I don't know when the offers and opportunities are going to run dry, when being a Bloscar winner is going to lose its shininess, I grab any of the offers that don't involve tofu hotdogs, gluten-free crackers, or anything remotely reeking of healthfulness. Hence how we have ended up at a table surrounded by chocolate *pot de crème*, truffles, and a slice of black forest cake.

"This one," Arianna whispers, as if writing this review is a top-secret mission, "is better than sex." She holds out the final bite of a chocolate stuffed with hazelnut nougat.

It is good, but it isn't better than sex. Perhaps better than some sex, but not better than sex with an attractive Spaniard after several years of a dry spell.

"Do you really think that anything but good sex is better than sex?" I ask, feeling badly for entering this line of questioning since I have had sex recently, and Arianna has been celibate for years.

"Sure. Back rubs. Back rubs can be better than sex," she says, reaching over for a scoop from the dish of chocolate ice cream with cayenne pepper. She fans her mouth and takes a sip of water.

"Back rubs cannot be better than sex," I scoff, knowing this is mean, since she went to a spa last week. I had sex, my best friend went to a spa. This is like dangling candy in front of a toddler, and I feel terrible—either from the last truffle I ate or from the fact that I seemingly cannot stop myself from rubbing my recent good sex luck in my best friend's face. "You don't orgasm from a back rub unless you're paying extra for a 'Happy Ending,' which means you're at a very different type of 'spa,' and then . . . well . . . you're essentially having sex."

"I mean a back rub given by the guy, not a massage at a spa," Arianna corrects. The owner stops by the table to see how we're doing, nervously pressing his hands together as if he's praying for some good press. I nod my head, my mouth full of cake, and he steps away from the table, disappearing into a back room. I wonder if he's checking his computer to see if I've already magically posted the review in the same way that I've been checking incessantly for Erika's message, despite the fact that she may not even have the proposal in hand yet.

"I've orgasmed from a massage," Arianna continues. She examines a white chocolate-covered slice of kiwi and sets it back down on the plate. "I mean, the guy was that good, that with just his hands on my back, and my hands nowhere near my nether regions, I was able to have an orgasm. Like a wet dream. Except I was awake."

I stare at her, my mouth partially open, possibly revealing the masticated crumbs from a forkful of torte. There are two ways this could possible go. Either Arianna is my sexual hero, able to achieve orgasms in a single bound, or Arianna has had such a dry spell that hands on her back are close enough to her vulva to cause tremors to occur. For my own ego's sake, I decide to go with the latter.

"You only did that because you haven't had sex in years," I tell her.

"How do you know that I haven't had sex in years?" she asks coolly.

The vase of chrysanthemums from a few weeks ago. The need for me to immediately return her favorite purse after my date. That's when I know for certain what I've been overlooking this whole time, what has been niggling me from time to time when I consider how good and kind and patient Arianna is, my personal Mother Theresa. Arianna is not a saint. Arianna can listen to my whining about Gael and my incessant chatter about my divorce because Arianna has been getting laid.

"Who? Who is it?"

"I'm not telling," she says. She doesn't look coy and happy. She looks clammy and over-sugared. I move the truffle plate away from her. "Not yet."

"Why? I thought we told each other everything. I'm your sister-by-choice."

Something in that phrasing makes her look even paler, as if she feels terrible for holding out on me when I've shared everything with her, and then I get this sinking feeling, this absolute certainty in my sinking feeling.

"Do I know this person?" I ask quietly.

"Rach, I don't want to do this. I'm not ready to talk about him. I'm not ready to have us all go out and double date and have you pick him apart."

"So it's not Gael?" I question, finally releasing my breath.

"No, it's not Gael! What the hell is wrong with you?" she admonishes. A couple at the table next to us stare for a second. "I would never have sex with your boyfriend."

My *boyfriend!*

"Then I don't understand why you haven't told me about him," I finally say.

"Because it's new, and I don't know where it's going, and I don't want to think about it too much. To overthink it. Not everyone is like you, Rach. I don't feel better after discussing the situation; I get more anxious. You get something out of blogging about it and picking it apart and considering it from all angles. I just get hives. I promise. I'll tell you when I'm ready."

"Fair enough," I say, pushing the truffle plate back towards her. "Is there any chance you'll bring him to my birthday party?"

I chew on the word boyfriend for a moment. I sort of have a boyfriend. I used to have a husband, and I was someone's wife for years. And now I'm a girlfriend. It's like being at a party and grabbing the wrong coat off the bed at the end of the night. It looks like your own, but doesn't quite fit. But since your own coat has exited the festivities, worn out the door by another friend of the host's, this is the mantle you'll need to wear home.

I'm just relieved to learn that we're on equal footing—two single women having sex, compatriots of a sort. It's hard when you're in the same circumstances as your best friend, but your progress differs. If we were dieting together, I wouldn't be able to crow about losing pants sizes, and if we were both actresses, I wouldn't want her to call me to talk about all of the parts she was getting. I know it makes me incredibly small, but I'm just relieved that we're both having sex.

"Not a chance," she says firmly. "Can we change the topic?"

"So, no picking apart Gael showing up at my apartment last night? Or my date with him tomorrow for Laura's party?"

"Let's scoot away from the topic of sex lest I have an orgasm over this mousse."

"Which would just prove that it's not the man's prowess but your own insane abilities to find release even with desserts."

Arianna pretends that she hasn't heard me. Eats the last of her *pot de crème*. Makes me wonder how I can ask her for lessons.

Gael buzzes up from downstairs right on time on Saturday night. I have been picking at a blog entry for over an hour, shifting the photographs around like I'm feng shui-ing the post. I hit publish and check my make-up one final time in the tiny mirror outside my bathroom, where the light is better.

I have put the cookbook he gave me on my bookshelf with the pages facing outward, though I hope he doesn't notice. At first, I had the binding facing outward, and then I couldn't concentrate. Either I was staring at the computer and wondering what Adam was thinking as he read my blog (because I could see that my sneaky, blog-lurking ex-husband was still reading) or I was staring at the bookshelf and thinking about Gael's thoughtfulness. I turned the book so that the ingredients-stained pages face outward. I don't even want to think about what I'm looking at—is it juices from tripe or chocolate from *churros?*

This time, I let him come upstairs and wait for the second announcement of his presence, a light knock to the door. I open it and smile grimly at him, as if we're on our way to the funeral of someone neither of us likes very much.

"I can't tell," he admits, giving me a quick kiss on the lips. "Are we happy we're going?"

"You know what," I tell him honestly, "we're enduring."

"Enduring. That doesn't sound good."

"No, it's fine. You know, it isn't as good as being excited to go, but not everything in life needs to be *crèma catalana* and confetti. Sometimes, you endure things just because you need to do it and then you can toast yourself on the other side."

"Wonderful," Gael says, rubbing his hands together. "A party and then drinking."

And then lots of sex, I finish silently in my head. I clear my throat and try to smile at him. "Should we go and do this and get it over with?"

I'm not sure why I've gone from being a little nostalgic when I got the invitation to practically dreading the cab ride over to her apartment. Laura is pretty much a fun person, and I have so few girlfriends left by this point in my life. It isn't like college, where people are pouring out of the woodwork. When you're an adult, you make your friends at work or in your neighborhood or through your children.

Being at home has cut off the work avenue, New York is just not conducive to knowing your neighbors, and being childless leaves the last door closed. I'm not sure where someone goes to make friends once they've left their workplace. It isn't as if the shul is holding a friendship schmooze and booze. The Jews are much more interested, it seems, in making sure you are married and on the road to getting knocked up than they are ensuring that you have someone to call at two o'clock in the morning when you are having nightmares about your divorce.

We take a cab over to her building, making small talk along the way. Gael points out a place where he once photographed a couple for their wedding, moments before their ring bearer vomited on the bride's gown. We both agree that the hotdogs are particularly good from one street vendor when we pass the empty space where his cart stood hours earlier during the day. As I've said before, it is easy to be with Gael. He is uncomplicated, he doesn't take himself too seriously. I feel my stomach unclench at some point during the cab ride. Laura is going to be very impressed with my beau.

And she is. I can see her eyes widen as she says hello to me but faces Gael, taking in his lopsided smile and carefully messy brown hair. She shakes his hand and accepts the house-warming bottle of wine that we purchased from the liquor store two doors down, before entering her apartment building. "And you're from Spain!" she exclaims, after she inquires where his accent comes from. "I love Spain! If I could move anywhere in the world, it would be Seville. I just fell in love with that city."

"Well, I am from Madrid," he corrects. "It's the middle of the country. Maybe six hours north."

"Of course!" she corrects. "Madrid is exquisite. I had a wonderful time going to the little tapas bars at night."

"Maybe you can talk Rachel into trying ham," he says, looking around the room. Even I can tell that he's bored, and I barely know him well enough to read his expressions. "I haven't had any luck."

"Rachel!" Laura practically shouts as if he has told her that I've been shooting tourists in Time Square instead of not partaking in meals made out of pig. She leans in close and whispers solely to me, "My boyfriend is in the kitchen right now. I need to tell you all about him. Un-be-liev-a-ble. By the way, I should probably tell you something," she begins.

We're interrupted by the doorbell ringing again, and Laura places one finger up to ask me to wait, though we're shunted towards the center of the room while another couple takes our place by the door to be interrogated by Laura. We give ourselves a self-guided tour to show that we're interested and also because we're nosy. New Yorkers are constantly mentally comparing apartments, worrying about where their own abode falls on the spectrum.

She has landed herself a small, two-bedroom, though the second bedroom is too small for a bed and serves more as an office. She has her office supplies neatly arranged next to her computer and several photographs of her cats in frames near the keyboard. It is as if she has recreated her workspace at home so she can play graphic designer in the same way that little girls play house. One of the cats rests on the table next to a picture of himself.

Her bedroom is plain and unassuming, beige walls and a crème colored comforter. But I am jealous of her doors—the doors that divide the two bedrooms from the hallway, even the door that divides the kitchen from the living room/dining room. It feels like she has moved up in the world while I have definitely moved down. Doors symbolize something—there has to be a reason why people work their ass off to move from a cubicle to an office to an office with a window. I am living a cubicle life while Laura has at least gotten the windowless office.

Gael leaves me in the living room to grab two beers out of the kitchen for us, and I sit down on the sofa next to a woman I vaguely remember from another office in the library. She confirms that she works in acquisitions, and we talk for two minutes about how she and Laura met by bumping into each other at the same deli every day and ordering the same thing: a turkey sandwich with lettuce and no mayonnaise. I look at the woman's left hand. She is also unmarried. I wonder if she keeps framed cat pictures on her desk. I wonder how long it would have taken for me to do the same if I had stayed in my job post-divorce. *The framing of cats is a difficult matter*, I sing to myself.

"I haven't seen you around though in a long time," the woman says. I realize that I've already forgotten her name. "Why don't you join us for lunch this week? You can always order something else."

"Actually, I don't do graphic design anymore," I admit.

"Oh, what are you doing now?" the woman asks.

"I'm writing," I say, trying it aloud with someone who I hopefully will never see again though knowing my luck will be the first person I bump into when I head back to my library job. "I'm writing a book."

"Oh, that's so exciting," the woman says, and I can tell that she genuinely means it. "Is it a romance novel?"

"No . . . more like self-help. A divorce guide."

"Oh, sort of the anti-romance novel," the woman nods. "I love reading romance novels. I probably go through two or three a week."

I see Gael coming out of the kitchen with the beers, so I excuse myself and make my way over to him. "Do you see what I mean at this point about enduring? You come and you drink a beer and you put another link on the friendship so you can call her up a few weeks from now for lunch and not feel awkward."

"I'm going to call her?" Gael asks, surprised.

"No, I was using the second-person, but I meant me. I'll call her to get coffee and catch up. But I wouldn't be able to do that if I hadn't come to the party. And I know a few other people here."

"Which ones?" Gael murmurs, his mouth barely moving.

I glance to the side and take a sip of my beer. "That man over there. By the kitchen door? He's Steve, and he also works in the design department. He steals stuff from the supply cabinet. Not just paper or tape but rolls of toilet paper. I'm sure he outfits his whole apartment in stolen goods."

Gael snickers, and I can see that he is watching a blond woman by the window that I've never seen. I wait until he looks back at me to continue, taking note how many times his eyes flick back at her.

"The woman on the sofa, I know her from acquisitions. She just informed me that she likes to read romance novels."

"Interesting," he comments. He looks at the blond again so I look at her too. She isn't that amazing. Really, the best thing about her is her cloud of blond hair. I casually shift my position, wedging myself in the sight line between the woman and Gael. He looks back at me again.

"Don't you have boring work functions in Spain?"

"We do, but you don't work with her anymore," he says. "You don't have to keep playing by the rules."

I am about to tell him that we can leave once we finish our beers when his eyes flick over my shoulder again. I am about to finally call him on it, say it loud enough to embarrass him, when I hear *his* voice, the last person I ever wanted to bump into tonight.

How has New York gotten so small that my ex-husband and I are at the same party?

"It's a relief that I'm out of it," I hear Adam tell another man. "I was so miserable towards the end."

He was miserable? Excuse me, *I* was the one who was burning a hole in the couch waiting for him to come home from the office each night. *I* was the one completely being ignored. I don't even have the sense to close my mouth before he turns around. He glances over his shoulder and sees me gaping at him, and he instantly looks as if he has swallowed a thumbtack.

"Rachel?"

And this is how I end up seeing my ex-husband for the first time in over ten months.

This is exactly what I've been dreading. What I wanted for our first encounter was ample warning, dressed in something amazing (it doesn't have to be full-out couture, but I would have loved to have been wearing the navy blue cashmere sweater that he always told me made my breasts look impossibly round and luscious), maybe carrying a copy of my book.

I wanted him to see me mid-laugh, so he knew with absolute certainty that at that moment in time, my life was better than his. I wanted him to be wearing something that was stained with soup. Maybe sweatpants with a hole that he didn't know about on the ass seam. I wanted him to be dropping things, looking depressed, perhaps with an embarrassing breakout of acne across his forehead. One that he had been hoping beyond hope that I would never see.

Instead, he is standing there, looking perfectly respectable, no soup or ass-revealing rips in sight. He doesn't even look embarrassed about having just described the last day of our marriage as the best day of his life. His face is instantly composed to reflect tentative friendliness. Whereas I am standing there, my mouth half-open, my new boyfriend staring at some blond woman behind me. I am the embodiment of surprise, of speechlessness. I am not wearing anything incredible. I am not feeling anything close to incredible. I am fairly certain that I have lipstick on my teeth.

I stall for time by saying his name back. "Adam!" Now the verbal ball is back in his court. He looks over at Gael and back at me.

"I wondered if you were going to be here when Laura mentioned that she knew you. I didn't have a chance to ask her," Adam tells me evenly.

"I worked with Laura at the library," I tell him. "How do you know her?"

Adam pretends to look surprised at my past-tense reference to the library. Sneaky, blog-lurking ex-husband. He has become very cricket-like these last few weeks—first popping up on the blog and now popping up at a party. You just never know where he'll jump next.

"I met Laura through her brother."

Adam glances at Gael again, who smiles serenely at both of us, as if he's watching a particularly tasty morsel-of-a-scene from a Spanish soap opera.

"Adam," I say reluctantly. "This is Gael. Gael, this is Adam."

Gael immediately recognizes my ex-husband's name and behaves accordingly, putting an arm around my shoulder as he leans forward to shake Adam's hand. Adam's eyebrows rise with understanding, and his face slides deeper into unreadability. I focus on a curl of his hair resting right over his ear. He has grown his hair out a bit—it looks longer, less sculpted, more as it did when we were in graduate school except peppered with grey. I have to hold my hands behind my back because I have such a strong impulse to tuck it out of the way.

I am still attracted to my ex-husband even if he is happy to be rid of me.

I've known his face for so long that I can't help but allow my eyes to travel to all my favorite spots. It's like revisiting your old college and needing to grab a beer at the same familiar bar, check if your graffiti is still there. In our silent pause, I examine the small grooves on his lower lip, a scar of unknown origin on his jaw line, the stubble I used to love to scratch my finger against. I check to see if that small gap of eyelashes on his lower right lid still exists. If his ear lobes are still detached. I have this urge to tell a joke and get him to smile so I can check if his bottom teeth are still crooked, or if they've been Invisilined.

But he doesn't really look like he's in a smiling mood.

And I don't know any good jokes. Knock, knock. Who's there? Ex-husband. Ex-husband who? Ex-husband who I wish wasn't at the same party as me.

See, doesn't really work.

"You two probably want to catch up, and I just saw someone I want to speak to," Gael says, slipping behind me and making his way to the blond woman. Which just lost him several points. Perhaps European men don't know this, but you never *never* leave an American woman alone with her ex-husband that she's awkwardly seeing for the first time in almost a year at a mutual friend's party. Gael is supposed to stand there and remind Adam that I am desirable. I am wanted, even if he didn't want me. Instead, Gael's quick departure makes me feel even more ill-at-ease, as if someone has snatched my security blanket away. The blond woman laughs at something Gael says and touches his arm. Bitch.

"So, you're dating someone," Adam says.

I nod. I can't really ask him the same question back without looking too interested. He seems to be at the party alone.

"How have you been?" I ask instead.

"Fine," Adam tells me. "Taking some classes, and I've started running again. So you left the library?"

He's normally a terrible liar, the sort who looks at the ground as he tells you that he didn't eat the leftovers I brought home from the restaurant and told him specifically not to eat. But he asks this question as if he doesn't know the answer, coolly looking me in the eye. Excellent—I've become a cook and writer since our divorce. Adam has perfected the art of deception.

I want to scream at him, "You know I left the library, because you lurk on my blog all the time. So you know that I can now fry an egg, and I've won an award, and I'm writing a book, and I'm terrified of baking, and I don't want to go back to graphic design work. Just say it."

Instead I give a small smile and take a sip of my beer. "I may go back. I just needed some time off to figure out things."

"Can you wait here a second?" Adam asks me. "I just want to get a beer. I'll be right back in a second."

He slips into the kitchen, and I take this as an opportunity to disappear myself. I walk quickly and silently towards Laura's hallway, where she is cleaning up empty cups, dumping them into a grocery bag that she is using for trash. Leave it to Laura to clean up during the party; everything in its place. She smiles brightly when she sees me.

"Your boyfriend is really cute," she tells me. "I need to introduce you to mine. My brother set us up—you know, the one who works at the new private school in the Village. Anyway . . ."

Laura's voice drones on, gesticulating with a wet cup in hand so that I'm splattered with tiny drops of someone's leftover beer. It's the perfectly terrible premature end to a perfectly terrible night. As she's rounding on the tale of her third date, the mention of her brother finally catches up with me, and I realize that the reason Adam looks like he's there alone is because his date is the *host.*

He is dating Laura, the cat fancier.

This was obviously what she meant to tell me when we got interrupted at the door. Quoting her Shakespeare—of course!—and taking her on indoor picnics God knows where. My ex-coworker with my ex-husband. I am at a loss for words over this thought, instantaneously hurt beyond belief that he has moved on and is dating someone else, even if I've come with a date too. I cannot believe that he has chosen to follow-up our marriage with Laura, the framer of cats and loser of undergarments. It will make me feel much less guilty when I go in her bathroom and raid her medicine cabinet for a leftover Ativan.

She might not have known that he was my ex-husband when they first met—after all, he never attended work events with me. But he obviously shared the connection with her once he discovered she also worked at the library. She could have told me when I called to RSVP, sent me an ooops-I'm-dating-your-ex-husband email. And why the hell is she practically giddy over the idea of reintroducing me to my own ex-husband? Have litter box fumes fried her brain? And why, if he has really moved on so completely and is describing the end of our marriage as a relief, is he reading my blog all night?

I'm about to wipe the smile off Laura's face about her fantastic new boyfriend when Gael pops his head around the corner and grins at me. Laura beams at him and gives my shoulder a small friendly rub, sort of the same motion a guidance counselor uses when she needs to break the news that applying to your first choice school is a waste of your time. She grabs her grocery store bag of garbage and continues her empty cup collecting, oblivious to the fact that I am not smiling back.

I give Gael a modicum of credit that he has torn himself away from the blond and does not seem to have her phone number written on his hand. "So, that's your ex-husband?" he asks.

"Yes," I say.

"I could tell. The whole boring lawyer thing. He has that act down very well."

I laugh despite myself. I still linger in the doorway and Gael looks back towards the kitchen. "Are you hiding from him?"

"I am hiding from him, yes. I really can't believe that we bumped into him here. He's dating Laura."

"*No,*" Gael says, holding out the vowel for so long that it becomes a growl in his throat. He's practically giddy with the idea of the underpantsless cat fancier with my ex-husband. "How did that happen?"

"Someone introduced them. I don't really want to talk about it."

"Do you want his 'coordinates?' Is that how Americans say it?"

"Where is he?"

"He's by the kitchen door. He is looking around a little confused. He can't see you where you're standing right now. He looks like he wants to tell you how it was all a huge mistake. That he misses the way you make *crèma catalana* and can't stand cats—the musical *or* the pet."

"You can tell all of that just by the way he holds his beer? I've never cooked for him." I hope that this next part doesn't make me look too unhinged and middle school. "I know that this isn't very adult of me, but could you sneak me out of here?"

Gael, every inch a gentleman now that he's finished flirting with the blond, waits until Adam has tracked back into the kitchen, still searching for me, to signal that I should head for the door. He promises that it will be okay, that no one should have to happen upon their ex-husband at a party when they're not ready.

And here I was anxious about attending this party because I'd have to make small talk. Who knew that it would be so much worse? But even though Gael repeats how idiotic they are several more times in the cab on the way home like a self-help cheerleader—the idea of a bar long since dropped—I can't help but feel as if something has changed between us. As if he has finally gotten a whiff and can identify the ingredients that make up the meal. One-third of a cup of insecurity, two tablespoons of tongue-holding, four cups of doubt.

Life from Scratch

blogging about life one scrambled egg at a time

Even before I got a divorce, my least favorite part of a wedding was the cake. It's always dry. Always. And I recently read an article that said that most wedding cakes are not only baked months ahead of time and frozen, but that the cake part is actually just doctored-up Duncan Hines. Can you imagine? You're paying several thousand dollars for a cake that has instructions as deep as "Add oil and an egg?"

Instead of throwing the bouquet, we should create a new wedding tradition of throwing the cake. Since it's about as tasty as a bunch of carnations, and it would make for a gorgeous picture in the wedding album. A three-tiered, white-on-white wedding cake sailing over the balcony to the waiting bridesmaids. Splat.

There seem to be two kinds of people in this world— the fondant kind and the buttercream kind. There are those who want the fondant cake, and while it looks gorgeous, a fondant cake is more about the surface than it is about what's underneath. Fondant tastes like crap, and we all know that, but the couple accepts the fact that they are serving a disgusting-tasting cake to their guests in exchange for the ooohing and aaaahing about the cake that comes beforehand. Fondant cakes are gorgeous cakes. They are smooth and unblemished and even and perfect. Not a very realistic way to go into a marriage.

On the other end of the spectrum are the couples who put taste over appearance, serving a butt-ugly but delicious cake to their guest. Fine, buttercream-coated cakes can be pretty, and if the baker fusses with it enough, it can even look smooth and seamless. But the reality is that buttercream is never as pretty and perfect as a fondant cake. It doesn't scream "photo-op." And it's a wedding—the best day of your life according to some—so shouldn't even the cake be exquisite, as least to look at?

Please don't ask me which type of cake Adam and I had at our wedding.

Chapter Ten

Crushing the Garlic

I rip up Laura's change of address card the moment I get home. I write a long blog post about how husbands who don't mourn the end of their marriage are heartless assholes. Arianna suggests that I should take it down; stop baiting Adam. But I leave it up and let it collect comments expressing agreement. Damn straight I'm right. A person shouldn't feel relief when something ends after twelve years unless they're being released from a POW camp.

Six days after the party without a phone call, and I am ready to write off Gael, too, when he calls to remind me of my promise to help him at the wedding. "I'm collecting on my promise," he informs me.

"Really?" I say, stirring some rice into the melting butter at the bottom of my pan. "A wedding."

"And you need to dress up. You need to blend."

"So I should grab my big white gown out of storage?" I say dryly.

"Do you still have it?" Gael asks.

"Of course I still have it. In storage somewhere, but I still have it. Why?" I ask. For a moment I'm frightened that he'll suggest that we head off to town hall.

"I didn't know if that was the sort of thing you got rid of after a divorce."

His statement makes me pause. I'm not sure how I decided what I would keep and what I would leave behind, but suddenly, my big, cream-puff-of-a-dress feels like an unlucky talisman for any future relationship. It's like the literary monkey's paw—I need to throw it out before it causes something terrible to happen.

Though fate doesn't really work like that . . . right?

I still make a mental note to get rid of said dress on eBay and promise Gael that I'll be ready to go by two o'clock, dressed in something appropriate and understated. My hair in something more professional-looking than a ponytail. I hang up and return to my rice, willing it to brown evenly.

I haven't really given the task of helping him at the wedding much thought since he first proposed it. To be fair, we had just had sex when I agreed to go. I was in such a state that I probably would have agreed to anything—running off to the Bahamas, breaking-and-entering into my old apartment, cooking ham. Thinking about going to a wedding— even someone's I don't know—makes me feel a little numb. Most of my friends were already married before I went through my divorce, so it has been several years since I've had to hear someone say "I do." In fact, this will be my first time facing a nuptial aisle since my own divorce.

Listen, I tell myself, *it's okay to be sad for yourself even in the face of someone else's happiness. You don't even know this bride. You owe her nothing except to hold some cameras and pass Gael his equipment.* If I have to tune out the "I dos," and avert my eyes from seeing her big white dress, so be it.

Gael calls me downstairs at two o'clock. I've left my hair down, willing it into damp curls with a little gel. I'm wearing a standard black cocktail dress; knee-length. I add a string of pearls that my ex-mother-in-law gave me for my wedding. Gael has parked a van outside my front door, blocking the fire hydrant. The van's back doors are open, revealing a series of boxes and bags.

"There is someone else doing the video," he tells me. "We're just taking the still shots. We have to be there at three, but I thought we'd get there a bit early to set up, so I could teach you all the equipment. Bridal party portraits begin at four."

It feels like he's all business, as if I'm just a woman he has hired for the day, one he doesn't need to invest a lot of niceties in, since there is little chance that he'll see me again. I feel myself respond with my own coolness, and I get into the front seat without speaking, fastening my seat belt silently and hoping I remembered to put on the waterproof mascara as opposed to my normal, black-river-creating make-up.

He is tense as we drive through the city, barely speaking except for an occasional statement here and there. It is annoying to drive in the city, the stopping and starting and people passing in front of the car. There is a small lot by the synagogue, and we pull in next to the catering truck. Gael gets out and unpacks the trunk, bringing all the boxes and bags into the dimly lit basement hallway. Steam escapes out the synagogue kitchen, and as the door opens, I glimpse white-aproned women squeezing something semi-liquid out of piping bags onto grilled toast. My stomach lurches.

He opens a bag and points at a disassembled camera body, rattling off the names of various cameras and their lenses. He shows me how to set up the tripod, insert the cable release so the camera can be ready for the ceremony. How to use the external flash. I am barely registering half of what he is saying, knowing full well how important it is to get this right. He is here to capture moments. This bride may need these photos later on to remind her why she married the groom in the first place. What if we miss the kiss at the altar? Miss the first dance? Perhaps it will change the entire course of their marriage when she is sitting on the sofa late at night, waiting for her husband to get home and desperately needing a visual reminder that she does still love him.

Sometimes I forget that everyone is not me.

And I had those pictures to remind me, yet I still left Adam.

One of the bridesmaids comes giggling down the hallway, clutching a glass of champagne in one hand and a make-up bag in the other. Her eyebrows raise as she catches site of Gael leaning over one of his open bags, and she gives another glance over her shoulder as she disappears into a stairwell, presumably on her way to the bride. I catch Gael looking at the swish of taffeta we can still see through the small, square window in the door.

"Pretty," I say tersely. Even in mauve taffeta, the bridesmaid was stunning.

"Blonds are not my thing," he says.

"What about the woman at the party?" I ask.

"What woman at the party?" Gael asks, genuinely confused. He opens one of the cases and shifts around two lenses.

"The blond. By the window."

"Carly?" he questions, as if I'd know her name. "I know her from a wedding. I shot her sister's wedding in the fall."

"Oh," I say, suddenly relieved. "Oh."

"Apparently the marriage is already over."

"Divorce is en vogue," I comment wryly.

He looks up at me and shrugs. "I'm sorry, Rachel. Are you upset to be at a wedding?"

"No, no, really, no."

Except that I am.

"I didn't want to shoot this one," he admits. "I had no choice, I needed the money, but I dated the bride."

"Recently?" I ask, hoping that I've kept the gasp mostly out of my voice. "Does the groom know?"

"It was years ago. And I didn't remember her, actually. She

wanted my brother-in-law to photograph her wedding, but he wasn't available today, so he set up an appointment with me. Midway through the meeting, she starts asking about Madrid and reminiscing about this crazy day in Central Park, and the groom says, 'I think we have something in common.'" Gael repeats the groom's words in a perfect replica of a New York accent. "I am not excited to be here either. Let's just endure and toast ourselves afterwards."

I manage a weak smile and hoist two of the bags onto my shoulder, following him up the stairwell to the lobby outside the main sanctuary. A few bridesmaids are milling around, fixing each other's make-up and hair. One gives a startled glance when she sees Gael and gives him a small, awkward wave. He gives a terse wave in reply and we duck into the sanctuary, almost knocking into the wedding director overseeing the finishing touches on the *chuppah*.

"Did you date her, too?" I hiss.

"She's a friend of the bride. I think we had dinner together one night. With the bride, Rachel, with the bride."

I am itching to ask him a dozen questions, everything from how many girlfriends has he had in New York to how long he dated the bride, who is due to show up in the lobby within the next ten minutes for family portraits. But he is busy walking around the room, checking the lighting from all angles. I sit down on one of the chairs and watch the florist twist a final rose around one of the poles holding up the *chuppah*.

At this point in my own wedding, I was sitting with Arianna and my sister and Adam's sister in the bridal room, changing the polish color on my nails. I had gotten a manicure the day before, and the color was still bothering me. Arianna told me to fix it; it was easy to switch the color and have it be perfect. I remember holding my hands flat on the table between us. I thought the nail polish color was important back then. No one probably noticed it.

One of the bridesmaids opens the sanctuary door to peek inside. "Hey Gael," she calls out. "Amanda is down here now, if you're ready to get started."

He gives me the smallest glance and mouths the word "endure," though it looks as if he is just puckering his lips. I follow him out into the hallway and help him arrange the various formations of family and friends, the bridesmaids giggling through the whole exercise, the bride radiant in the center of each picture.

She is small and blond—so much for his lack of interest in

blonds—with thin lips and hairless arms and blond eyebrows waxed into a look of perpetual surprise. She looks like she could still be in high school, except that her mother keeps referring to her as Doctor Flaum to anyone who will listen. I try to picture her with a stethoscope draped around her neck, but Gael whispers that she has a doctorate in literature. I try not to laugh and drop the flash the next time I hear her mother address her.

"Hey Rachel," a voice drawls, and I turn around, half expecting to see Adam sporting a new voice—almost like the monster that keeps jumping out at the heroine in the horror film—except that it's Polar Pete of dinner party fame. He takes my hand limply, shaking it as if he's rattling a piggy bank. His skin is still cold and strangely white. "Funny seeing you here."

He is obviously one of the groomsmen, formally attired in the same tux and cummerbund combination as four other men. He tells me that he has known the groom forever. He looks bored by the friendship. "How do you know Amanda?"

"I don't," I admit, wondering when New York got so small that you could bump into Polar Pete and your current boyfriend's ex-girlfriend all at the same affair. "I'm here with Gael, helping with the photographs."

"Oh, so you finally decided on a career," he says. "Photography."

"No, this is a one time deal. Just filling it for his usual person."

"I thought you had followed your brother's footsteps into photography."

"No, no, nothing like that," I say.

And then I realize that I have nothing more to say to Polar Pete. We both stand there awkwardly, waiting for Gael to call the groomsmen into the shot. I examine the stained glass windows depicting various Bible scenes, and try not to be blinded by the bride's dazzling smile. I busy myself with reading through one of the cream-colored programs that outlines the ceremony, including a final addition: "And after the kiss, Mr. and Dr. Flaum-Ravelstein are husband and wife!"

The bridal party disappears into a back room, and the groom and his men walk in the opposite direction to what appears to be a small coat closet off the sanctuary. The lobby begins filling with people who spill into the sanctuary, taking their seats on either side of the satin runner. I follow Gael up towards the *chuppah* and turn around, holding the lens firmly in my hands. With no bride to watch, all the eyes are on me, and I shift uncomfortably until the ceremony begins.

The music starts up and the groom walks down the aisle, flanked by his parents. He kisses them at the *chuppah*, his mother leaving a smudge of lipstick on his cheek that I'd desperately like to run forward and rub off. The groomsmen walk down the aisle, each with a bridesmaid on his arm. A flower girl tosses huge clumps of rose petals, finishing off the basket several yards ahead of the *chuppah*. A woman runs forward, scooping up a particularly large batch on the satin runner, and tosses them towards the groom's feet.

And then the music changes.

The doors open for a final time, and the tiny bride begins the walk towards her groom, and my vision blurs. This is the happiest moment of her life on the happiest day of her life. She is walking for the last time as a single woman. We all believe, when we take those steps down the aisle, that it will be our last time as a single woman. After all, if we thought otherwise, why would we ever take that leap of faith?

When I took that walk down the aisle I felt lucky. I felt like my chest was going to burst open from all of the pride bubbling around like a newly opened bottle of seltzer. Now I feel queasy watching the bride beam at the guests, turning her head from side to side to smile at friends and relatives, her gaze always returning to the groom waiting for her at the end of the aisle.

The groom, waiting.

Not the bride.

That day was the last time I wasn't waiting for Adam; that he was waiting for *me*.

I whisper an apology to Gael, set the lens on the floor and slip discreetly out a half-open door next to the ark. I am in some type of darkened chamber that holds a desk, two chairs, and a few books on a mostly empty shelf. The only light coming into the room streams in through the window, but it's almost dark outside. Winter in Manhattan.

I cry as quietly as possible, even though I had the forethought to close the door lightly behind me as I slipped out of the ceremony. I am now stuck in this room until the wedding is over. I can hear the dull murmur of the rabbi intoning the blessings, and honored friends reading passages in English. I put my hands over my face as if I'm trying to hide the fact that I'm silently sobbing, and when I move them away, they carry with them two identical streams of black eye make-up. So much for streak-free mascara. I can only imagine what I look like.

I hear the shattering of the glass marking the end of the ceremony, the cry of joy from the audience and then wild Klezmer music accentuating a long kiss. I am waiting to hear the buzz of guests exiting out the sanctuary, when a quiet but urgent knock comes on the door. I expect to see the rabbi's bald head telling me that I've defiled the holiness of this chamber, but it is only Gael.

"I have to work the cocktail hour now, but I wanted to make sure you're okay."

"You probably think I'm crazy," I blurt out.

"Not crazy," Gael says fondly, giving me a quick kiss on my forehead. "A mess with make-up all over your face, but not crazy. Remember—*endure*. I need you in the cocktail room, *mi amor*."

I nod, indicating that I'm about to pull myself together. "I'll be in there in a second. I'm just going to slip into the bathroom."

The bride has set up baskets in the bathroom containing everything a person could possibly need at a wedding, from tampons to a new pair of stockings, and, thankfully, small tubes of make-up remover. I scrub my face clean and pat it dry with one of the hand towels. I toss the towel into the laundry basket, feeling badly that I had stained it with remnants of my make-up. One of the bridesmaids is reapplying her own make-up and watches me in the mirror.

"Are you okay?"

"Me?" I ask. "I'm fine. I just don't do well with weddings."

"Sucks that you're a wedding photographer," she says.

"I'm not. I'm just helping the photographer today."

She points out that there are little tubes of lip gloss in the basket. I take out one and apply it with a Q-tip.

"I don't do well with weddings either," she confides. Bathrooms have a way of starting conversations like this. There is something about bathroom tile that brings out a woman's darkest secrets. "Always the bridesmaid, never the bride. Seriously, *never* the bride. And I'm going to be thirty-five."

"I was married," I admit. "Now divorced. And now my ex-husband is dating a friend of mine, can you believe that?"

"I'm so sorry," she says and hands me a Kleenex, as if she expects me to start crying again. I tell her the whole story, acutely aware that Gael is probably struggling under the weight of the camera bags and juggling lenses as we speak. I finish my story with seeing Adam at the party and how I couldn't speak coherently around him. She clicks her tongue sympathetically in all the right places. She squeezes my hand,

and we both exit the bathroom, the nameless bridesmaid to pretend to be happy for her friend while I hunt down Gael, who is snapping pictures of guests.

"Where have you been?" he questions, handing me one of the bags.

"Cleaning up. It takes time to get all that make-up off my face."

I snap a grapefruit martini off of a passing platter, and Gael gives a sigh, shaking his head slightly as if he doesn't know what to do with me. He takes dozens of pictures, sometimes asking for equipment out of the bag. Most of the time, it's faster for me to simply open the top, and let him poke around to find it. As he moves through the room, making sure to photograph every guest, I watch the bride. She is radiant, with her veil casually pushed back from her top of her head and her tiny stick arms flailing in the air as she hugs everyone who enters her path. She is so happy that it seems as if the happiness should linger around for hundreds of years to come, almost like an echo in a cavernous room, continuing to bounce off the walls. I drink way too many martinis watching her and end up sitting on a bench in the hallway, the room tipping a bit from side to side.

After the wedding, Gael packs up the van and then tells me that we can leave it in the lot for a bit. We walk down the street until we hit a bar, a forgettable sort of place with round tables and movie posters on the wall and a clichéd dart board in the corner. The people drinking there look like the antithesis of the bride, drunk on depression.

Gael orders a beer for himself and a soda for me and returns to the table. I have kicked off my heels and placed my feet on one of the empty seats.

"Talk to me," he says.

And I guess that's the point; I can talk to Gael. I can tell him what's on my mind, meet his open expression with my own. He may not be perfect, but his face doesn't make me swallow everything I'm thinking. The words tumble out of my mouth, an old story that I've never told anyone beyond Arianna.

"I didn't know I was going to leave him the night we separated. And I'm aware that this is going to sound really stupid; not a good reason at all," I say, taking a sip of my soda. I deeply regret the grapefruit martinis. "But there was a cockroach in the bathroom. The super had sprayed roach stuff the day before, and now the cockroaches were coming out to die. Most of the time when you see one, they run so quickly that it's hard to kill them. But these were lingering around, strolling across the counter as if they had all the time in the world. And one was sort of hanging on the wall, close to the ceiling."

Gael watches me without saying anything. He reaches over and squeezes my ankle.

"I'm usually not that squeamish about killing them, but for some reason, I couldn't bring myself to hit this one up by the ceiling. Maybe I secretly just wanted Adam to come home and take care of me. I convinced myself that if I hit it and I missed, it was going to land on my head. So I sat on the edge of the tub, watching it, and waiting for Adam to come home and kill it for me. I called him at work, but he told me that I was 'bothering' him, and once he said *that* I couldn't very well admit that I wanted him to come home to kill a cockroach."

I wipe the condensation off the outside of the glass with my finger. "I sat on the edge of the bathtub for . . . hours. I probably sat there for *four* hours watching this half-dead cockroach on my wall. I didn't want to leave the bathroom because I was scared that I wasn't going to be able to find the roach again if it moved. And I didn't want to sit in the bathroom staring at a cockroach because . . . well, I'm sure you understand."

"I do," Gael says simply.

"I picked up the phone and set it down a dozen times. It's an awful feeling; not being able to be truthful with your husband. To just admit that you're scared of a bug, that you want him to come home and take care of you. I could never tell him what I needed, because I couldn't find the words. They shriveled up inside of me whenever I heard that tone that told me that I was *bothering* him.

"I know I sound like I'm crazy, but it wasn't about the cockroach. I mean, it *was* about the cockroach because I convinced myself that it would fall on me if I tried to kill it. But it wasn't about the cockroach. It was anger at myself for being unable to tell Adam what I needed, and it was anger at him because I had this strong sense that if I *had* found the words, he wouldn't have cared.

"I just had this sense that if I called him to say that I had fallen down the stairwell and had broken my leg, he would have told me to call an ambulance instead of coming home. Or if I had told him that someone had followed me home and was now in our building and I was terrified, he would have told me that he had a brief he had to write. He always put work before me. I never felt like he had my back."

"I see," Gael says gently.

"A little after midnight, he came into the apartment, and he called out to see where I was. I told him I was watching a cockroach in the bathroom, and he didn't come in right away. I could hear the water running in the kitchen and hear him changing his clothes. Finally, he came in the bathroom, smacked the cockroach with the heel of his shoe, and then walked out of the bathroom without saying anything. He just went into the bedroom to go to sleep."

"So you left?" Gael asks.

"I told him that I wanted to separate. It was the first time I used that word—separate. Isn't it crazy? I couldn't find the courage to ask him to come home and kill a cockroach, but I heard myself tell him that I wanted to separate. It was sickening to say it, but once I used the word it also didn't feel right to take it back. We had crossed a line. We had one of our usual talks about my expectations and his schedule. And how he 'worked so hard for me,' which was why he was angry that I was also bothering him at the office. But it wasn't about the bug, his schedule or his rationale for working all the time. I knew at that point that we weren't going to reconcile. That was it."

I wait for Gael to suggest that we head home, cut the evening short. Anything to get away from the crazy cockroach lady who cries at weddings. But he nurses his beer, taking his time.

And I like him for listening.

Give yourself a day to feel bad.

First I write that advice in my book and then I follow it myself and have a twenty-four-hour mope, setting a time limit rather than giving myself a drill sergeant pep talk about bucking up that I'm not going to listen to anyway. Twenty-four hours to cry at sad movies and eat fattening food and not shower. A twenty-four-hour cleanse, like an emotional colonic, to get over the garbage feelings I put in my body by attending Amanda Flaum's wedding before I was ready. I'm not sure I'll ever be ready for taffeta and tulle again.

I spend the day alternating between bed and the kitchen. My sister calls and informs me that I sound depressed. She rattles off a list of three psychiatrists she would recommend, a few anti-depressants she thinks I should try, and finishes off with an invitation to Penelope's ballet recital all the way out in Park Slope in the same tone of voice one would use if giving a sibling a free vacation to Hawaii.

"Do you think that could also be the cure for my depression?" I ask. "Dragging the spinster aunt to see young girls with their lives ahead of them prance around an auditorium stage? I'm not depressed; I'm allowing myself a twenty-four-hour mope."

"You're becoming very sour," my sister informed me with some detachment. "I thought you'd have a wonderful time visiting us. You don't have to take it out on Penelope."

I instantly feel terrible, because when it comes down to it, I am the worst aunt in the world. Despite the emergency babysitting I provided a few weeks back, I rarely attend any of Penelope's various recitals and performances—ballet, piano, or mini-debate team. With the exception of the dollhouse, I usually fail to buy her cool gifts, and I've never taken her to an American Girl store. I don't even slip her forbidden candy, for fear of my sister's wrath. I literally wouldn't be surprised if I discovered one day that Penelope had started a blog called *Worst Aunt* that cataloged all my transgressions.

"Please tell Penelope I'm sorry that I'll miss her recital. I actually already have something scheduled that day," I lie. "I really do want to be there." I'm not in the mood to tell Sarah that I bumped into Adam at the party and hear her thoughts on that. She hangs up after muttering some sulky things about the dinner party Arianna is throwing for me.

The thing with a twenty-four-hour mope is that it has time limitations. As long as I don't answer the phone during the time period or leave the apartment, I don't even need to involve others in my pity party. It really is a healthy alternative to get it all out in one big vomit-of-a-depression. I watch romantic comedies from the 1980s and scream at the screen. I use my sleeve as a tissue. I avoid my blog at all costs, because nothing good can come from tearful blogging.

I make foods that are fattening. Chocolate mousse. Fettuccine alfredo with huge pats of butter and a mound of extra, grated, parmesan cheese. Broccoli with flecks of hazelnut. I eat the whole meal—four or five helpings—in front of the television and polish off most of the mousse.

There is something about high-fat food that can comfort better than even a manicure and hand massage. I stare at the television, not really seeing the image, while I dream about becoming a recluse in the apartment, eating fettuccine alfredo from morning until night, until I become so large that the paramedics cannot lift me off the sofa.

Adam would read about me in the *New York Times*, his eye catching on my continuing use of his surname: *Rachel Goldman of Murray*

Hill discovered she was stuck to her sofa late Sunday afternoon when her knees refused to bend. Goldman says, "I was essentially part of the furniture in my old life, therefore, it's fitting that I actually merged with it in this life."

I don't bother to wash the dishes in the sink. Nor fill the dirty ones with water. I let the alfredo sauce congeal on the sides of the bowl. Even my kitchen looks depressed.

Arianna stops by with Beckett and asks me to hold him for her while she untangles herself from the Ergo carrier. It's her fault that I'm indulging in my twenty-four-hour mope. *She* is the inventor of the productive mope, the person who taught me about setting pity party time limits. You would think that she would be smarter than to set foot over my threshold while she knows I'm detoxing on romance movies and mousse.

I start sobbing wildly, scaring Beckett into his own crying jag. "I'm a divorceeeeeeeeeeee," I cry, dragging out the final sound of the word.

"You are," Arianna agrees, bouncing Beckett on her knee until he calms. He eyes me suspiciously, so I ball up my Kleenex against my face so I can stop freaking him out.

"But that is old news. You need to pull yourself together. It wasn't even the wedding of someone you know."

"I still have eight more hours," I tell her. "You need to give me my full twenty-four-hour mope. I still have *Sleepless in Seattle* to watch."

"For the love, sweetie," she tells me, cleaning up some of my used tissues with her bare hands. That's a true friend.

"Do you know what I don't get?" I tell her after she promises that she'll grant my remaining eight hours in exchange for turning off the movies and doing my dishes. "Why Adam couldn't tell me that he is reading my blog. I feel like if he had been honest with me at the party, I could have been honest with him. But it's his lack of forthcoming that makes me too nervous to tell him anything real. It was like that in our marriage and apparently, we still haven't figured out how to be honest with one another. I don't think he told me anything real in the last five years of our marriage, and I think I followed his lead."

"Maybe he was scared," Arianna consoles. "Maybe he was just as nervous as you were; just as thrown off to see you there at the party when he didn't expect it. You don't know; maybe he came to the same realization and changed his mind, but there wasn't time to show you. Maybe he went to get a beer in the kitchen so he could collect his thoughts and talk to you about your blog, except you left the party without giving him a chance."

"You think I should have given him more time?" I ask incredulously.

"No, hell no," she adds hastily. "You should do it on *your* terms. You've done too much already on his terms."

The phone rings, and I let the answering machine pick up. I hear a young woman clear her throat and haltingly tell me that she read my book proposal and loves it. It sounds as if she is reading another, unrelated piece of paper while she speaks, her mind pulled in two different directions. She clears her throat a few more times. She has made a few small tweaks to my proposal that we can talk about when I call back. She will email me an agency agreement, and we can get started once I mail it back.

I dive for the phone, but she has already hung up, so the answering machine whirls and clicks off as the message ends. I hit redial, but I get voice mail where I tell her in what just might be the shakiest voice she has ever heard that I am thrilled that she will be representing the proposal.

I can't believe this is happening.

I let out a shriek the moment I set down the phone.

And then I dance around the living room, swinging Beckett through the air, laughing for real as I willingly toss away the last eight hours of my mope, all thoughts of Adam and Laura temporarily out of my mind.

After I call my siblings and let them know that I'm about to be a published writer—perhaps a bit premature, since all I have is an agent, a low hurdle to clear—and I chat with my mother about how I can now legitimately call myself an author-to-be, and I even call my grandmother down in Boca Raton, making her late for her Yiddish Club, so I can tell her about my huge accomplishment. I post the news to my blog and collect several hundred comments of congratulations as well as an arm-load of unsolicited advice about the writing process.

My mother may be a talented lawyer and my sister may be a brain surgeon, but being a writer with a book in Barnes and Noble trumps both of those, at least in my mind. For the first time ever, I don't feel like the black sheep of the family insofar as accomplishments. Now I am more like the glittery star atop the Christmas tree of professions.

Ethan stops by with copies of his latest photographs. The coffee seeping into the cracks of a table; a carpet of sugar collecting on a coffee shop floor. He refuses to take my bait when I ask him how it feels to be the only rudderless Katz, now that I'm about to become a famous author.

He is completely content to live hand-to-mouth, barely scraping by, and taking photographs that most people will never see. I would love to study his brain, boil down the essence of what makes Ethan tick, makes him confident that each idea is a great idea. I'd like to bottle it; drink a little myself. As the gracious, soon-to-be-published older sister, I endure listening to how his coffee table book is going to revolutionize the world.

"It's meta. It's a coffee table book about coffee on tables. Think of the possibilities for other projects after this one. A book about paper-making made out of paper that was made through the paper-making recipes in the book."

"Do you really think people want to buy that kind of book?" I ask. I'm not saying it to be cruel, but to understand how he can dump his eggs into this very strange basket.

"Probably not. Which is why I've taken on other photography work to earn money. And why you'll hire me to do the photos in your book when it comes out. I've been practicing with food."

"Maybe I'll hire you to do the cover," I say generously, not entirely sure this is how publishing works.

"So, Ari said that you bumped into Adam at a party?"

"Seriously, she's *my* friend. Why are you talking to her?"

"She was just making small talk," Ethan insists. "I saw her at Starbucks."

Now that I'm finished with my twenty-four-hour mope, I have no desire to rehash what got me into the mope in the first place. But Ethan has paraded out his kindly brother face, and I can tell that he's going to make me listen to all the advice he has to offer, whether or not it's helpful to me. I might as well just dive in and get it over with.

"Yes, I bumped into Adam, and it was all kinds of awkward. He didn't admit that he was dating someone, even though he was there as the host's new boyfriend. Who, yes, is my friend Laura, from work. He pretended that he isn't reading my blog and that he has no clue what I had been doing with my life all year. And that made me . . . I don't know. *Revert*. It made me revert back into the old Rachel, who could never tell people what she wanted."

"Why do you let him have that power over you? Who cares, Rach?

If he wants to waste his time checking your blog, let him. Ignore it. You're over him."

"I *am* so over him. Wait, why is reading my blog a waste of time?"

"It's not a waste of time. You know what I mean. I know you say you're over him, but really, you need to stop caring. What he does is his own craziness. Even if he showed up here tonight, admitting that he reads you all the time and wants to get married again, would you do it? At the heart of the matter, do you trust him? Could you trust that it would be different this time?"

I hold one of Ethan's photographs, the question hanging in the air between us, giving it intense thought even though this really is a conversation I don't feel like having at this moment. Ethan is killing the author-to-be buzz that I've been on for the past two days.

I stare at my brother, still fumbling for my answer. As attracted as I was to Adam's face back at the party, I try to imagine what it would be like to actually reconnect with him. Would I be able to bring what I learned on this leg of the journey back into our marriage, or would we forever return to our old roles as I did at the party?

Ethan's question jars an old memory. On the night that Penelope was born, Adam and I took the subway out to Brooklyn, giddy as we sat clutching a baby outfit we had purchased the week before. A pink number with a fake tutu around the waist. When we got to the hospital, Sarah, doped up on painkillers but still in control, with her hair tightly back in a bun and her face scrubbed before she allowed company into the room, let us hold her—Baby Penelope—and Henny-Penny was so tiny, so perfect, so fragile that my heart shattered into a million pieces inside my body.

At that point, Arianna had been trying for a while to have a baby, and here was this one, easily alive and miraculously here. It is a wonder that anyone is born at all, when you consider all the things working against conception.

As we held Penelope, Adam bent down and murmured to me, "One day, we'll have our own," and it was that moment, during a time that was already becoming strained with arguments, where we entered into synchronicity with each other's mood, fit into each other like puzzle pieces. Where, in the very same moment of time, we felt the very same amount of love for one another. And though the imbalance of love was the more common state of our marriage—him more in the beginning, me more in the end—the fact that we could achieve that equilibrium makes it difficult to let go of the marriage as I cross ever closer to the one-year mark.

I have, for the most part, succeeded in making a home for one—it can be done. But it's much harder to live as a single person within a marriage? What if I was the only one who has truly changed over these last ten months? And how could we ever get to that place of equilibrium if I was returning because I missed *him*?

I missed the way we argued over the best section of the *Times*. I missed the way his back felt when I rested my hand against it in the middle of the night when I awoke from a nightmare. Seeing his presence on Sitestalker and bumping into him at the party has dialed up the sense of missing him. Increased the volume on my internal radio station tuned to longing.

Despite the evidence that he might actually miss me if he was spending time on my blog, I couldn't imagine *what* he missed about me when he barely noticed me while we were married. Did he miss having someone to do his laundry? Surely he could take it to the cleaners, or Laura would happily throw in his boxers with her cat-hair-covered sweaters. Did he miss having someone around to water the plants while he went on business trips? There were people you could pay; neighbors you could ask. Perhaps it simply came down to the fact that for some people, it is better to be able to say that you have someone and feel that appearances have been kept than it is to find that meaningful relationship—the one that will make it worth leaving the office at six and hurrying home for the intimate, homecooked meal. Maybe Laura is his stand-in for me, and he is still looking for what we had, because we *did* have it at one point, at least in the beginning.

The one thing I know at this point is that I want to roast my own chicken. I never want to go back to being the helpless woman who doesn't know how to boil water and needs to order-in even her steamed rice. Being in the kitchen makes me feel like a Titan, like I'm literally taming my life. And there is no meal that has made me prouder than the one I made a few days earlier to celebrate getting an agent.

I roasted an entire chicken. I followed the recipe step-by-step, rubbing the skin with butter, sticking my hand inside the cavity and stuffing inside a lemon and vegetables and sprigs of aromatic herbs. It felt like I knew a secret every time I opened the door to baste the bird. From the outside, it looked like a normal bird. But inside, there was this feast going on. This infusion. And how could you go back to eating plain, rotisserie chicken from a deli after you've cooked one in your own oven?

But would Adam get that? Would he agree with me when I told him how important it was to be able to cook for myself, regardless of what my mother taught me about women being enslaved in the kitchen. Once in front of him, would I be able to hold onto my own voice, state these words? Would he tell me that he's proud of me, celebrate this new side of my being, or would he merely endure it? Would he cook *with* me, become the sous chef to my executive chef?

I hand Ethan back his photograph, not trusting myself to speak. But of course, I don't have to. My face says it all. Damn brother killing my authoring buzz.

A little voice calls at six a.m. on Saturday. "Aunt Rachel," she begins, solemnly stating each word as if it is the most important message she has ever had to convey. "You forgot to take me with you when you went to pick up the dish."

"Henny Penny? What time is it?" I ask.

"Mommy and Daddy are still sleeping," she admits.

"You should be sleeping. I thought you weren't allowed out of bed without an adult coming in the room."

She ignores this fact and repeats her message. "You said you would take me with you."

"I will," I say, sitting up in bed, now fully awake despite the hour. Shit. I left the dish back in the store in Brooklyn. It is probably gone by this point. "I just haven't gone yet."

"What about today?" Penelope suggest brightly. "You could come out here and make udon noodles in your udon noodle dish."

It is difficult to get frustrated with a voice that is this cheerful despite the early hour. I promise to leave the apartment within the hour and come to breakfast. "Mommy can get us whole wheat pancakes from Flipped!" she promises with undeserved excitement.

I debate calling Gael, asking if he is up for an early morning date to Park Slope so I can introduce him to my sister and show him off. See the orchids at the Brooklyn Botanic Garden. He has been noticeably more reserved since the wedding disaster, as if it was a major turn-off to watch your girlfriend behave in a crazy manner after seeing her ex-husband, have a breakdown at a wedding, and then confide that a roach is why she filed for divorce. Just imagine how quickly he would have run if I had brought up The Dating Diva's blog. Gael, and I have only had sex once since that night in the bar, during which, we barely spoke.

Which makes me set the phone back down without dialing.

I take my time getting out to Brooklyn, the sun fully rising as my train passes over the river. The buildings start sparkling, the water shimmering as they reflect the light and the icicles hanging under the bridge. I pass back underground, the darkness rocking the train until I almost fall asleep waiting for the doors to reopen in Park Slope.

I hold my coat closed as I walk up the street to Sarah's apartment. I can see Penelope's face pressed to her window, and it feels so nice to see someone watching for me, caring about when I arrive, that I give a small wave and look around to see if any of the stores are open so I can duck inside and bring her a gift. A bar of organic chocolate, a book, a shoe horn.

My sister is now awake and buzzes me into the building, and Penelope greets me at the door, two dolls in hand because she would like to recreate our earlier Julia Child storyline at the dollhouse. "I forgot to pick up my dish," I explain to Sarah, glancing at a Styrofoam delivery case holding a small pile of gritty, grey pancakes in the kitchen.

"Unfortunately, Penny has a creative movement class at ten a.m. and then Japanese lessons after lunch, followed by a nap," Sarah says. "I'm not sure today is a good day for paint-your-own-pottery."

"No, I just have to pick it up," I say, removing the ticket from my pocket. "It's ready in the store."

"It's a happy dish," Penelope explains to her mother. "It's for udon noodles."

"I needed a serving dish," I finish.

"Well, we can walk with you to the store before the class so Penelope can see it," Sarah relents.

She goes into her room to wake Richard and get ready, and I check the ticket for the store's opening time. I settle onto the floor in Penelope's room, and she sits down so close to me that she is practically in my lap. She laughs and falls onto the floor, playing silly for a moment, which is a nice change from the Penelope I usually get when my sister is around.

"At creative movement, we put our feet in the air like this," she says, flailing her legs in the air and narrowly missing my cheek bone. I grab her socks and lower her feet back towards the floor.

"Do you do somersaults?" I ask.

"Only if an adult is watching," she tells me. "'Protect your neck.'"

"When I was little, we did somersaults down a hill. Better to pick up speed that way."

She stares at me with her wide eyes, disbelieving that someone would so foolishly risk their life for fun. *Oh sweet Penelope, when you are older, I will tell you about drinking games and dizzy bat and truth or dare,* I think to myself.

"What else did you do when you were little?" she asks.

I think of the most benign life possible. "I read books and played pin-the-tail-on-the-donkey and ate whole wheat pancakes."

"Just like me," she says proudly.

"Just like you," I repeat.

"Aunt Rachel, I missed you."

She says this not as a guilt trip or because she wants something, but as a simple declaration of fact. I was here and then I was gone and now I'm back; and in between, she missed me. She had hoped I'd come along for one of their panini jaunts, but I wasn't in Park Slope, and in turn, she missed me. I know that I am grinning like an idiot when I tell her that I missed her too, even though it isn't quite true. Even a four-year-old is better than I am when it comes to honesty, with stating her heart.

Sarah pauses in the doorway to Penelope's room, watching us with her coffee mug in hand. "Mum says that you said that you wanted to host Passover this year," she comments.

"I do," I agree. "No more take-out from Jerusalem's Catering. I'm going to make turkey and a brisket and a kugel—the whole thing."

Sarah doesn't say anything, but she purses her lips in such a way that she clearly conveys that she thinks cooking is a waste of time.

"I guess you'll be back at work then," she says.

"I don't know. I don't know what I'm going to do about that yet," I admit.

"I thought you were planning on going back to graphic design at the library."

"I was, but now that the agent is shopping my manuscript, I'm thinking about seeing if I can make writing my job for a few more months. Maybe start trying to get freelance work at a magazine or something like that," I say, pulling this idea out of thin air. Being with Sarah is at least good for exercising my creativity.

"Do you know what you need to do?" my sister begins. But for the first time ever, a considerable feat considering that these lectures began during our high school years, I hold up my hand and answer the question for her.

"I need to stop thinking about what I need to do, and just do it."

This is a completely reasonable answer, one that even Sarah can't argue with, and yet because she doesn't know exactly what I intend to do, it leaves her squinting and gaping for her next piece of advice.

Penelope grins up at me, waving her doll against mine as a reminder that we're playing house. I move my doll back into the kitchen, making her open the tiny refrigerator while I continue my thought to myself. I need to not feel so apologetic for my nervous breakdown after the wedding, but learn from all my mistakes with Adam and tell Gael what I need. Maybe change back my name.

I need to write my damn book and take my own advice and not feel any trace of nostalgia. I need to make my real life just as exciting and funny as my blog life. And I will start right after *The Real Dish* gives me my sunny, happy, hand-painted udon noodle bowl.

My blog's first anonymously-left comment slips into the inbox between a publicity pitch and a self-help newsletter. I wasn't even aware that comments could be left anonymously, having dodged the harsh responses that plague bloggers writing about more emotional subjects. I mean, how much hate can someone muster for a how-to post on browning beef or musings on whether you need to use filtered water when cooking? I've had a few people tell me that I'm a pussy about baking, but they're right, so it hasn't exactly been hurtful. But now there is my first anonymous comment, staring up at me from my inbox, daring me to open it.

The comment was left on a post about adding avocado to fresh mozzarella sandwiches. Why would anyone hide behind an anonymity function on a post as innocuous as making grilled cheese?

"Sneaking bites of avocado?" the comment read. "I thought you didn't like avocado."

I quickly yank up Sitestalker and scan through the recent visitor activity, trying to match the comment to an IP address. I switch back and forth between the email to check the timestamp and the visitor log until I triumphantly land on a single possible visitor. One who happens to be from Brockman and Young. Adam!

The pride in my expert detective work quickly returns to fury. How dare he imply in a comment that he knows anything about me anymore? So what if I didn't like avocado years ago? In the last few weeks I have tried it again and discovered that, when ripe, it actually isn't bad at all.

People change, I want to write back in all caps.

Instead of being a man and admitting at the party that he's dating someone new and he reads my blog, he leaves an anonymous comment, knowing full well that I would check and figure out it is him. A coward's choice.

It's as if he believes that by reading my blog he has somehow bridged the chasm between us, knows something new about me. But all he knows is my catalog of recipes, a handful of opinions on New York restaurants or cookbooks, a few musings about my life before and after him. He doesn't know the real me. Even Gael has a better sense of who I am in this moment.

Adam may have known my past, but he certainly doesn't know my present.

After his anonymous comment, I squelch whatever small amount of doubt I had about my decision to put him out of my life for good, to fully close the door. He certainly won't know my future.

Life from Scratch

blogging about life one scrambled egg at a time

I am really not a fan of birthdays. Like most people, I quake at the idea of growing old. Secondly, you can never plan something good enough to do, and even if you do have the most kick-ass plans, there is always a chance that something sucky will happen that day. I hate my thirty-fifth birthday even when I'm not being reminded by every women's health magazine that this is the date that my ovaries are shriveling up into dusty crumbs of womanhood. Even when it's not several weeks before my first divorce anniversary.

Arianna, God bless her little heart, has planned a fantastic birthday dinner at Quiddity, the new molecular gastronomy place in Tribeca. While I'm looking forward to trying freeze-dried grapes, it doesn't stop me from lolling about on my bed moaning out the infamous words of Prufrock: "I grow old, I grow old."

Instead of attempting the angel food cake again, I have embraced my pussiness about baking and bought a chocolate malt cake from Momofuku. Insanely good. Insane. I popped a candle in it and sang myself the birthday song a few days early. Just because I felt like it. I decided I need to leave goals for myself. I've accomplished so much at thirty-four— divorce, life after divorce, macaroni and cheese. Baking is a good thing to save for thirty-five.

Chapter Eleven

Trussing the Chicken

I invite Gael over for pre-birthday sex. Thirty-five seems like such a momentous age that it is worthy of a multi-day celebration. He rolls over in bed afterwards and looks at me. "You don't look like you are turning thirty-five."

"I don't?" I ask, fishing for compliments.

"You look like you're about forty, maybe forty-two," he teases, and I punch him in the shoulder. "No, *mi amor*, you look like you are thirty, tops."

"I wish I were thirty," I sigh. "Life was pretty good at thirty."

No, it wasn't, I remind myself silently.

"Tell me about thirty. What did you do for your thirtieth birthday?"

"I didn't have a party. Adam and I talked about having a party, but we never pulled one together," I say, staring at the ceiling. Even before my post-wedding breakdown, I felt awkward reminiscing about my marriage with Gael. I put myself in his shoes; I would never want to hear about past birthdays with his ex-girlfriends, but even knowing that, I can't stop myself from talking. "We went to London."

"That's romantic."

"It was. I mean, I know Paris is the more romantic option, but we went to London and visited all these places I wanted to see. Buckingham Palace, the Tate. That was our last big trip. I mean, we did small vacations around New York, but we never went overseas again."

"That's sad," he simply says in agreement.

"It is sad. I wanted to travel more, but after London, Adam could never get away. I wanted to go to Australia. I've never been there."

"I haven't been there either."

"Next honeymoon," I tell him as I stretch. "For the next one, I'm going to Australia. For a month. And I'm going to go scuba diving. I don't know how to scuba dive, but I'm going to learn."

"Do you want to get married again?" Gael says, and I notice that his voice has gotten more careful, more cautious, as if he is creeping towards a particularly hairy spider to get a closer look.

"Yes," I admit, tucking my chin towards my chest so I can avoid looking at him. Even I know better than to look at a single man who is asking me questions about marriage. "One day. I liked being married back when it was good, and I think I could do it better next time."

"What would change?"

"I'd cook," I tell him, and he laughs. I glance at him to show that I'm serious, while not taking myself too seriously. "I would. I know it sounds like a small thing, but I want to take care of someone. I'd make really good food, and my husband would help me, and we'd both make excuses to leave work early rather than stay really late."

The air in the room feels very heavy, as if we are Dorothy and Toto in reverse, moving from a world of color into the land of black-and-white. I lighten the mood by rolling onto my side and tossing my hair over my shoulder, looking demurely at him through my lashes. "And I'd wear a lot of sexy clothes. I'd cook in a merry widow and stiletto heels."

And even though he laughs, even though he rolls me onto my back so he can have me again, for some reason, his face looks incongruent, as if his mouth and his eyes and his cheeks have all ceased to work in unison.

I decide definitively that I like being a writer, like sitting in front of the computer for hours at a time, like the way my mug of coffee looks on my desk, like the numerous sticky note pads I have lying around the apartment in case inspiration strikes while cooking or peeing.

It's a life I could definitely get used to living.

It doesn't feel like real time, and it is easy to look up at the clock and realize that I have been working for ten or more hours and still feel like I could keep plodding forward, not because it needs to get done now now now, but because I'm actually excited about the work. I'm excited to see words form into sentences and sentences form into paragraphs, and I keep glancing down at the tiny reminder on my Word document to see how much I've written, how it would translate out to pages in a real book.

My official birthday therefore creeps up on me gently, even though I'm not a big fan of marking time passing. Even though I'm now officially of "advanced maternal age," if I decide to attempt procreation. I am in a higher risk group for genetic issues. A higher rate of pregnancy loss. These cheery thoughts flicker around in my head like little birthday candles. Thank you, women's health magazine articles, for the birthday wishes.

Arianna calls to say that she is on her way with croissants and coffee. Penelope calls separate from my sister and whispers the words to the *Happy Birthday To You* song into the phone, as if she's worried about startling me into aging. My brother calls to see if he can bring over croissants and coffee too, but declines to join us when I tell him that Arianna already has it covered. He tells me he'll see me that night at the birthday dinner.

I check email after I've showered; before Arianna arrives with breakfast. Last night, I put up a blog post about turning thirty-five, and my inbox is now clogged with thousands of well-wishers leaving comments. It's easy to write the requisite "Happy birthday," so even the lurkers come out of the woodwork. Nestled amid all of the emails is a single, anonymous birthday wish, laden with an enormous amount of hidden meaning: *"I really do want you to have a happy birthday today."*

I immediately file it within my email account so I don't have to see it again in my inbox.

I will have a good day, I decide, *with or without Adam's blessing.*

Arianna shows up without Beckett but with a bag of croissants and two coffees. I take her over to the computer and search through my email to find Adam's message. She reads it and shrugs her shoulders. "You have always known that he's not willing to open up about his feelings. I mean, he wouldn't even sit down and talk to you straight about the problems in your marriage."

"Right," I agree.

"Remember that time that you tried to plan a cruise? You thought that if you got him onto a ship, there would be few places where he could run away and do his own thing? You'd be forced to spend time together. And what was his response?"

Adam had refused to even look at the cruise ship brochure, sighing that he couldn't believe I thought he could take a three-week vacation. "He wouldn't talk about it."

"Or the time you wanted to take him clothes shopping for new suits after he landed a major deal for the firm, and he couldn't even explain to you why he wouldn't give you one afternoon—not couldn't, but *wouldn't*—of his time. He was so secretive; he shut you out."

Arianna sounds far angrier than necessary. She asks me if I'm going to delete his email or figure out a way to block him from leaving more comments, but I shrug my shoulders. I can't imagine deleting it any more than I can imagine looking at it again. It's sort of like The Box in the closet, resting in emotional purgatory.

"I would delete it," she insists. "I wouldn't let him have that power over me or leave reminders of himself in my space. Your blog is your space, Rach. And insinuating himself into it through anonymous comments, reminding you that he's still around without actually connecting with you in a meaningful manner, is just a power play. You're letting him have power by not deleting his comment from your blog."

"How is that letting him have power? I think it's much more powerful to leave it there and not react. Why are you so angry?'

"I don't like the way he treated you. What if he was leading a double life? Had a girlfriend on the side? Didn't you ever wonder?"

Of course I wondered. I had wondered about it all the time, which was why I called his workplace so often, hoping to catch him away from his desk so I could confront him on my theory that it wasn't all work that kept him away from home. But no matter how many times I called, no matter how many times I searched his pockets looking for a forgotten receipt, or sniffed his collar for leftover perfume, I never found anything worthy of a confrontation. I'm not sure which is worse—the idea that there's another woman or the idea that I'm not worth spending time with.

I log out of my email account, not making a decision either way on what to do. Arianna must sense that her anger is getting on my nerves, because she softens her voice, returns to talking about the new milestones Beckett has hit, and sets up our breakfast with dishes from my cupboard.

There is a strange tension in the air, as if time is slowly working its magic, aging me, graying my hair and crinkling my eyes. And I can't explain why, but part of me doesn't want to go out tonight, to mark the event. It feels like electricity. Like the moments before a storm.

That night, Gael picks me up at the apartment. When I open the door, he is standing with his hands behind his back. He walks into my apartment strangely, twisting himself so that I can't see what he's holding.

"Is it a present for me?" I ask, trying to sound cute instead of greedy.

"It might be," he says, his smile even more lopsided than usual.

"Is it small?" I question.

"Well, it can't be that large if I'm hiding it behind my back," he laughs.

"Maybe you should give it to me later, after the party. I don't want to be late. Guest of honor and all."

"I want to give it to you now," he says, suddenly looking serious.

The change in expression makes my heart start pounding—and not in a good way. In an everything-is-starting-to-sound-tinny-and-faraway-because-all-the-blood-is-rushing-away-from-my-head sort of way. I can't help but think of our conversation a few days ago, how he asked me if I ever wanted to get married again. Was he asking for himself because was planning on proposing? We haven't even been dating for very long. It doesn't help when he confirms my engagement fears by pulling out a small box. A small, robin-egg blue box unmistakably from Tiffany's.

"Oh my God," I hear myself say. "You shouldn't have. I mean, you really shouldn't have."

"I wanted your birthday to be special. I know you're not happy about turning thirty-five, but I wanted to make this a day to celebrate too."

When Adam proposed, it was like this huge sigh of relief, like finally fitting that last piece of the puzzle in place. It wasn't a surprise, I knew it had to be coming, we had discussed it enough times. But it didn't make it any less romantic when he dropped down on one knee and fumbled through the question after I got out of the shower because he was too anxious to wait another hour until we were at dinner.

I remember the drops of water staining the shoulders of his shirt as I stood over him, and how we took a second shower together after we made love on the towel I threw over the tiles in the bathroom. That proposal felt like completion, like crossing through the first event in a triathlon.

But this moment feels entirely wrong.

I want to tell him that he's crazy, that we haven't even said "I love you," yet—that I'm honestly not in love with him yet—but he is standing there, so earnest with the tiny box, that I have no other option than to take it out of his hands.

In all honesty, I don't want to be remarried yet. I don't even want to be engaged with the pressure of setting a date removed. Because I'm not sure Gael is the one. The One. He is gorgeous and sensual and thoughtful and moves slowly, showing me that I am allowed to have as much time as I want. But now, with the moment possibly before me, I wonder if that is enough. I said I want to be married again, but do I? All of my thoughts jumble on top of each other, smothering each other, and I can't even really hear myself think after a bit because my heart is literally pounding in my ears.

And then I open the box.

And I stare at the anti-engagement ring—a hideous silver lobster pin with eerie turquoise stone eyes. It is so terrifying and my relief is so great, that I actually make a sound, something akin to a groan, as I remove it from the box and try to smile to show how much I love the gesture.

Gael helps me pin it on, watching my face for signs of how I feel about it. Part of me wants to smack him, explain everything that went through my head as I saw that robin-egg blue box. And the other part of me feel foolish admitting that I thought he was about to propose.

"I know you don't like to eat shellfish, but I thought you might enjoy *wearing* shellfish," he says.

"It's fantastic," I enthusiastically agree, to cover up for the fact that my hands are still shaking. "It's unusual. No one else at the party will be wearing something like this. But you really shouldn't have," I say, seriously wishing that I didn't have to attend my own birthday dinner wearing a lobster pin. Tiffany's or not, no one wants to walk around wearing a crustacean, unless perhaps they are vacationing in Martha's Vineyard and have a penchant for pastel pants suits.

"Do you remember that first dinner party?" he asks. "The lobster dish you used for the salad."

"Right," I say, wondering if this is his ill-fated way of being romantic. Can you teach someone romance?

"I knew you must like lobsters. Lobster-shaped things. I figure I also owed you wages for helping with the wedding photos."

He is staring at me with such a strange expression on his face that it's a little unnerving. "Payment in lobster pins," I repeat.

"Did you think it was something different?" he questions, which makes me think that I'm being set up somehow. That he knew that I would have a reaction to the robin-egg blue box and this was a trick to rope me into admitting that I have been secretly punching holes in our condoms in order to snare him into having a baby with me. Damn that marriage talk earlier in the week. It just confuses everything.

"Nope," I say. "Well, I mean, I was worried you had chosen from the Tiffany's cute animal collection, but it was a big sigh of relief when I saw the lobster. Little claws. Good in butter."

We stare at each other with mutual suspicion until I remind him that I don't want to be late for my own party. The atmosphere feels unusually thick in the cab.

Little did I know that the lobster pin would be the best part of my night.

Quiddity, the molecular gastronomy restaurant Arianna picked out of *Zagats*, is impossible to find. There is nothing at the address, no sign, no marked door, no attractive host standing outside to welcome us to the home of tiny plates. We spend a good five minutes walking back and forth over the same patch of pavement, trying to figure out which unmarked door leads into the restaurant—the locked one marked with the name of an insurance company or the locked one with the scratched-up, frosted-over window. I am getting more agitated as we search for the door, and I am aware that Gael is watching me as if he's waiting for me to explode, tell him that I thought he had been about to sink down on one knee, and realizing that he is waiting for me to say something only makes me clam up more. Gael is acting so strange that it is unnerving, he is making my stomach twist up into itself. We finally find our way into the building and greet the others, who are waiting for us at the bar.

Perhaps wrongness is catching, passing from person to person like a virus, because everything feels off at the bar, too. Gael slips away to the end of the bar after giving Arianna a kiss hello and Ethan a firm handshake. There is a weird tension between Ethan and Arianna, as if they had been fighting before I arrived. Sarah is looking in the opposite direction from Richard and smiles tensely at me while saying her birthday wishes through clenched teeth. It is shaping up to be a delightful evening.

Arianna hands me an appletini while we wait to be seated, and I survey the room, and it feels so incredibly wrong. Like having your birthday in a museum. Even the other diners look like they're chiseled out of marble. The only people who look at home are Sarah and Richard, who are standing stiffly by the bar, identical gin and tonics in hand.

But I can't complain because Arianna has put so much work into the evening, so instead I smile broadly, drink my appletini, and follow Gael's gaze to the stunning brunette sipping a glass of scotch by herself at the end of the bar. We all hear her unmistakable Spanish accent at the same time, and Gael slips away to chat with her. I watch her surprised expression soften into a smile and listen to them exchange a rapid conversation in Spanish.

My boyfriend is chatting up another woman on my birthday.

I grab a second appletini, answering Richard's awkward questions about the book and trying not to notice that Gael is now laughing, brushing the woman's hair off her shoulder—in a casual manner, but for the love of God, he's touching her, nonetheless. On my birthday.

We are finally led to our table, and like my first dinner party back in the apartment, we start a game of musical chairs, trying to keep all of the couples together, when I hear Gael jovially ask the waiter if there is room for a seventh chair.

Gael has brought the small brunette, who is holding her glass of scotch and grinning at us broadly. "Valentina's date didn't show, so I told her that she could join us."

"If it's too much trouble, I could just go home," Valentina offers, in a lilting Spanish accent.

"That's silly," Gael says, answering for all of us. "You're here, you waited a long time for the reservation. Just join us. The more the merrier, right?"

The more is definitely merry, though the rest of us are silently staring at her in disbelief. Valentina positions herself between Richard and Gael, and I am shunted to his other side, at the end of the table, so it is difficult to speak to anyone else. I am positively livid that my boyfriend has invited along an extremely beautiful and Spanish-to-boot third wheel.

This is gearing up to officially be the worst birthday ever.

Despite the strange angle of my chair, Arianna and my sister attempt to pull me into the conversation, but I allow the others to carry the discussion, answering each question curtly. It is obvious that everyone is embarrassed for me, and that thought is even more embarrassing than having my boyfriend—soon to be ex-boyfriend— snag another woman at the bar at my birthday dinner.

As I swallow the first course—a single leaf of lettuce floating on what appears to be a pool of butter—I am filled with nostalgia for Adam. I know, it feels like whiplash to be so angry with him in the morning over the email and missing him by the evening, but there is something about birthdays that take a person on a wild roller coaster of emotions between nostalgia and fears for the future.

Adam may take hours to kill my cockroaches and be relieved to be divorced from me, but at least he didn't embarrass me like this.

I morosely continue to get drunk, my belly empty on the small portions but filling with appletinis, which are magically brought to the table at regular intervals despite the look of perpetual worry creasing Arianna's face. I tune out the conversation at the table, staring dully at the salt shaker.

My mind is on my thirtieth birthday, when Adam and I went to a tiny sushi bar in Notting Hill. He gave me a ring that we had seen on Portobello Road the day before; he had secretly doubled back to get it when I was busy inside a bookstore. It was a gold band, someone's old wedding ring perhaps, and inside the band it was inscribed with what turned out to be a Henry Wadsworth Longfellow quote: "All things must change to something new, to something strange." We had laughed at the time because it seemed like the most unromantic inscription of all time, but now, considering it against the lobster pin, it feels strangely fateful that those words came so incredibly true.

I miss Adam.

I miss my home.

I want all the things I have now—minus Gael—in my old home. It doesn't matter if Adam's now with Laura; he can't be that happy with her if he's still curious about me. I want all the knowledge I've gained, the insights, the blog fame, the agent, even the wider thighs and graying hair that are surely just around the corner, but I want it while sitting across from Adam. His anonymous comments are like finding our dishtowel pattern in a store and realizing how much I miss our kitchen.

I'm like a college student who longs for her parents, forgetting all of the screaming and door slamming that went on during her tumultuous teenage years, how they stifled her and gave her a ridiculous curfew and frustrated her. Suddenly, she only remembers how they gave her the Barbie doll she wanted for her eighth birthday. And, even though I'm getting progressively too drunk to remember this part too, I admit that the college student usually remembers why she was thrilled to move out in the first place when she returns home for that first Thanksgiving. It is that knowledge, that I can't go home, that home will never be the fantasy home in my head, again, that makes me burst into tears. At my birthday dinner. With everyone watching.

"I was just thinking about Thanksgiving," I mumble as if this is enough of an explanation, taking the napkin that Ethan offers. I note that Gael does not make any move to comfort me, sending me into fresh tears while everyone sits there silently. He says something in Spanish to Valentina.

"Perhaps she is drunk," Valentina offers as an explanation.

"I think that should be your last appletini," Ethan agrees.

"Don't tell her what to do," Arianna counters, even though all evidence points to the fact that I do not need to imbibe one more apple concoction.

"I'm not telling her what to do, Ari. I'm just agreeing that Rachel has had enough, and we should probably ask for the check."

"But we haven't even eaten dinner," I gasp. "I've eaten lettuce soaked in butter. And you haven't given me presents or sung *Happy Birthday* or had the waiter bring me out a piece of cake with a candle in it."

Ethan makes the universal sign for the check, and I struggle to get up to my feet, waiting for Gael to stand up and help me and when he watches me, with a look that straddles being bemused, concerned, and mortified simultaneously, I steady myself and totter into the bathroom, followed by Arianna. She finds me by the sink, splashing water onto my face.

"This birthday really sucks," I tell her.

"I'm sorry, this restaurant was a terrible choice," Arianna agrees.

"It wasn't the restaurant that was the terrible choice. It was my second first date who sucks. And my first ex-husband. All men suck."

I am not nearly as drunk as I would like to be. I test the counter for dryness and then lift myself butt-first onto it, leaving my legs swinging underneath the marble shelf. Arianna leans against the stall door and watches me.

"I'm spending the rest of my birthday in here. In the shitter. It's fitting, you know, to spend this birthday in the bathroom."

"Gael sucks," she agrees.

"Did you think he sucked before this?" I question. Could anyone have predicted that this evening would go this horribly wrong?"

"No, he seemed fine . . . great, in fact, at the dinner party."

"He *was* great. He was a great guy, until we saw Adam at the party. That fucked up everything. Everything changed. Seriously, what kind of boyfriend picks up another woman at a bar during his girlfriend's birthday dinner? *Your* boyfriend is giving you orgasms through backrubs and mine is picking up random Spaniard señoritas."

She looks distinctly uncomfortable with this, but I can't stop myself. "Am I that unlovable, Ari? That men don't want to come home to me or even eat lettuce dipped in butter with me?"

"You are very lovable, sweetie. You're just having a run of bad luck with men."

"Where did you find your boyfriend? Was it a set up?" I ask.

"Who would set me up?" she questions.

"Well, where did you meet him? What does he do?"

"Rach, I don't want to talk about him."

"You've found this great guy. Are you going to marry him?" I ask.

"I don't know. It's really new."

"What's his name? Can I at least know his name?"

She squirms around uncomfortably, making some excuse that we should get back to the table because Ethan will have paid the check, and we can all leave to get some real food somewhere else. And with perfect clarity, I see her eyes moving back and forth from the door to my face, and I know.

My best friend is dating my brother.

"You're dating Ethan? Ethan fucking Katz, my brother?"

"Yes, I'm dating your brother."

"And you didn't tell me?" I screech incredulously.

"Honestly, we didn't hide it. You've caught us together a thousand times. I didn't think it would take this long for you to put two and two together. We didn't keep it secret to hurt you . . . it just happened."

I want to shout out a long tirade about friendship, loyalty and brothers being off-limits unless she asked for my blessing up-front, but even in my drunkenness, I'm mortally embarrassed by how self-absorbed I've been for the last few months, how I've somehow missed that my best friend and brother have hooked up. Were clues really dropped in my path? How could I have missed all the signs?

All right, I *know* how I missed all the signs—I was too busy obsessing about myself and Gael and Adam. My fixation on my ex-husband turned me into a terrible friend. The worst sort. One who doesn't even notice that her friend might have something she wants to talk about too.

I never get a chance to tell Arianna everything that is running through my mind in a matter of seconds, because I have just enough time to gurgle a bit then hop off the sink before I am vomiting up four appletinis and a piece of lettuce into the toilet with Arianna holding back my hair. That is a good friend; someone who will hold your hair while you vomit. I am a terrible friend who doesn't keep track of what is happening in anyone else's life, and she is a wonderful friend not even commenting on the amount of alcohol money that is literally being flushed down the toilet.

We don't say anything else while she helps me clean myself up, and we leave the bathroom. I am too embarrassed to even start my apology; I don't know where I'd begin.

I go out into the main dining room to pick a fight with my soon-to-be-ex-boyfriend. Who is standing next to the table, thankfully without Valentina, who has miraculously disappeared in my absence. This fact alone, though even more so coupled with the fact that I have vomited up a large portion of the alcohol, makes me feel better.

Though, by better, I mean seething mad. And I finally find my voice.

"You are taking me home," I tell Gael.

"The others thought that maybe we'd do better at another restaurant. There's a place up the street . . . "

No one else looks as if they want to accompany us to another location and be privy to the argument that is about to go down. They shuffle towards the door, muttering things about babysitters or needing sleep. I don't even bother responding, I just link my arm through my sister's elbow and totter unsteadily towards the door, wishing I hadn't consumed quite so many appletinis because I do my best fighting when slightly buzzed. No inhibitions about shouting out the truth, and the alcohol haze dulls any unkind words tossed back. My brother hails us a cab, and Gael enters docilely, giving everyone his lopsided smile as a goodbye.

I don't talk to Gael for the whole cab ride back to my place. I would be hard-pressed to come up with a worse birthday, including the time when I was eight and missed my own party due to chicken pox. Even through my appletini smog, I'm so livid I can't even look at him. I read the taxi driver's name over and over again, thinking of a hateful word for each letter of his name. Monstrous. Offensive. Shithead. Evil. Sorry-assed-loser. The poor cab driver did nothing to deserve this abuse of his name, but I know that if I pick apart Gael's name instead, I will start flinging the words I come up with directly at his skull.

Moses delivers us to the front door of my building. The

unpromised land where the lack of definition to our relationship howls around in my heart like a maelstrom as Gael pays our cab driver. I don't even bother taking out my wallet and pretending that I'll split the cost.

Laidback, I sniff, thinking about how I described Gael in the past to myself. More like "commitment phobic." He'd never even given me a date when we'd go to the Guggenheim. Looking back on our relationship, we didn't go on *any* of the dates I wanted, the kind he said he liked, too, when we first met—the spontaneous plans formed by what seats are on tap at the TKTS booth, the concerts, the people-watching in Central Park. Fine, the last one may not have been the best idea in the dead of winter, but the others were supposed to have happened by this point. Gael was supposed to be like Adam 1.0 before Adam became Adam 2.0. Instead, Gael and I have spent the majority of our time together either eating or screwing.

I should have been more suspicious of the fact that he never took me to the Kandinsky exhibit.

I should have bought a freakin' ticket for myself.

He waits until we're in my apartment, after I've slammed down my keys on the kitchen counter and kicked my heels off angrily so that one slides half under the bed. I jerk the faucet on and fill up a cup with water, not bothering to offer him one. I only take one sip and then spill the rest down the drain.

"Why are you so angry?" he finally asks.

"Are you kidding? It was my fucking birthday party. And you invite someone at the bar to our table?"

"I didn't think it was a big deal," he stammered, as if he had predicted an entirely different reason for my anger.

"Well, it is a big deal. In America, we don't invite random women from the bar to join us at our table and then proceed to flirt with them in a language that no one else at the table speaks."

"Her date stood her up. What was I supposed to do when she said that? Tell her 'Oh, bad luck,' and then go on my way?"

"Yes! Yes, that's what you're supposed to do. Or not talk with her in the first place," I yell. I am certain that we'll hear my neighbor knocking on the door in a moment, reminding me for the one-thousandth time that she has a baby, and that we have woken him up.

It feels good to yell, like the beginning of a run when you have lots of pent-up energy. It has been so long since I've actually argued with someone, told them how much they've hurt me.

"Well, I'm not like you," Gael tells me. "I'm not going to ignore someone just to make you happy." He sits down on the edge of the sofa, as if these words have ended the fight. "Besides, that's not why you're angry."

"Why am I angry?" I ask. "You tell me, because apparently I don't know why *I'm* angry."

"You're angry because of the lobster pin," Gael informs me.

"Because I don't like shellfish? Don't you remember? I have a lovely lobster-shaped dish—that's how much I love crustaceans," I say, forcing him into admitting that the whole thing was a set-up. I knew it, I knew he was trying to force the issue. He can't claim I didn't like the gift when I have endured being seen in it all night.

"You thought it was an engagement ring and then you were angry when I didn't propose."

Hearing him admit to it makes me burst out laughing. He looks hurt, as if he can't quite translate my reaction but knows that we are not heading where he wanted us to go.

"Why would you think that I wanted to get married?"

"*You* brought up getting married. The next time I go on a honeymoon . . . remember that?"

I have vague memories that he was the first one to broach the topic of marriage, but maybe I did bring up the topic of honeymoons. I am too drunk and tired and hungry to untangle it all in my mind.

"You're pushing everything too fast, Rachel." My name no longer sounds melodic as it spits off his tongue. "We're just having fun and then you're bringing up marriage. I don't know what you think this is, but we never defined it, never said that we weren't going to date others."

He crosses his arms over his chest as if he is admonishing me for allowing my imagination to run to future places based on a few nights of sex. And this is, of course, what attracted me to Gael, this attitude of being in the moment. That's what you get with a commitment-phobe who can't even set plans to see an art exhibit. I am just a woman he is dating.

The robin-egg blue box is still on the table, and I sink down onto the sofa as if I'm wilting like a daisy in her final moments, and in one graceful—albeit drunken—movement, I snap the pin off my shirt while scooping up the box and chuck both at his forehead. The pin misses, and the empty box ricochets off his hairline. He ducks, more out of habit than danger. "Why the fuck did you do that?" he shouts.

"You're crazy."

"I *am* crazy," I agree. "And you set me up. You wanted me to think that you were about to propose to test me. What the hell is wrong with you?"

This was obviously not how he thought this argument would go. I'm assuming he thought I would admit how much I wanted to be married again, and he would be able to untangle himself gently from this relationship by reminding me that he was a free spirit, commitment-phobic, or whatever euphemism he wanted to use to explain why he was so terrible at considering another person's feelings.

"You're not crazy," he backpedals, maybe because it's my birthday or maybe because he's scared that I'll start crying and make this even messier. "But I just don't think this will work out. I want fun, Rachel."

"I actually wanted fun too. But, you know, you sometimes need to plan to have fun. Some things require reservations."

Breathing deeply, staring at the robin-egg blue box on the floor, I am filled with reservations and regrets. I should have demanded that Adam see a marital therapist with me rather than throwing myself back in the dating pool again. I should have told him what was on my mind instead of hoping that he'd guess it. He may have stayed late at the office, but I am the one who failed to communicate.

It is strange how I can pour my heart out to strangers on my blog, but I never sat down with my husband—who obviously still cares somewhat about me if he's reading my blog and sending me emails—and told him exactly what I needed before I told him that I wanted to separate. Thinking about this in my appletini fog makes it sound ludicrous.

I slammed doors and fumed. I never just turned to him and said, "You mean more to me than anything else in the world, and I want to work through this together. I want you to spend more time at home because I love you and I love being with you. Tell me what I need to do." Instead, I only told him what he needed to do to keep me. And that isn't a partnership, as much as I thought I was doing things right.

I loved Adam. I loved my imperfect, workaholic Adam.

Now I close my eyes, rocking a little bit as the room goes dark for a moment. As much as I thought I wanted to bring the elements of my new life back with me to the past, what I really want, more than any other birthday wish I've ever made, is to meld what I know now with what I had then and build something entirely new in the process, to change Adam and I to something new, to something strange.

Something potentially wonderful, again.

Except that when I open my eyes, Gael is still in front of me.

And I'm not really making a very good argument against the fact that I'm not crazy.

I realize what good blog fodder I will get in the future from this breakup, somewhere down the road when the facts can be changed so the innocent can't recognize themselves. I let him down gently, allow the fish to wiggle off the line.

"You're right," I say simply. "But it's me; it's not you. I really think I need to be alone for a bit to work out everything I'm feeling about relationships. I'm still carrying a lot of baggage with me from my divorce."

And this allows Gael to slip into the part of the perfect gentleman, reminding me how much he really has enjoyed our time together, how he wishes me nothing but the best, how he hopes we can still see each other from time to time. Perhaps catch a future exhibit at the Guggenheim.

And then he leaves.

And that is how I spent the thirty-fifth anniversary of the start of my life.

Life from Scratch
blogging about life one scrambled egg at a time

Four appletinis and no food and I should be snoring in a pool of my own vomit, but instead I have insomnia and I'm drunk blogging. Computers should come with a special lock key so you can't blog while buzzed.

Except if you can't be honest on a blog, where *can* you spill out your inner thoughts without qualms?

Once when I was little, my father told me to hold my tongue while he was on an important phone call, and I literally stood for a full three minutes pinching my tongue while saliva dripped down my chin until he turned around and shooed me out of the room. I remember that little muscle under my tongue felt raw after being stretched in wordlessness.

I have done nothing but talk since I started this blog, but I still haven't said the most important stuff—here or to the people in my face-to-face world. It's like starting with dessert and never moving on to the protein-laden part of the meal. And while dessert tastes good, woman cannot live on cake alone.

I'd like to record what I've learned by age thirty-five in case I forget it before the morning: that there is no point in saving face if it makes you lose everything else. That you should stick your heart, raw and beating on the table and hope that the other person picks it up; and if they don't, deal with the consequences of having your heart outside your body rather than never letting it leave your chest. Sometimes the most messed up things can be fixed, but you only know if that's true if you try. Failure is a possibility if you're trying hard enough.

And now that the room is properly spinning, I think I'm going to go to bed.

Chapter Twelve

Sprinkling the Pepper

I barely sleep after I return to bed that night, and avoid checking my blog comments the next morning. I can't bear the idea of everyone running from my blog, screaming in fear at my enormous neuroses, as if they're tearing apart the city like Godzilla while even Adam squirms in his office in the face of my raw emotions. And he *knows* me; he knows how neurotic I really am. He knows that my blog post doesn't even scratch the surface, from his experience.

I wait until close to seven a.m. to slip my coat on over the yoga pants and sweatshirt I'm using as pajamas. I walk through the bitter morning cold to Arianna's apartment. I have the front desk call her to say I'm on my way up, and she leaves her door open a crack so I can walk right in. I find her in bed, the sound of Beckett's deep breathing crackling through the baby monitor, and I slip into bed beside her, wondering only for a second if my brother occupied this very spot before me.

My parents had a rule that we could never share their bed. If we were sick, they would sometimes sleep in our room, but we were never allowed to sleep in their bed, this strange island, this unknown land. I feel like a child as I rest my head on Arianna's other pillow and she strokes my head in a motherly manner.

"I read your post last night," she tells me. "I couldn't sleep, and then Beckett was fussing. I think he's getting teeth. It was very good, your post."

"I'm not even entirely sure what I wrote. I was in that post-drunk place where you're not really sober, but you're not buzzed."

"You posted around two? I read it around four in the morning, and you already had over 100 comments."

"I did?" I ask.

"People like honesty," Arianna tells me.

"Were any of the comments from Adam?" I question.

"I looked. There was nothing there. But maybe he hasn't read it yet. But I thought you were over and done with him."

I look up at a stain on her ceiling. It's in the shape of a teddy bear. Beckett snuffles in the next room, and then I hear the squelching sound of the binky. I don't wish I was a baby again, but I would sure love to have some of his internal peace.

"Was Adam the failure you were talking about?" Arianna asks.

"One of them," I admit. "I suck as a friend. I'm sorry about that, too. I'm sorry that I didn't push you to talk to me about your relationship with Ethan."

"I was sort of waiting for that," she admits. "I'm sorry, too. It was wrong of us to be secretive; completely wrong. We should have come out and told you instead of dropping bread crumbs and waiting for you to notice and call us on it."

"How long has it been going on?" I ask, breathing deeply as I catch of whiff of a smell that is comforting. Home-like.

"I guess it started after that dinner party you gave. I took the elevator down with the boys. Gael immediately said goodbye and walked off in one direction. And the other guy sort of lingered around talking to us for a bit, and then he went to the subway. And then Ethan offered to walk me home. I guess I never thought much about him before; he was just your little brother. But he came up, and we spent the night talking and when he kissed me . . . it just felt right. Is this too weird? Is talking about this too weird?"

"I'll tell you when it gets too weird," I promise. "Just stay away from talking about back rubs."

We both look at each other and start laughing hysterically, the kind of laughter that you need to do simply to clear the tension from the room even though nothing funny has been said or done. "Ethan Katz," she gasps, tears streaming down her face as I snort. "I'm in love with Ethan Katz."

"You're in love with him," I repeat, suddenly serious again. Arianna is not one to throw around the word "love."

She wipes her eyes with her sleeve and nods her head. "I am. Is that crazy? I don't know where it's going, but he's wonderful with Beck, and he's wonderful with me. He makes me eggs in the morning."

"My brother makes you eggs? But Katzs don't know how to cook."

"He uses that recipe you posted on your blog a few weeks ago for scrambled eggs with herbs. He brings me flowers. And he changes diapers. What more can a single mum want? I think I'm getting easier to please in my old age."

"You still have months before *you're* thirty-five," I tell her, trying to steer away from learning more intimate facts about my brother. We will need to tread slowly with this topic, baby steps, even if I am happy for her and him. And I'm not just saying this because it's the right thing to say when your best friend has found happiness with your brother. I'm saying it to myself because it is true. Everyone should find that someone worth making eggs for, worth waking up next to, and Arianna has been waiting a long time. "You're young," I tell her.

Arianna looks at me with gratitude over the fact that I am not strangling her, calling her a liar for keeping this news for so long, or demanding she choose one of us because she cannot have the whole Katz set. None of those things sound like good options, though I am aware that my reaction is tempered by the fact that too many other thoughts are competing for my attention as well as the fact that she held my hair while I vomited last night. Holding my hair during a drunken puking session goes a long way.

"So what happened after you got back to the apartment last night?" she asks.

Again, I catch the smell in the air, like sourdough bread, the tang of yeast. I sniff at the blanket but I can't find it again. "We ended things. Like civilized adults."

"How are you with that? Is Gael the failure you wrote about last night?"

I stare at my hand, at the ring from Me&Ro. It has started to meld with my hand, to form an imprint on my finger from daily wear. The tan line from my wedding band is nearly gone.

"I know that you have every right to hit me when I say this, Arianna, considering how many nights you sat up with me after the divorce while I cried. But I miss Adam."

"I know you miss Adam, sweetie," she says.

"No, I mean I really miss him, and I wonder if I've done the right thing, and I feel like we should have another go at it."

"*Rachel*," she begins. And actually, that's also where she ends. As if my name is enough of a statement to convey how terrible an idea it would be to call up my ex-husband and attempt to reconcile.

"Listen, I've learned a lot this year. A lot about myself. It sort of snuck up on me, the learning about myself. I am so terrified of failing that I never really tried to save my marriage. But this is a theme with me, isn't it? Before I let the marriage fail, I never tried to have a baby with Adam because I was too scared to push it because I thought

Adam might say that we're not on the same page about parenthood. I never tried cooking not just because my mother scoffed at women who bother with learning their way around the kitchen. I never tried because I was terrified of failing at it. In creating huge kitchen disasters because I had no one to help me learn. I didn't trust myself to be a good-enough teacher for me. I never told Adam what I needed to tell him because what if he didn't listen? What if he didn't give it to me?"

"What if he did?" Arianna asks.

"Well, that's the problem with being scared to fail. You usually end up failing in the end by default, because you don't grab what you want. Somehow I talked myself into the idea that it would mean more to me if he came to all the right conclusions by himself. That it would mean less if he spent more time with me because I asked him to, rather than because he wanted to. I know that he hasn't told me in a straightforward manner that he misses me, but he obviously hasn't moved on if he's reading my blog and sending me messages."

"*If* it's him reading your blog," Arianna says. "What if there's a newly-divorced woman at the law firm who's desperate for your advice? Remember how you used to read blogs about relationship problems? What if your mystery reader turns out to be a fifty-year-old legal secretary?"

Beckett begins his morning cooing through the monitor. We listen to him talk to the mobile above his crib as if he is asking each stuffed figure a series of important questions.

"But if I find out definitively that he misses me and is thinking about me, then wouldn't it be worth trying a second time?"

"Rachel, you were so miserable in that relationship. Don't you remember all the nights you sat on the sofa and waited for him? And were frustrated and waited for him? And waited for him and waited for him and waited for him?"

"I do," I admit. "But I never told him how much it hurt, not clearly and passionately. I just withdrew more and more, as he did the same. I feel like I called it quits too soon. I made myself fail so I could get the failure part over with quickly. And what I should have done was work my ass off..." And this is where my throat catches.

Arianna returns to stroking my hair, and the smell crosses in front of my face, and that is all I need to start crying. Beckett hears me and starts his own wail, and I motion to Arianna to get him. I have a good cry in her bed while I'm waiting for them to return. She sits down on the bed and pops a warm bottle into his mouth. He watches me over the rim of it with interest, and I rub the bottom of his foot. It is incredibly smooth, like a stone that has been washed by the ocean for a thousand years.

"People make mistakes," I try again. "He made mistakes but so did I. I need to acknowledge that; I need to tell him, then either move on or go backwards and try to correct it. And knowing that he is still thinking of me while I am thinking of him makes me want to choose the latter. The former. I never get those words right. Which is the one that means that I want to go try to fix my mistake?"

"The latter."

"Do I have your support?" I ask. "Will you be here for me with ice cream and tissues if it all goes to hell?"

"Of course we'll be here," she says, motioning a bit to Beckett to indicate that they're both on my side.

The smell again, something so familiar though I can't place it. It is like a former place you lived, something fresh from an oven, warmth.

"What am I smelling?" I ask.

Arianna sniffs the air and shakes her head. She sniffs her sweatshirt, her hair and the back of her hand. Finally, she holds out her wrist. "This? It's formula. Beckett spit up on my hand last night."

Knowing that it's spit-up makes it ten times less romantic, but I shake that out of my mind in order to cling to the wave of drama I've been feeling since my birthday. There is something about having an almost-tangible reminder of time that lays the past bare. The fact is that somehow my life has gotten off course. I am supposed to be holding a child too and be happily ensconced in a relationship. And now that I've picked up a few life skills and a modicum of self-confidence, it's up to me to get my life back on track even if that means showing up at Adam's office and placing my own damn heart on his desk for him to do with what he will.

I go home to shower and put on a navy blue cashmere sweater that I had hoped to be wearing when I bumped into him for the first time. He always loved the way it fit my body, and I agreed with him, though now, my body almost a year older and a little wider, it is different. Hopefully more like something new than like something strange.

I am having one-thousand doubts that I'm doing the right thing, but I squelch them, knowing full well that I will not feel at peace no matter which option I choose. Staying in the apartment or going. Calling him or showing up at his office.

I am terrified of the way my stomach is already lurching while I swing by the carryout kiosk on the corner, ordering a grilled cheese sandwich with avocado as a tongue-in-cheek ice breaker that I hope conveys immediately that I know he has been skulking around on my blog so we can get that part over with. The accusations, I mean. I hope to skip straight into the passionate love-making on the floor amid his legal briefs, his declarations of undying love, his promise to come home by six p.m. every night.

I take a cab instead of the subway, giving an enormous tip to the driver, as if that will bring good luck for my endeavors. I take the elevator up to the eighteenth floor, four below his office, and get off with a set of young magazine interns who must additionally be students at NYU, based on their conversation. The girls look so young, so confident. They make me want to place my arms around their shoulders and tuck them in close for a little older-sister advice session. Or at least scare the shit out of them by explaining how life will really turn out so they stop looking so damn confident while I'm quaking in my boots.

I slip into the stairwell, which is cavernously silent. One year, when I wanted to surprise Adam with a birthday cake at work, I was told that the eighteenth floor has a back passage that connects the building's two stairwells—the public one accessible to people like me, and the private one to be used by personnel traveling between floors for multilevel offices. I walk down through the narrow walkway, prepared to climb the last four flights in order to avoid having the receptionist at the law firm's front desk notify Adam that I'm about to descend upon his office.

As I climb up the stairs, I rehearse everything I'm about to say aloud. I'll begin with an apology. I'll keep it simple. "I'm sorry," I'll tell him, my words hanging in the air between us until he accepts them. And then I'll state all the things I'm sorry it took until now to learn: that I'm not the world's best communicator but I've found my voice now. That I should have told him not just to spend more time at home, but *why* I wanted him there. That I missed him when I was sitting on the sofa by myself.

But now I have that passion he talked about, for my blog, my writing. I will understand his career demands, and he will understand mine. I'll support him with meals and homemaking, not as a bribe or a submissive role, but because I am good at it. I'd like a chance to put into effect all of the things I've learned this year—not just about cooking, but how to make myself happy for the times I need to be alone. I want to tell him that I now understand how a person can lose themselves in work, have hours pass without them noticing. It has happened to me with the blog and the book. I couldn't understand it until I experienced it myself—how work can sometimes be as satisfying as being with someone you love, and how you can derive your happiness, and your self-esteem, from both.

All of this will be told to him as directly and concisely as possible. As honestly as possible. And if my heart gets shredded in the process, if I leave not with the words I'm hoping to hear, but an answer that is unpalatable, I will still know that I did my best, I gave it my last effort.

I drink up the false bravado, swallow my placebo of confidence, and push open the heavy door down the hall from his office. They've replaced the carpeting, turning it from a threadbare navy blue to beige, and I glance at the door number to make sure that I have the right floor. The names on the nameplates are still the same. I pass by Gardner, Finnegan, and Sharpstein, all their doors thankfully closed. I pause outside of Goldman. The door is, luckily, open.

I peer inside, first trying to catch a glance at him. I do a double-take, because since the party, Adam has dyed his hair blond. And had it thinned out. And put on about forty pounds, judging by the heft of his shoulders. And become a short, goyishe, ham-sandwich-eating-at-your-desk man. With pictures of children on his desk, and a new wife beaming from the photo frames.

And a new last name of O'Connor.

I jump back, almost dropping the Styrofoam container of grilled cheese, even though it would hardly matter if Mr. O'Connor caught me sneaking around his door. I hadn't counted on Adam switching offices in the past year, and this definitely throws a wrench in my surprise-it's-your-ex-wife plan. I glance around at some of the doors in the area, searching for his name.

"Can I help you?" Mr. O'Connor's secretary calls out from her desk.

Her eyes move from my Styrofoam box to my face and back. I lean in close to her desk to minimize being overheard.

"I'm looking for Adam Goldman. This was his old office. Do you know where they moved him?"

"I'm sorry, I don't think anyone by that name works here," she tells me.

"He's a lawyer," I try again. "Adam Goldman. Maybe he's on a different floor?"

"That's possible," she admits. "I'm new here, and there are a lot of lawyers in this firm. Why don't I look it up on the computer?"

"Thanks, that would really help," I tell her.

I watch her face as she scans through the directory, and she finally shakes her head. "No, there's no one named Adam Goldman."

"Brockman and Young? I am on the right floor?" I question.

"Yes, this is Brockman and Young, but there's no one who works here with that name."

Seriously? Can this woman not spell Goldman? It's times such as these that I wish I had a Blackberry so I could go on the Internet myself and check the firm's website for his office number. I thank her and duck back towards the front desk, hoping that the receptionist doesn't ask how I've come from the opposite direction. So much for a surprise attack.

There is also a new receptionist at the front desk, a blond Amazonian woman who looks like she'll break my arms if I don't answer who I've come to see in the building. I set my grilled cheese sandwich on the counter and attempt to look friendly.

"Hi, Lisa," I say, checking her nameplate. "I'm here to see Adam Goldman, but I believe he has moved offices since my last visit."

"We don't have anyone here by that name."

I'm finally beginning to believe them, but my mind can't keep up with the news. If he's not here, then where is he? Especially if he was here as of a few weeks ago. How is it that no one remembers him even if they've only been here for a few months? Have all the employees of Brockman and Young been clocked on the head?

It dawns on me that maybe law offices pretend the lawyer isn't there so that people can't deliver a subpoena. I've seen it on so many television shows that I can't believe I've forgotten this fact. I am about to admit to Lisa why I'm there and how she can trust me with his office number when I hear someone calling my name.

Except it isn't Adam.

It's Rob Zuckerman of Bali-traveling fame. My first first date.

"Rachel!" he shouts and awkwardly gives me a hug, as if we've had several encounters rather than one date. "What are you doing here?"

"I came to visit a friend," I lie. "But he's not here. Anymore."

"What have you been up to?" he asks. "I've been thinking about you. I wanted to get together again. It's just so busy here. You know how it is. I don't think I've been home before two a.m. in weeks. It's brutal."

"It sounds like it," I agree.

"And when I'm home, I'm just tied to my Blackberry," Rob says proudly, holding up the electronic device as if it were an Oscar statue rather than an instrument of communication.

As much as I can now understand Adam's love for his job, that pulse of energy doesn't translate well for Rob. Maybe it's like the difference between being in love and wanting to be in love.

"What have you been doing?" Rob asks. "You know, I never heard back from you. Did you get my messages?"

"I didn't," I lie again, despite my desire to fill my day with stark honesty. "I'm so sorry. I wondered why I hadn't heard from you. Well, now I know. I have to get my stupid phone fixed."

"Well, maybe we could go out this weekend," Rob says. "If you're not busy working on your book."

"I am, actually. I'm pretty busy working on something right now."

"Well, maybe another time?" Rob says, looking at his Blackberry again. "I think I still have your number. Should I call you?"

"Yes," I tell him. "Give me a call tonight, and we'll make plans."

It takes me until he gets a few steps down the hallway before I wonder how he knows that I'm writing a book. I'm about to call out to him, despite the evil looks coming from Lisa, who perhaps is harboring a secret crush on Rob Zuckerman, when he turns around and says, "Hey, did you see my comment this morning? I finally figured out how to add my name. I think I'm something like number four-hundred. Your blog sure is popular."

I smile because if I don't, I'm going to start crying. And I'd at least like to get to the elevator bay before that occurs.

Rob Zuckerman. Overworked lawyer. Brockman and Young. My name is plastered all over my blog.

I almost run down the hallway, Lisa be damned, to give Rob Zuckerman a piece of my mind for making me think he is Adam, even though that isn't his fault, but I am too broken-hearted. I skip both the subway ride and the cab to walk the entire way home, dumping the uneaten sandwich in a cigarette ashtray in the lobby of the building.

Adam *doesn't* read my blog. Adam has made no effort to keep up with my life. Adam doesn't love me.

He doesn't think about me or pine for me or want me back at all.

He is dating Laura and probably blissfully stroking her cats right now.

Since this is New York, where people barely notice the torments of others—they'll even step over a mugging victim who is bleeding to death in the intersection—I walk and cry at the same time, not even bothering to duck my head, but allowing all my grief to hang out around me, like an entourage of friends. People walk around me like blobs of oil floating through my vinegar. I promise myself that having two twenty-four-hour mopes in a single month does not make it a habit.

When I get back to my apartment, I spend a good ten minutes allowing myself to truly wail, a scary sort of cry that even keeps my neighbor at bay though I am certainly waking her child from one of his numerous naps. I cry in that way that gives you a headache and makes your eyes puffy for days and sends you into a deep, headachy sleep.

And then I stop.

It isn't a conscious decision, and I am certainly still just as sad as I have been since I stepped over the threshold into my apartment, but the crying stops, and I sit down at the computer to check my blog. Over seven-hundred people have posted since last night, thanking me for my honesty and admitting their fear of failure too. It seems to be a popular cause of low self-esteem. Seven-hundred-plus people, and none of them named Adam. Though, scrolling down through the four hundreds, I pause at Rob Zuckerman's comment.

He probably thought that I had read it this morning and ran straight to his office to declare how much I wanted a second date. If only it could be as easy as "You get who you get and you don't get upset."

But I really am still in love with Adam.

And I wanted Adam to want me back, wanted Adam to not be over me or our marriage. I know that you can't believe everything you see on a computer, that you should ask the source, but I thought it was so clear, so unquestionable.

I go to the Brockman and Young website, search for Adam's name, and the search window comes up empty. I try again with just his last name, and it pulls up a nebbishy sixty-something with light shining off his bald spot. Marc Goldman. I Google Adam's name, and it shows me a host of articles by a writer named Adam Goldman, a LinkedIn profile for an engineer, a teacher at a private school, an Amazon wish list. I click down the list, bypassing a rock singer, a Facebook page, and a doctor of cardiology. My Adam has seemingly disappeared, which is not a difficult feat when you have a common enough name. The name Adam Goldman is the "John Smith" of the Jewish set.

For old time sake, I go back onto Sitestalker, and there is Rob Zuckerman, still hitting refresh, somewhat more frequently than usual, perhaps because he has just seen me. But all of that is sort of beside the point.

I don't really know what to do with myself. I am not in the mood to write a blog post, especially not after last night's. I'm not in the mood to peck at the book manuscript or eat a meal. I'm not even in the mood for Arianna, and I can't remember the last time I wasn't game for a good, old-fashioned pity party with her as host. I wander around the apartment, picking up objects and setting them down, mostly in the same place, until it occurs to me that if I don't scratch this itch, it will just continue to surface indefinitely.

This isn't pathetic, I convince myself. This is the emotional equivalent to calamine lotion. This is about fighting for what I want and not caring about the possibility of failure.

I grab my purse and head back towards my old apartment. Soon I am walking past Hunan Chow's slightly sketchy storefront and the new cupcake bakery and my old subway stop and Morty's (which at one point was our favorite diner). I walk past the Christian Science Reading Room and the restaurant where I once got food poisoning. When I round the corner and can see my old apartment building, I dial my old telephone number and listen to the phone ring and ring until the answering machine kicks in. My stomach clenches as I hear my own voice informing me that we're not home right now.

Fine, I may have never changed my name back, but he never changed the answering machine. Instead of leaving a message, I settle myself on the bottom step after ringing the buzzer to ensure that he's not home. It is a brisk February afternoon, and my jeans immediately feel soaked through with cold. I consider doubling back to the diner and waiting for him there, but part of me thinks that sitting on the step as penance sends a stronger message to how much I want to speak with him.

I am either deeply committed or deeply crazy, and I hope he thinks the former rather than the latter despite the closeness the word "committed" negatively shares with mental health. People walk around me into the building. It's less than a year later, yet there is no one I recognize. It is strange how much can change in under twelve months.

I rest my head against my knees and keep my eyes focused down the street. And finally, some time after it is starting to get dark, probably two hours since I planted myself on his doorstep, I see Adam returning home, in jeans and a sweater and a new brown coat. He's wearing a baseball cap that makes him look ten years younger and carrying a paperback book in his hand. He pauses when he sees me and furrows his brow.

"Rachel? What are you doing here?"

It's not quite the welcome I was seeking, and it makes me promptly forget all of the opening speeches I practiced inside my head. It's like those terrible movies where time starts moving in slow motion and your heart just breaks for the main character's humiliation. How could she ever have thought it was a good idea to put herself out here? I am literally cringing for myself.

"I can make a whole roasted chicken," I blurt out. It just like how I used to daydream in math class, asking myself crazy "What ifs." What if I jumped on top of my desk right now and started singing "The Star Spangled Banner?" What would happen? Would it scar me forever socially, mark me as brave or label me the nut job who burst into song while Mrs. Alba tried to teach theorems? What if I pulled down my pants and turned a cartwheel in the aisle? What would happen to me?

What if I show up at my ex-husband's apartment—which used to also be my apartment—and sit on the step outside for several hours until he comes home and then tell him that I know how to roast a chicken? What would happen? I twist my Me&Ro ring on my finger to gather up strength to say what I need to say.

"That's great," he tells me. He shifts the book he's holding from one hand to the other.

I try again. Reboot.

"Could we go get coffee?" I ask.

"Where?" he questions suspiciously, as if I've just asked him to enter a pit of snakes.

"I don't know. Morty's?"

"The diner? I don't think so, Rach."

We continue to stare at each other, and I mentally will him to give me a chance. Perhaps I am more skilled in ESP than I think, because I see his shoulders relax a bit.

"I wanted to talk to you at that party, but you disappeared," he points out.

"I know," I say simply. There really isn't an acceptable excuse. I never thought when I ditched the party that I would be seeking him out a few weeks later. "I want to explain and tell you some things. We can go somewhere else. Really, Adam, I need to talk to you. Please?"

Adam's brow visibly unfurrows, and he shrugs his shoulders. "Fine, let's go to Morty's. I'm not in the mood for Angelo's."

This is our shorthand; every relationship has abbreviations and code. Angelo's is too crowded, too loud, non-conducive to privacy or even hearing one another. Throwing me Morty's is a step in the right direction. I have been forgiven, I decide, for the party slipaway.

We walk the few blocks to the diner not really talking. I picked the diner, of course, because it reminded me of our marriage—of the early days in our marriage—where we would get coffee and pancakes at Morty's on a Sunday morning. We lost that tradition when Adam started putting in Sunday hours at the office, but the weekends used to be about reading the newspaper and bitching about the Style section and drinking endless refills of coffee. I'm hoping that sitting in this familiar space will somehow transport us emotionally back to those early days of the marriage, when things were worth saving.

But as we double back the way I came, I wonder if the ulterior motive was to get him to take a few steps away from our old place and towards my new apartment. While I can't see it tucked behind all of the other buildings in the way, I know it is out there. Our old life and our new life and then this space in between.

I know in that moment that I'll be fine—that whatever happens at Morty's, I'll live through it. That I'll still have so much, even if I don't have Adam—the blog, the book, Arianna, my siblings. Tiny Penelope and her whole wheat pancakes. If I can't be a mother, I'll be the best damn aunt in the world. I internally promise Penelope that I'll do better with this aunthood thing. Whatever happens, I'll live through this, and that fact is comforting, like a small loaf of bread newly tucked into the oven, slowly expanding.

Morty's is the type of place that no one ever thinks to enter, and for the first few months of living in the neighborhood, I walked past it without noticing the sign on the door. It was Adam who first suggested that we go in to get out of the rain when the skies opened up on our way home from the subway. And somehow, it became ours—sticky tabletops and chipped coffee cups and all—like an ugly dog from the pound that only the two of us could ever love. But because it is the receptacle of our joint love, and our joint love alone, it becomes more special, more enticing, like the ring from Portobello Road that was discarded by its first owners. I hope he feels the same energy that is coursing through my body as we step into the restaurant and are greeted by the smell of French fries under heat lamps and tart coffee spills.

The place is almost empty, so we slip into the booth of our choosing—a middle ground, one that we've never used before. The waitress tries to hand us menus, but Adam doesn't even open his menu to be polite. He asks for a chocolate shake, extra thick. He says it emphatically, as if this is the only choice he could possibly make, and I wonder how well it bodes in changing his mind about us. I examine him closer, without the jacket in the way. He has lost weight.

"A milkshake," I comment, after the waitress leaves with my request for a cup of decaf. I use what I hope is a casual tone, but coming out of my mouth, it sounds judgmental.

"I felt like having one. I got one here a few weeks ago, and it was really good."

On a date with Laura? I want to ask. This isn't really the sort of place you bring a date. It's the sort of place you bring a spouse. Or a wife-to-be. I stop considering his love life and start rolling and unrolling the edge of my paper napkin to give my hands something to do. "Because you actually look like you've lost weight."

"Maybe," he says. "I started running again."

"Again?"

"I ran before law school. So, what do you want to talk about, Rach? Is there something you want to tell me?"

I had wanted to jump into the conversation *before* he asked that question, because the reality is that after that question has been asked, whatever comes next better be pretty good. I really don't know how to begin, so I look at my slightly ragged napkin for answers. The paper serviette is silent.

"I left that night at the party because I was really thrown-off seeing you there," I admit, deciding immediately that honesty is the only way I'm getting through this.

"I was too," he offers. "I didn't know if Laura invited you, if she was even in touch with you anymore."

"I wasn't, not really," I tell him again. "But she invited me to the party, and I thought I should go."

He doesn't seem keen to discuss her. "But you're not working at the library anymore?"

"No," I say, taking a deep breath at the same time. "I left that job about ten months ago. I needed to do something totally different. My whole life had been turned upside down so it seemed like the right time to shake out everything in the process. I wanted to choose something that didn't resemble my old life at all."

"What did you pick?" Adam asks, and I can tell that he's genuinely interested. Perhaps he's only curious to know what I thought was missing from our life, but I'm hoping it's because he actually still cares about me somewhat.

"Nothing. That's sort of the funny part. Now I think I'm going to go back to the library."

"That's funny?"

"No, I just mean that I realized this year that the change I thought I needed wasn't the change I needed. I spent the year learning how to cook and writing a food blog, and I got an agent who is shopping my book proposal."

"That's great, Rach. So you became a writer?"

"Sort of. I mean, yes, I'm writing, but there isn't real money in it, so I'm going to go back to the library. Which is okay, because this year wasn't about finding a great new career. It was about finding things that make me happy. Finding my voice. Standing on my own two feet."

He's silent for a long time, long enough for the waitress to return with his milkshake and my decaf, long enough for both of us to take several sips before we speak again.

"I was trying to remember if we ever cooked at home. I guess we didn't," he says. "What is the book about?"

I suddenly feel shy admitting this to him. "Divorce. Cooking. It's called *The Divorced Woman's Guide on How to Cook Your Life from Scratch*. So that's what I've been doing. But I guess you didn't know any of that," I conclude.

"No, I had no idea. Congratulations, Rach, it sounds like you've had a great year."

He hasn't tried to find out about me. He hasn't inquired. He doesn't care anymore. I'm trying not to think those thoughts.

I want to tell him that despite all of that, I haven't had a great year. I've had a terrible year, and as we approach the anniversary of our divorce in the next few weeks, I have only been more filled with longing rather than healing. That it doesn't really matter what I've accomplished this year in the face of what I've lost. I've lost him. I've lost him. I've lost him.

I believe him when he says that he didn't know. He looks too bewildered, too thrown off that the Rachel he knew could become a writer. Stepping back, it does seem strange and out-of-place, like seeing a friend for the first time with colored contacts. A small part of me is a little insulted that he's so shocked by the accomplishments, but wasn't that the entire point of the Year of Me? To rub it in his face how little he knew his wife once he started spending all of his time at the office?

"Are you still at Brockman and Young?" I ask even though I know the answer.

"No, I left my job too. Maybe it's the post-divorce thing to do," he says, somewhat dryly.

"Are you working at a different law firm?"

"No, I'm an English teacher. I teach high school English and composition at a private school. That's actually how I met Laura— through her brother, who works with me at the school. You don't need a teaching degree to work there, but I'm taking some additional classes regardless." He has placed the book on the table, and I stare at the spine as if it contains my response. *Candide* by Voltaire. He looks down at the book too and moves it slightly closer to himself. "I actually have you to thank. If you hadn't left, I wouldn't have stepped back and seen how unhappy I was being a lawyer. I really only practiced law for you, and without you there, I didn't need to do it anymore."

"For me?" I exclaim. "But I never told you to be a lawyer."

"I know you didn't. I chose that myself. But, come on, Rachel, you knew I wanted to be a teacher. I was only doing law school to make my parents happy—I had no desire to practice law. But how could we have lived in this neighborhood on a teacher's salary? Even now, I'm only doing it on savings. At some point, I'll be pushed out to one of the outer boroughs."

"We didn't have to live in this neighborhood!" Our conversation is beginning to skate a little too close to an O. Henry story, and I stop savaging the corner of the napkin to look him straight in the eye. "You loved being a lawyer. You loved it so much, you never came home."

"I never came home because I had to work ridiculous hours to support the lifestyle you wanted!"

We're getting progressively louder, and other diners have peeked over from their respective booths. I recognize one table from our old apartment building, an elderly couple from the fourth floor who bought cat food by the case and needed someone to help schlep it upstairs each week. They give me a disapproving look, and I note the clump of cat hair clinging to the bottom of the woman's coat before I return to my argument with Adam.

"What kind of lifestyle did you think I wanted?"

"Cruises. You were always talking about cruises. And private school for our future children."

"I wanted to go on a cruise because I wanted you to be trapped on a boat with miles of water around us and no Blackberry service, where you couldn't sit in the room working and leave me swimming on my own, like you did on every single vacation."

"I had to work like that because I needed to make money to pay for those vacations. I had no time to do anything *I* wanted to do. God, Rachel, until I became a teacher, I hadn't been to a museum in years. I was so relieved the day I walked out of that office," he spits out.

I am so stunned I can barely breathe.

He worked those hours because he thought I wanted a lifestyle that it never occurred to me to want. And I only placed out those ideas for vacations in order to get him away from said work schedule and grab a little time for us as a couple. Now I realize how I sounded to him: whining for cruises, begging him to let me take him clothes shopping, booking us nights at expensive bed and breakfasts. I expect to see O. Henry sitting at a nearby table, twirling his handlebar mustache and nodding at our ridiculousness.

"You bought me combs, but I sold my hair," I tell Adam.

Maybe because I have spoken to him in his language, using words from a short story, his body visibly relaxes, and he starts laughing. So do I. We're both laughing without taking a step back to look at the fact that we're cracking up over the demise of our marriage. It just feels good to laugh after so much tension. His hand slaps the table a few time, and I watch his fingers come down against the edge. The ringless third finger on his left hand.

And that is what pushes me over the edge, that image of his hand without the reminder of me around his ring finger. My laughing crosses over to real tears, and I am crying as I did in the apartment, except this time with an audience staring at me inquisitively. It is almost as if he is seeing me cry for the first time, a train wreck that he can't help but gape at from across the table. He doesn't reach out for my hand or offer me a Kleenex or get me a cup of water. He just watches me cry, as does everyone else in the coffee shop.

"This," I try catching my breath, "this is the first time you have opened up to me in years. In years."

"Can we go back to the apartment?" he asks. He glances back at the cat couple. "Are you okay going back there?"

He pays for both of our drinks, grabs his copy of *Candide*, and helps lead me out of the restaurant. I keep my head down, nose running, as we exit through the frosted glass door. I want to tell him that I still love him, that I want another chance, but since we just shared a laugh about the end of our marriage, it doesn't seem the appropriate desire to admit. He keeps his hand on the small of my back until we are on the sidewalk, and it feels like an anchor, a small stone keeping me here, keeping me mentally here instead of floating backwards through memories or moving forward to sitting alone in my apartment after this.

His key sticks in the front door lock just as it always did, and he bumps the door with his hip, just as he always did, and I walk past the mailboxes, over the threadbare rug, holding my breath as if I am passing a graveyard. Mailbox gravestones. It has been months since I've been back in this building, almost a year.

He opens the door to our old apartment, and I can see that he has changed very little. Everything I left behind is still here. The only thing new is a bookshelf housing an assortment of used books. The shelf where I used to leave my purse is now lined with several pots of cheery, yellow crocus plants. The doors to the bedroom and bathroom are closed. The kitchen still looks unused except for two empty and washed out beer bottles sitting to the left of the sink on the counter. The Picasso poster is still hanging in the living room.

He doesn't offer me anything to drink, and I choose the sofa to sit on and cry while he grabs the box of Kleenex out of the bathroom. He sits down next to me, waiting for my tears to burn themselves out, but they keep coming and coming again, like *Alice in Wonderland*.

"Rach," he begins softly. He was always good at calming me by speaking softer and softer, until I had to quiet down simply to catch his words. "Why did you come here today?"

I know he is asking me why I acted on whatever impulse flitted through my mind, but without being able to put that into words, I tell him the story of Rob Zuckerman and the case of the wrongly accused cyberstalker. I take a deep breath and set my heart down on the table. "I wanted the reader to be you. I wanted it to be you missing me as much as I have missed you."

Then he takes my heart and squeezes it through his fingers until it is just a mess of pulp and gore. "I'm dating someone, Rach." I stop breathing for a moment; I am literally holding my breath, but I only notice this when I gasp out all of the air I've trapped in my lungs. It doesn't matter that I already knew that he was with Laura. It still hurts to hear him say it aloud; to know that perhaps things are actually quite good with her. "And so are you," he adds.

"I'm not," I tell him. "I'm not anymore."

"So is that what this is? You've broken up with someone and you don't want to be alone?"

His voice isn't accusatory; it's simply inquisitive. Questioning. I shake my head, looking around the room for signs of Laura. A picture of her cats, an object they've purchased together. But the room reveals nothing. I realize how little I actually know about her beyond her stories about panties and incredible alcohol consumption. Maybe she's really someone Adam can discuss Voltaire with over manicotti at the Italian restaurant on the corner.

I want to form an argument for myself, ask him to choose me over her. But without knowing anything more about her beyond her design work and cats, it's hard to form an argument. How can I point out myself to be the better woman when I have no idea whether or not I am actually the better woman?

I'm well aware of how hypocritical I'm being after carrying on a relationship with Gael, but while the image of myself in bed with Gael has been put to rest, I am immediately haunted by the new image of Adam rolling around with Laura, bringing her to orgasm (because, in my imagination, she's the type of woman who orgasms every single time—from sex, from backrubs, from him looking at her from across the room. She puts Arianna to shame.) In my old bed. In *our* old bed.

He continues to watch me, his hand tucked behind his ear, his elbow resting on the back of the sofa. It is the way he used to read books, the pages held in front of his face. I imagine all the times we've sat on this very couch, reading books together. And now he reads books with Laura.

"I wanted to see you because I thought I finally understood something," I hear myself say. What the hell am I doing, giving him more ammunition for my ultimate embarrassment? "How you could love work so much that it becomes your whole life. I thought you weren't coming home from the office because you had these expectations of wifely duties that I wasn't fulfilling. That you wanted me to take care of you. To support you. Well, now I know how to take care of someone; to make chicken soup when they're sick and make pancakes for breakfast. And the only person I want to take care of is you."

I stumble onward, unable to stop talking. "I used to sit in this room alone. Every night. I used to watch the clock and yell at you when you walked in the door. I thought that if I pointed out the time to you enough times, loudly enough, you would come home earlier. I didn't want to just *ask* you to come home early; I thought it meant more if you thought of it yourself. That's all I wanted, Adam, just your time. You gave me more of your time when you were in law school, even when you were studying for the bar and you had *no* time. You always found some and gave it to me. I knew how precious your time was, and the fact that you would give it to me spoke volumes."

I start crying again, and Adam proactively hands me a Kleenex. "But now I know my nagging was just one more thing you thought I was asking for—you thought I wanted your time and your money and something had to give. It's too late, but what I should have done is make you *want* to be here. By taking care of you, too. And I should have *asked* for what I wanted rather than waiting for it to occur to you."

"Where did you get this idea about wifely duties?" Adam asks, genuinely confused.

"You said it! You said I never was supportive."

"Of me wanting to be a teacher! I didn't care if you cooked or didn't cook. If you did the laundry or if we sent it out to a service. Rach, I was talking about the fact that you knew I wanted to be a teacher, knew I loved the world of literature, but you never told me that it was okay to go that route. I thought if I didn't work as a lawyer, give you the life you wanted, that you'd be disappointed in me."

"I didn't *know* how much you wanted to be a teacher. I'm sorry that I overlooked that; that I missed that. It never mattered to me what job you held. I thought you loved being a lawyer so much that you wanted to be a lawyer more than you wanted to be with me."

Adam is silent for a long time.

And finally, he says, "I'm sorry."

It's not enough. It's not nothing, but it's not enough. The fact that he's dating Laura, coupled with those sole words, sort of shuts the door on more conversation. There is nothing left to say or do; even his eyes flicker towards the door as if he's subconsciously telling me to go. I scoop my heart off the table and place its mangled remains back in my chest. I gather my purse and say vague supportive comments about having a good future and thanking him for allowing me to get these thoughts off my chest.

He watches me collect my things, not stopping me, which shreds my heart a little more. But that's sort of the thing about time—once it passes, you can't move backwards. And while it is nice that I realized all these things about our relationship, it is now too late. The time to have done this hard thinking was years ago, and I can only move on from here, keeping in mind all that I learned.

Except that I'll be alone forever, I think dramatically, while he'll have Laura and their cat babies.

I say goodbye, and Adam tells me feebly to wait, but I know it's just a pity "Wait," one of those "Waits" you say when you can't think of any other word to say and you know one is expected of you. I don't wait. I just give a really cringy smile and dump my Kleenex in the garbage can that *I* purchased at the Duane Reade. I twist the knob on the door that *I* painted a few years back and step into my old hallway. *This is the last time I will ever be here*, I think.

I go back downstairs, sniffling the whole time. This is the worst part about gaining knowledge—what's the point in doing all this mental work and coming out with these answers when it's too late to use the information?

Now it just feels like torture to finally know the right response but also know that there is no chance to use it. I push my way back out onto the street. During the time that we've been inside, it has gotten dark and cold. I pull my jacket tightly around my chest and begin walking back towards the subway.

I start composing blog posts in my mind. *Adam has moved on without me. He and Laura are probably talking about me as I write, drinking their wine out of the glasses that my Aunt Leah gave us for our wedding.*

"Rachel!" I hear Adam call from behind.

I turn around, and Adam is jogging towards me, just like in a movie. He is slightly out of breath, as if he has leapt down the stairs two at a time, and he leans on the railing by the subway stairs to catch his breath. A man playing saxophone nearby starts wailing louder on his sax, nodding at us and half-smiling at the same time. I toss some change from my coat pocket into his case and wait for Adam to speak.

"There is no one," he tells me.

"What about Laura?"

"I'm not dating Laura anymore. It was a brief thing."

"You just said in the apartment that you're still dating her."

"Laura is dating some teacher at work now. Her brother set them up after I broke up with her. Rach, I'm not dating Laura."

"You broke up with her? When?"

He bit his lower lip. "Right before I saw you at her party. When I found out you two knew each other. She was dating the teacher by the time we saw each other at her apartment. "

"Why did you say . . ."

"I thought you were still dating that Spanish guy you brought to the party."

"Gael? I broke up with him. But . . . at the party . . . I heard you tell someone that you were relieved to be divorced."

"I never said that," Adam insists. "I'm relieved to be out of the law firm. I was never relieved to be out of our marriage."

Adam squints at me, somewhat distracted by the saxophone and the people pushing past out of the subway. We both stand there awkwardly, as if we've run out of shocking truths.

"I thought about you a few weeks ago," he admits. "Before I saw you at the party. I was teaching a poetry unit to the kids, and the anthology we were using had that Longfellow poem in it. Remember that ring I got you from London with the inscription in it?"

"Bizarro wedding band," I say.

"Right. I decided to read it with the kids. And one of the kids asked the etymology of the word 'strange.' So we looked it up online. I don't remember the whole thing—maybe it's from Old French—but part of the definition of strange is 'Someone who has stopped visiting.' And I thought, *That's what I became to Rachel.*"

My husband the stranger, I once called him when he walked in the apartment. Isn't this the way it always works—that the answers are with you the entire time, sometimes even entwined around your finger, and you just don't see them until it's too late.

"I never told you what I was thinking because, as I said, I never felt you wanted me to be a teacher. I always wondered if you married me for the money—my family's money or the salary I could pull in as a lawyer," he continues. "I would have shared all of that before this point if I had thought that you would hear it and . . .do something with it."

He waits again. I'm not sure if I like his new habit of circumspection, pausing after every two sentences. But we can work on that now that Laura has fizzled out like static on a television.

Adam says, "I want a chance to talk again. With no promises, Rach. Just a chance to think all of this out."

"We may still reach the same conclusions," I warn tearfully, but smiling.

"We just need to have the conversation that we never had last year, and see where it takes us."

It will really suck, I want to joke, *if we discover that we could have worked through all the misunderstandings without needing to divide all of our property and pay two divorce attorneys.* But perhaps we could have never ended up here, leaning close to each other on the railing of the subway stairs, if we hadn't gone through the divorce and rebirth. He wouldn't have shown me who he really wants to be. I certainly would have never found my passion for cooking, or my confidence in the kitchen. I wouldn't have found my voice as a writer or connected with an audience through the blog. I don't think we could have ever moved forward until I found something for myself, a small passion. Like the filling inside a pie. Without the apple slices and cinnamon, a pie is only an empty shell.

And that's what I was when I used to sit home by myself, thinking that he didn't care.

"Can I take you out for dinner tomorrow night?" he asks.

"No," I say firmly. Then, quickly, to dispel the disappointment flickering in his eyes, I explain, "Let me make you dinner."

He smiles. "At your apartment? Tomorrow night?"

I write the address on a small slip of paper from my purse. We stare at each other for a long time, not saying anything, and then he gives me a small kiss on the cheek.

I hear him whisper another apology under the wail of the saxophone.

I whisper one back.

Life from Scratch

blogging about life one scrambled egg at a time

My mother has agreed to let me cook the Passover seder meal this year. Which doesn't sound like a big deal, but since she has protested this the last few times I raised the idea, it feels like a small victory. She still tells me that she doesn't see the point in me cooking when the caterer can produce a perfectly lovely meal. But it means something to me.

I can finally call myself a cook. A home chef. I've graduated from the basic cooking books and borrowed a new slew of ethnic cookbooks from the library. And before you twist your underpants in a tizzy, it doesn't mean it's the end of the blog. Oh no, dear readers, you're stuck with me. I will always find new recipes to write about, new lessons to learn, new neuroses to unload. My hope is that I can keep this level of honesty in everything I'm touching—

this blog, my food.

I declare this the start of my Honest Food Movement.

Honesty + food = if not something good, then at least something without regrets.

In honor of landing the Passover meal, tonight I'm making a meal combining everything I learned this year—from roasting to basting to baking (gasp!) to sauces. I have tried to incorporate every type of knife cut and ingredients from all four food groups. It wasn't difficult. The choices were clear. Second-nature. I only hope it tastes as good as it looks.

195

But in the tradition of the great cliffhanger, a critique of the meal will need to wait until the next post, because I just heard the buzzer I've been waiting for from the building's front door.

Chapter Thirteen

Pinching the Salt

Unlike the first time I cooked for Gael, I am not nervous when I hear the buzzer announcing Adam's arrival. I feel shy; I feel anxious to hear his thoughts on the meal; I feel a fluttering sensation at the base of my throat, somewhere close to where it meets my stomach. I am anything but hungry. But I'm also at peace. Having the strength to pull myself off of our sofa and walk out of our apartment without the promise of a next meeting has filled me with confidence. I will get through the next phase, this night, whatever "this" happens to be.

While I was cooking, I checked Sitestalker for old time's sake. And there, most likely for the first time, was Gael Paez. He stayed on only for a few minutes, and I have no deep feelings about his visit. It was like Alice catching a glimpse of the Mad Hatter while she does her toiletry shopping at Target. She has moved on from Wonderland; her experience there helped her find a new way to be happy in the real world. It's nice to see the Hatter over there by electronics, but she doesn't need to follow him through the store, understand why he's there, or search for greater meaning.

Goodbye Mad Hatter. Goodbye March Hare, and Red Queen.

Before Adam arrives, Arianna and my brother call from her apartment. Ethan promises me that Adam has always been his favorite brother-in-law, despite all the times he cursed him this year. Even though they are an odd couple, I can already tell there is something about Arianna and Ethan that works, a comfortable give-and-take where they finish each other's sentences and move with a fluidity that cannot be learned or faked. He ducks off the phone call to take care of Beckett, and Arianna whispers a final "Good luck," and tells me to call her the second Adam leaves.

I have made Adam the meal that, for me, embodies home. My grandmother used to make it the first night we came to visit, and it always made me feel as if she had been thinking about me the entire time she was waiting for me. Making this meal makes me feel like I can honestly say that I really know how to cook for someone I love.

To roast the chicken, first I peeled the onions. I juiced a lemon and placed the rind inside the bird's cavity. I melted butter and rubbed it lovingly into the skin, my Hebrew school teacher's voice be damned. I prepared the thyme, de-stemming the leaves. I snapped the carrots, rondelled the celery, cubed the potatoes, and chopped the parsnips. I splashed wine into the roasting pan, added crushed garlic cloves before trussing the chicken's leg together with cooking twine. I sprinkled pepper and pinched the salt.

And after all of that is done, I hear the buzzer.

Smiling, I open the door and welcome Adam in.

Acknowledgements

Despite being a writer, it is difficult to sum up into words the enormous gratitude I feel towards the people who made the book possible.

Thank you to Deborah Smith and Debra Dixon at BelleBooks (as well as the rest of the BelleBooks team) for taking a chance with me and for loving Rachel with your whole heart. Seeing the book through your eyes made me fall in love with the story all over again. I could not have asked for a warmer, effusive, and inclusive team to bring this book into print.

To Katherine Fausset, the most patient agent in the world, who always knows the right thing to say at the right time. And to Jay Neugeboren, my mentor, who believed in my fiction before *I* believed I could write fiction.

To my sister, Wendy, who is nothing like Sarah in this book, especially since her cooking would make Martha Stewart weep with envy. Thank you for lending me your daughter's name, and for not only being an incredible mother, but passing along your lessons learned to me. To Jonathan, the anti-Richard, for your enormous heart. And, of course, to Olivia, who gave me my first foray into aunthood and is the coolest ten-year-old I'm lucky enough to know.

To my brother, Randall, who is only like Ethan in the sense that he always has my back and has, on many occasions, dragged boxes of books up and down stairs for me. For all your advice and notes; I could not have done this without you. And frankly, I wouldn't have wanted to do it without you.

Thank you to my parents for being nothing like the Katzes (except that you store much of our stuff in your basement). You always make the time to listen to me, and you've given me the space to write. Without your help, these books would just remain in my head. A special thank you to my mother, who taught me how to cook and ate that first loaf of uncooked French bread simply because she loves me. And to my father who passed along his imagination and way with words.

My most enormous thank you goes to my husband, Josh. Without him, you would not be holding this book. He is the one who knows with a simple look that I am in need of a hug, who makes me ice cream in the Espresso Royale mug, and who plucks the solutions out of thin air. Thank you is too small a word to give to him in exchange for all he has given me. I love you.

And lastly, to my children. It is no secret that I struggle sometimes with letting you grow up, but it is only because I love you so much, and you change so quickly. It feels like every day is a goodbye and a hello. I love the silly faces you make and the dances you do when you burst into my room while I'm writing, and I always pause to take a mental snapshot. Those moments capture your true selves—your uninhibited laugh, your curiosity, your creativity. I know you need to grow up, but please also hold on to the people who made me Scoobee, the paper vampire, and rocket clocks.

About the Author

An amateur chef and popular blogger herself, Melissa Ford is the author of the award-winning website, Stirrup Queens. Melissa completed her MFA at the University of Massachusetts-Amherst. She is also a contributing editor at BlogHer. Ford lives outside of Washington, D.C. with her writer husband, Joshua, and their twins. She is currently at work on the sequel to *Life From Scratch*.

LaVergne, TN USA
30 January 2011
214551LV00004B/38/P

9 781935 661986